ChangelingPress.com

Maddog/Archangel Duet

A Bones MC Romance

Marteeka Karland

Maddog/Archangel Duet

A Bones MC Romance

Marteeka Karland

All rights reserved.
Copyright ©2026 Marteeka Karland

ISBN: 978-1-60521-973-8

Publisher:
Changeling Press LLC
315 N. Centre St.
Martinsburg, WV 25404
ChangelingPress.com

Printed in the U.S.A.

Editor: Jean Cooper
Cover Artist: Marteeka Karland

The individual stories in this anthology have been previously released in E-Book format.

No part of this publication may be reproduced or shared by any electronic or mechanical means, including but not limited to reprinting, photocopying, or digital reproduction, without prior written permission from Changeling Press LLC.

This book contains sexually explicit scenes and adult language which some may find offensive and which is not appropriate for a young audience. Changeling Press books are for sale to adults, only, as defined by the laws of the country in which you made your purchase.

Table of Contents

Maddog (Black Reign MC 10)
A Bones MC Romance
Marteeka Karland

Who knew we'd get ambushed by the cartel on our way to a village deep in the Amazon jungle?

Holly: I was sick as a kid. Leukemia. Felt like someone always had to drop everything to take care of me. Hate being dependent on people now, so I try to do everything myself. When my best friend takes up with a creep and won't believe me when I tell her something's not right with the man, I decide it's safer (for her) if I go with her on a trip to Columbia he's organizing. Bad news: I'm right. Fortunately the most annoying man I've ever come to count on thinks it's his job to rescue me. This time, I might just let him. And that's where the trouble starts...

Jax: I've known Holly nearly all her life. I've been her protector and the person she wants most when things go horribly wrong, which they do, more often than not. To say we have a contentious relationship is an understatement. I put a claim on Holly she never accepted, but it's time to force the issue. Not because she doesn't love me. Because she's afraid history is doomed to repeat itself. She's wrong. I'll always come for her when she needs me. Like it or not, Holly's more than my responsibility. No matter the cost, she's *mine*.

Chapter One

Jax

"Let me get this straight." I pinched the bridge of my nose, trying to stave off the headache threatening to split my skull open. Funny how that worked when I talked to Holly. "You're *voluntarily* going to a country with a *level four travel advisory*. Unarmed. With a bunch of college students. With no security to speak of. Have I got that right?" I tried to keep my voice low and even, to fight my way through the rage that she'd be so cavalier with her life.

"Sweet God, could you be a bigger buzzkill?" Holly, ever the little ray of sarcastic sunshine, sounded like she was exasperated with me. Or, quite possibly, like she thought I was being unreasonable.

"Answer the question, Holly." If I let her distract me, she'd talk her way around the point I was trying to make and hang up before I could forbid her from going. Not that it was going to help. Holly always did what she wanted. Usually, only her mother was able to knock some sense into her.

"You do realize you're not the boss of me. Right?"

"I realize that, when you're considering putting your life in danger for no good fuckin' reason, someone has to rein you in. I'm surprised Wrath even considered letting you go, much less gave his blessing." The silence on the other end was deafening. "You didn't tell him." It wasn't a question.

"Again, not your business, Jax. This is my life and I'm living it. If I get into trouble, I'll accept the consequences."

"Even if it costs you your life?" I tried to go for a matter-of-fact tone, but my words came out a low growl.

"Even if it costs me my life."

Neither of us spoke for long moments, the silence so long I was afraid the call had dropped. Then she sighed.

"Look, Jax. I've got a sat phone. Even if there's no cell coverage where we're at, Shotgun will be able to see where I am. He and Esther are great with that shit. If we get into trouble, I can call him. They can either send someone to come get me or let me work it out myself. I'm only agreeing to any of this so my mom doesn't worry."

"Did you at least tell Celeste? Because I don't see your mother letting you do something like this at all."

"No one lets me do anything, Jax." Holly's tone was hard and firm. She was barely out of her teens, yet I'd never met anyone more in control of her life. Which was to say she lived in utter chaos most of the time, but that was exactly the way she liked it. "But yes. I told her what I was doing. She's not happy about it, but she knows she can't talk me out of it."

"Did you ever stop to think how your mother and father would feel if you got hurt or killed? I realize it could happen anywhere, but going to Columbia increases those chances exponentially over anywhere in the U.S. She almost lost you once and gave everything she had to keep you alive. Don't you think you're being incredibly selfish?" I winced. Yeah, this wasn't my finest moment. Had I been trying to push her away I couldn't have done a better job.

"Go fuck yourself, Jax." She disconnected the call.

"Motherfuck!" I hissed the expletive under my breath. I knew better. I fucking knew better. The best way to get Holly to do *anything* other than what you wanted her to do was to tell her she had to do it. Pushing her into doing what you wanted was even worse. Trying to lay a guilt trip on her? Yeah. I'd just guaranteed Holly's heading straight to Columbia on that humanitarian aid expedition.

I pressed her contact and waited for her to answer the Facetime call. She let it go to voicemail once, so I tried again. She picked up this time and… yeah. She hated me right now.

"Got nothin' else to say to you, asshole." I recognized that mulish look on her face. She thought I was going to try to talk her out of going again, but I knew better than that.

"Can you give me two days, Holly? Two days and I'll go with you. You can still do what you do with your college friends, but I can make sure you're safe."

"We've got plenty of security. There's no need for that."

"Holly. Two days."

She shrugged one delicate shoulder, a look of indifference and disinterest on her face. "Sorry, Jax. I don't make the schedule. Plane leaves tomorrow morning at six."

I wanted to throttle the younger woman. She was constantly bucking me, doing exactly the opposite of what I wanted her to do. To be fair, I was twelve years older than she was, and had decided she'd be mine long before I should have. I'd been sixteen when she came to the compound with Wrath and Celeste. She'd been a precocious but sickly child of four. She'd survived leukemia like a champ, never letting anything get to her. No matter how sick I'd seen her from the chemo, the girl had no "quit" in her. I knew because I'd been with her for the last few treatments. Which she'd *not* appreciated. I'd insisted, because she'd been so mad at me she hadn't focused on all the needles and unpleasantness. I'd been happy to take her wrath then, even if what remained of the kid in me had been slightly hurt that she hadn't accepted me as her protector.

Even when she was so young, I'd been drawn to her. She was this little pixie who'd absolutely cut you if you displeased her, but needed someone looking after her. I'd taken that task on my own, growing into a man protecting the girl until she'd started becoming a woman. The plain truth was, it scared me the first time I caught sight of her in a bikini at the pool. Freaked me the absolute fuck out. Once I'd come to terms with my feelings for Holly, I'd inserted myself into her life but kept playing the part of mean and annoying older brother. Why? Because I knew if she learned to stand up to me, she always would. And if she could stand up to me, she could stand up to anyone.

"Holly, I'm half a fuckin' world away right now. All I'm asking for is two fuckin' days. It's the right thing to do and you know it. I may be a bastard, but I would never let anything happen to you."

Her expression didn't change. "I don't need your protection, Jax. Shotgun and Esther have my back. I'll be fine. Besides, the father of one of the students going is a senator. They always have security."

"And their priority will be the senator's kid. They won't give two shits about you or the others."

"And if you were with me, you'd give a shit about the others?" Oh, the sarcasm was strong with this one…

"Of course not. But I'd care about you. I'd be the one protecting you and I'd do it with my life."

She snorted, scowling at me over the video. "Dramatic much?"

"Holly --"

"No. You listen to me! Nothing's going to happen. And if it does, I'll deal. I don't want or need your help, Jax."

"You're wrong there, baby. You need all my help you can get. But I'm telling you right now, if you don't wait for me, when I find you, I will turn you over my knee and blister your bare ass until you don't sit for a fuckin' week."

Oh, that got her attention. The resolution of the new phones Shotgun had gotten from Argent Tech recently was so great, I could actually see the sweat erupt on her brow. She sucked in a breath and her face and neck flushed a becoming pink. The pulse at her throat beat like mad. All of which, of course, meant pissed her the fuck off something fierce.

"Go find something to do and stay out of my life. Mm'k?" She gave me a saccharine smile before disconnecting the call again.

"I'm really gonna spank that little brat when I see her again."

"Didn't know you had a kid, Jax." Loki clapped me on the back as he walked by. The grin on his grizzled face told me he was fully aware I didn't actually have a kid.

"You know better." I fell into step beside him as we made our way to the transport back to the States. We were headed home from a high-profile protection detail with ExFil. Thankfully, it had been an exceedingly boring assignment. I knew Holly had been planning something but hadn't figured out what it was when the assignment came down. So, of course, she waited until I left before letting anyone know she was going.

"Hmm. Woman, then."

"Isn't it always?"

Loki appeared to think about that, giving it serious consideration. "You know. I think you might be right about that."

There was a beat of silence before we both chuckled. Again, Loki clapped me on the back and we boarded the big troop carrier headed back to South Carolina and ExFil.

I strapped myself in and pulled out my phone. I shot a text to Shotgun, needing him to look into what the fuck was going on. If Shotgun wouldn't help me, I'd take it to Holly's daddy. No way Wrath approved of this or would allow it. I'm surprised El Diablo hadn't put a stop to it because no way he didn't know.

Me: What outfit is Holly going to Columbia with?

Shotgun: Holly's going to Columbia?

Me: What she said.

There was a long pause before the dots signifying Shotgun's reply appeared.

Shotgun: There's a charter flying out of Miami International. Fifteen passengers, including one VIP. Looks like she's a passenger.

Me: When's it leave?

Shotgun: 6PM tonight.

The little witch had lied to me! Probably hadn't expected I'd be thorough enough to actually check myself. She knew I was out of the country. She also knew how these tours worked and the timeline. Little hellion likely thought I'd wait until I got back to South Carolina. The flight was only ten hours, so when I landed I'd still have a couple of hours before she was supposed to leave.

Me: Find out if Wrath knows. Stop the fuckin' plane.

Shotgun: On that already, but they already left. They were ready early and there was a window for them to depart.

I was truly going to beat her ass when I got to Holly. Right there in front of God and everyone. Her daddy'd have to get over it.

Me: Get details. I'll talk to Samson and see if he'll get El Diablo to approve transport to her.

Shotgun: He will. What would you do if he didn't?

Me: Steal something and go get her myself.

Shotgun: ?????????

Me: Smartass!

Cain, our boss at ExFil, didn't spare any expense to keep us all safe. As a result, we all had a personal sat phone. It's how I'd been able to contact Holly before, and now Shotgun. I debated my next move. Shotgun would contact Wrath. But if he heard this from someone other than me, he might think I would avoid coming to him with something to do with Holly.

"Fuck." I swore as I pulled up Wrath's number. It went to voicemail, so I tried again. He picked up on the third ring this time.

"What the fuck do you mean Holly's run off to Columbia?" his voice roared through the phone and I winced. The Bluetooth was connected to the headset in my helmet, so there was no way to get away from a very pissed-off Wrath.

"Don't yell, you bastard," I growled. "I'm on my way back to headquarters."

"Why didn't you tell me the second you found out about this?"

"Because I found out about it ten minutes ago. The first five was spent loading my gear onto the transport, the next five texting Shotgun for information. You were my first actual call. Jesus!"

"Shotgun's preparing you a flight plan. What do you need?"

That kinda threw me. "You're sending *me* after

her? Voluntarily?"

"Who the fuck else would I send after her? Are you saying you don't want the job?"

"Oh, I was going whether or not you wanted me to. I just didn't expect you to actually agree with me."

"Dumbass. You've loved Holly since you first saw her when she was four. Only person who has as big a reason for needing her safe as Celeste and I do, is you."

I took a couple of deep breaths before I spoke next. "To be clear, Wrath. I do love your daughter. The claim I already put out there still stands. I intend to make Holly my old lady."

"Yeah? Then you might want to start calling her by her road name. No daughter of mine is gonna sit by passively while her man takes care of every little thing for her. Not unless that's what she wants. And we both know Holly isn't the shrinking violet type."

"I can see your point. And it's a small price to pay to soften her up for me." I couldn't keep the humor out of my voice. "Maddog, it is."

Chapter Two

Holly (Maddog)

The second Dad started blowing up my phone was the second I decided I really was going to kill Jax this time. Slimy bastard had ratted me out! Like I was four or something! I wasn't about to answer until there was no way they could turn the plane around, or my dad would threaten to kill anyone he had to for them to head back to the States. So I turned my phone off. All that buzzing would wear down the battery. Yeah. That sounded good.

About six or seven hours later, we landed in Simón Bolívar International Airport in Rodadero, Columbia. The second we stepped outside, the heat hit me like a shockwave. It felt like I'd opened an oven door and got my face scalded. "Fuck me," I hissed.

"Anytime you want, Holly." Chris Alistair the Third purred in my ear. The guy was a fucking creep. He was also the reason I was here in the first Goddamned place. He was dating a friend from school and I had the feeling he was up to something. Since I couldn't talk Andrea into not going, I decided I was going with her. It had seemed to delight Chris that I was going, which made me incredibly uneasy.

I gave him the side eye. "Not if you were the last man on the entire fuckin' planet, Chris."

He chuckled but backed off. Bastard had been making comments like that the whole trip. Now that we were in a place it wasn't safe to navigate on my own, I was beginning to rethink not waiting on Jax. I'd actually been going to ask him to come with me when I'd called him. Then he'd gone and been the Jax I've known most of my life. Asshole Jax. So I'd let my temper get the better of me. Which was when I remembered my sat phone was still turned off.

I stuck my hand in my jeans pocket where I'd tucked my phone and turned it on. I didn't want Chris knowing I had a working phone. Most everyone had cell phones, but where we were supposed to be headed outside the city didn't have cell service. I was thankful I'd set the device to vibrate. If he was listening for it, he'd probably be able to hear it buzzing, but it was crowded and noisy outside the airport and he wasn't close to me at the moment. The longer my dad kept trying to call without me answering, the sooner he sent someone after me. Shotgun could pinpoint my location as long as the phone was on. Though Chris gave me the creeps, I hadn't realized how nervous I was around him until this very moment. Yeah. Turning off my phone had been stupid. And not a mistake I'd make again.

Andrea was cuddled up to Chris as we waited for the bus taking us to the village. I wanted to barf. Problem was, it wasn't because I found them disgusting. I was jealous as fuck. While I knew Chris was a bastard, Andrea obviously thought she was in love. I wanted that. Not with Chris, obviously. He was a swine. No. When I thought about cuddling up with a guy, the only man I saw was Jax. Which wasn't acceptable at all.

Jax had seen me at my worst. When I was so sick all I could do was puke and sleep. He'd been with me when I'd fought so hard during the last couple of treatments. Sure, I'd just turned five at the time, but even though I didn't like him back then -- I was a kid and he was a teenager who didn't want a little girl hanging around him -- I'd taken as much comfort in his presence as I had my mother's.

The rest of my life had been one series of medical

tests after another, trying to catch any sign of a recurring cancer as soon as possible. Even though he claimed not to like me, that I was a pain in his ass, he always seemed to be in my line of sight. Trying to prove to Jax that I was tough was the only thing that got me through some of it. But while I practically idolized him, Jax saw me as a kid. To be fair, I was twelve years younger than he was. It would probably creep him out if he knew, every single time he threatened to spank me for being a brat, it turned me the fuck on something fierce.

I tried to keep someone between me and Chris every time we moved around. There were fifteen people in our party, so it wasn't too hard. What was hard was letting Andrea too far away from me. Afraid as I was for myself, I was even more so for her. Because whatever happened, when it did, she'd never see it coming. At least I had a heads up and could take precautions. Late though they might be.

We boarded a bus to take us to a village about six hours outside of Rodadero. My phone had been buzzing every half hour since I'd turned it on. It buzzed again, then the calls started coming every couple of minutes. I wanted to turn on the GPS on my watch but had to use the phone to turn the damned thing on.

Anytime I took a trip of any lengthy distance where cell coverage was questionable, my dad and Shotgun agreed to give me at least twelve hours before losing their Goddamned minds. It hadn't quite been that long, but I was hoping and praying that Jax had gotten tired of waiting and they were finally going to activate the GPS remotely. And as much as my mom and dad loved me, I knew it would be Jax who would force the issue because Mom and Dad always tried to treat me like a responsible adult and abide by the agreements we made regarding safety. If Jax thought they needed to contact me earlier, he wouldn't hesitate to ride roughshod over that agreement and do exactly what he deemed best for me.

To my tremendous relief, there was one long, continuous buzz for fifteen seconds from my watch. That was my signal that help was on the way. The phone had linked up with my watch to turn on its satellite GPS features. Now, if my phone got separated from me, Shotgun could still track my watch. It had been designed to save the battery. The satellite link would only turn on if I activated it, or Shotgun told it to.

Not a moment too soon either, because the bus braked hard. The driver gave a shout right before we slammed into something. My head hit the seat in front of me and knocked me silly. My ears rang and my vision blurred. There were screams all around me and a flurry of Spanish. A gunshot sounded in the confines of the bus. I cried out as my ears popped. There was a wet spray across my face and someone fell on top of me, pinning me to the floor of the bus.

"Everyone off the bus, now!" A male voice speaking in heavily accented Spanish shouted over top of all the screams and cries. There was more commotion as people moved down the aisle in a hurry, shoving and tripping over each other.

The weight on me shifted and I realized the person who had fallen on me was being dragged away. I fought to clear my head, to push through the hazy fog that had settled over my brain. The rapid pounding of my heart echoed in my ears while my chest constricted in panic.

I forced myself to open my eyes, wincing as the

harsh sunlight hit me where it shined in through the broken bus window. When I could focus, I saw a pair of rough boots in front of me in the aisle.

I didn't dare move. The man standing in front of me dragged me roughly to my feet and shoved me toward the back of the vehicle where the rear door was open. I stumbled forward and tried to brace myself to jump to the ground, but I was shoved, landing with a cry in a heap.

"Get up, bitch." Again, I was manhandled, the guy dragging me to the rest of the group and shoving me hard. I tripped and went flying into the people in my party. I'd lost sight of Andrea and Chris, but figured I needed to worry about myself at the moment. Chris would take care of Andrea. If not, I'd do what I could, but I had to face the fact that I might not be able to save her. Or myself for that matter.

Around me, the chaos continued. The air was filled with the terrified screams and pleas for help. The heat felt like it intensified tenfold as fear and adrenaline coursed through me. I tried to stand but found myself dizzy and disoriented, falling back onto the ground. When I rubbed my face with my hand, it came back sticky. Blood streaked my fingers and the palm of my hand, but I didn't think it was my blood. Which was when I remembered the person who'd fallen on top of me.

My gaze found the bus as they rolled a body out the back and onto the dirt road. Men were speaking Spanish to each other. Though I knew some Spanish, I couldn't keep up with these guys. They gestured to the dead girl they'd shoved out the back of the bus, obviously upset for whatever reason. One of them was angry, the other on the defensive, but I couldn't catch what they said.

"Get down! Get down!" I was certain that was the bodyguard with Chris. When I turned my head toward his voice, the large man had shoved Chris into the dirt. He had a small handgun out, tracking the guys who'd attacked us but not firing. The bodyguard seemed to be reluctant to shoot anyone and was more than a little scared. From the looks of things, he was panicking as much as everyone else.

One of the attackers turned to when the big guy yelled, aimed, and shot. I jumped as brain, blood, and bone splattered over the dirt road. Chris gave a terrified yell at the same time everyone else screamed, but didn't move to get out from under the dead guard. I saw Andrea huddling at the front of the bus next to the tire. She screamed, covering her head with her hands and tucking herself into a ball.

During the chaos, all I could do was sit there and gape at everything happening. It was like I was frozen to the spot. My limbs were heavy and everything felt like it was happening in slow motion. I shook my head, trying to clear it and get my wits back.

"I said get down on the ground! All of you!" This guy spoke unaccented English, unlike the others who seemed to only speak Spanish. He was the one who seemed to be calling the shots. He had a confident stature, straight-backed and unflinching in the face of the chaos he caused. His jet-black hair provided a stark contrast to his icy blue eyes that were scanning the area for any signs of rebellion. A thin line of sweat trickled down his temple, but he made no move to wipe it away. In his hand was a semi-automatic, the sight of which sent chills down my spine.

No one defied him, myself included. I stayed put, my hands out in front of me, shaking like a leaf. A frightened whimper left me and when the guy turned my way, I ducked, keeping my hands up and prayed he wasn't looking to kill us all. Didn't these types of things usually end up making ransom demands? We were being kidnapped. Right?

"Muévelos a todos aquí. Mantenlos a todos juntos." He gestured to all of us in a sweeping gesture with his arm. I thought he said he wanted us all in the same area. Kind of like he was corralling us to better keep us contained.

Andrea still huddled in front of the bus, visibly trembling, a look of abject terror on her face. Chris was still underneath his dead security detail. The gun the guard had dropped when he fell lay next to him, well within Chris's reach. I thought Chris might reach for it, but he didn't even try to move. For a moment, I was afraid he might be dead. Of the fifteen in our group, five had been killed. Much as I thought he was a creep, I didn't want him dead.

There were seven men around us, all of them armed with automatic rifles. All of them pointed at us. Someone pulled Andrea up by her hair from where she huddled at the front of the bus and tossed her in our direction. She stumbled and fell before crawling the five or six feet to me where I huddled. I reached for her, pulling her to me and wrapping my arms around her while she sobbed, as terrified as I was.

The conversation among our attackers was a cacophony of rapid-fire Spanish. They were obviously arguing, but my brain couldn't translate quickly enough. The guy in charge scanned those of us who were left. Two of his men pulled the bodyguard off Chris and shoved Chris into the group of us. I thought Andrea might go to him, but she stayed with me, looking around her fearfully.

The leader stared down every one of us, studying

all of us intently. Turning his gaze toward me, he paused. A chill ran down my spine as I huddled with Andrea on the dusty road, my throat dry as I tried to swallow.

I could feel his gaze on me as I stayed as still as I could, keeping my head down so he didn't think I was challenging him. My only thought was to keep myself as safe as possible until Jax came for me. Because I knew it would be Jax who came for me. My heart pounded in my ears and still shook uncontrollably, but it was only a matter of time.

Chapter Three

Jax

When I got Holly home safely, I was gonna blister her ass. If Wrath had spanked her more as a child instead of coddling her because of her cancer, she might take her safety more seriously. And yeah. I get why Wrath coddled the little princess. I coddled her too. And despite my bravado now, I'd continue to fucking coddle her. Why? Because the thought of losing Holly for any reason made me want to lose my Goddamn mind.

Mechanic gestured toward the screen where he was tracking Holly. "She's not moving." Since he'd landed our Osprey as close to Holly's position as he reasonably could given the size of the aircraft, we'd been following her movements and heading steadily in her direction for the better part of an hour. The Phantom Badger we were using was loaded to capacity with men and equipment. Which was to say, me and Razor and some serious hardware.

Holly's group had been headed toward a small village about six hours south of Rodadero. Which was bad. With the heavy traffic from Rodadero and Santa Marta to the U.S., there had been increased drug traffic south of Rodadero. The whole general area was considered very high-risk for traveling. ExFil had been hired to extract more than one goodwill mission.

"Have they reached their destination?" Razor was native to the area. He studied the screen from our end same as Mechanic did back at the Osprey. "See if you can zoom in. There's a dirt road in that area they should be following to the village. It's been a couple years, but that road is in exactly the wrong spot if they want to live."

"Yeah." I snagged a weapons vest and shrugged into it before checking my sidearm. "Bettin' they've been stopped." My vest had several extra clips as well as some grenades. "How far are we from her, Razor?"

He shrugged. "We can get there in the Badger in less than five. They'll hear us, but as long as they've been stopped, that might be a good thing."

I gave him a crisp nod. "Let's move. Mechanic, have Iron and Tank ready in case we come back hot."

"We expectin' trouble, Jax?" Razor spoke softly, raising an eyebrow.

"With Holly?" One side of my lip curled up in a half grin. "Always." I was trying to lighten the mood, but the truth was, my insides were screaming at me to get to her. I wasn't as seasoned as some of the guys in Black Reign, but I'd done my time with Special Teams. The most important lesson I learned was to always trust my instincts. It had saved my life more than once. Now, I was counting on it to save Holly's.

The ride took less than five minutes. Even before we got there, we could hear gunshots. Normally, Razor would have stopped before we got too close so we could scout the situation, but that wasn't happening.

Without prompting from me Razor hit the accelerator hard, and we charged through the forest until we burst onto the road. Razor managed to maneuver the vehicle to a skidding halt between the small group of people and gunmen. We were practically on top of them, and even though we weren't expecting to take fire and hadn't put the roof on the Light Utility Vehicle, I was glad for the bulletproof glass on the door of the Badger.

I stood and fired over the window, taking down two hostiles. Razor got another one and the rest fled.

"We may have to ditch some ordinance." I spoke

through my throat mike to Mechanic, back at the Osprey. "Got at least ten civilians still alive."

"Copy that. Dump it, then destroy it on your way out. It'll have the added effect of takin' out their road."

"If you do that, you'll cut off the village from supply trucks." That was one of the women in the group. "We should leave."

"I can't fit all of you in this vehicle unless I drop equipment in the back. If I do that, I can't let the locals take that equipment. My only option is to destroy it where I drop it." I tried to be patient, but I needed to get Holly and get the fuck outta here.

"Can't you drop it somewhere else?"

"Look, lady," I snapped. "Either I dump the shit and destroy it, or I leave you here. Don't care which. But if you stay, they will come back and they *will* kill you. Eventually." I dismissed the woman as I scanned the group until I found Holly.

The lady protested or something. I dismissed her, but her voice was like a buzzing gnat in my subconscious. The only thing that mattered right now was Holly.

She sat huddled with her friend against the side of a large rock. Both women looked terrified. Blood streaked down Holly's temple and she looked a little dazed. Her gaze locked on mine, and she let go of her friend and shoved herself to her feet, half running, half stumbling toward me. When she threw herself at me, I caught her with one arm, my pistol in the other as I tracked the area for threats.

"Jax! Oh, God! Jax!"

"I've got you, baby. Gonna keep you safe. But you're gonna have to let me go so I can dump some stuff to make room for everyone. OK?"

She stiffened, then shoved herself away from me.

"I'll h-help." She clasped her hands behind her back and took a couple steps backward, a not-so-subtle retreat. "What has to go?"

"Everything, honey. Anything in the back of this vehicle needs to be offloaded." I hated not being able to comfort her like I knew she needed, but we didn't have a lot of time. And if worse came to worst, I'd grab Holly and take off. I would not hesitate to leave every single person in the fucking group behind if it put Holly in unreasonable danger. If that happened, she'd never forgive me. Or herself.

"Got it." And she went to work. Honestly, the work would help her focus on something other than what had just happened or what would happen next.

It didn't take me, Razor, and Holly long to completely empty out the bed. While we did that, the group gathered their dead to take with us. Only one or two of them didn't help. Both were in obvious shock.

The second the last of our weapons and ordinance was unloaded, the group started loading into the truck. They managed to get all but one of their dead in the back before we left. They'd argued for a few seconds before Razor put the vehicle in gear and sped off. Most of the group yelled and screamed at us to stop and go back, to get the last of the bodies, but Razor and I were in silent agreement that we needed to get back to our transport. Pronto.

Holly was between me and Razor. I had my left arm around her waist, my gun still firmly in my right hand as Razor pushed the vehicle as fast as he could. She trembled but said nothing. Holly gripped my thigh with one hand and the hand around her waist with the other. Seconds later there was a deafening BOOM! as the ordinance detonated behind us. Hopefully, even if those guys came back with reinforcements, the destroyed road would at least slow them down.

"We can't leave the village like this!" A young man a few years older than Holly leaned forward from where he'd piled in the back with the others. "We have a responsibility to fix what we broke!"

"Report it after we've gone," I snapped. "Or I can toss you out here and you can fix it yourself."

"I'm not tucking my tail between my legs and running home! If you're military, you should know I'm Christopher Alistair the third, United States Senator Alistair's son. My Secret Service detail was killed, so you have to act as my detail. That means I'm in charge."

"Ain't military, kid. We're in the private sector, and we're here for her." I indicated Holly. "Only reason you're with us in the first place is because it wasn't in her best interest to leave you behind. If that status changes, you'll find yourself on your ass on the side of the road, no matter who your daddy is."

Up ahead, the Osprey was powering up. Razor approached it and skidded the vehicle to a stop several feet away.

"Everyone out!" I yelled, tugging Holly out my side of the vehicle. Never letting go of her hand, I trotted with her to the transport while Razor drove ahead to pull the vehicle into the Osprey. I urged her to the front of the plane and the troop seating. When I would have helped her fasten her seatbelt, she brushed my hands away and did it herself. I knew then she'd be all right. For the first time since Wrath had told me what was going on, I felt the band around my chest ease up a little. It wouldn't be completely gone until we landed safely in the Black Reign compound with Holly safe and sound.

ExFil had arranged for a midair refuel for us to

head home. Once the refueling was complete, all there was left to do was wait. Mechanic and Razor had the bird well in hand. They'd let me know if they needed me. In fact, I expected Razor would be back with us soon. Once they got everything settled from the refueling and all the other pilot shit they did, Mechanic wouldn't need Razor until we got closer to our destination.

I turned slightly to look at Holly. She still gripped my hand, but didn't meet my gaze.

"Hey, baby. Look at me." She sucked in a breath and blinked several times, like she'd been startled awake. She obeyed, looking up at me with wide, vulnerable eyes. "That's my girl. Are you hurt? Did you get hit?"

She looked slightly confused, then stiffened. "I-I hit my head." Her voice was high-pitched and slightly husky. "When the bus wrecked."

"Do you know what happened?"

"Not really." She frowned, rubbing her temple as though she had a headache. If she'd hit her head, she likely did. "The bus swerved, and we hit something. I'm not sure when those men got on the bus. But I don't think it was too long after we wrecked."

"You're right. This is what the cartel does."

"But… no one uses that road other than supply vehicles. And those only come once a month at most. The villagers know to stay off the road and it's the wrong time of year for the cartels to be moving their products north." She rubbed at her head. "This should have been relatively low risk."

I had to bite my tongue to keep from telling her that no place in Columbia was "relatively low risk," but didn't think now was the time. Once she'd had time to process everything that had happened, and accepted my claim on her, I'd have plenty of time to address her life choices. And I was afraid this one wasn't going to go away any time soon. She'd taken ten years off my life.

Instead, I leaned in to brush a kiss on her forehead, wrapping an arm around her. She rested her head on my shoulder, but didn't quite relax. She still didn't let go of my hand, but other than that small gesture, she didn't move. I thought she might be close to falling asleep, but she slowly pushed away from me. With a sigh, she let go of me and laid her hands in her lap.

"Talk to me, Holly. I'll make everything all right if you'll tell me what you need." I meant it too. She was breaking my fucking heart.

"This is all my fault." Her voice was barely above a whisper.

"What's your fault, honey? You're not making sense."

"That you're here. This plane. All that money everyone spent. This time because I did something stupid." Tears had been streaming down her cheeks in a steady flow since I found her. The only time she seemed to be able to fight them off had been unloading the Badger.

"Honey, I'm here with all this shit because I will always come for you. By any means necessary. Bad choice on your part or not, I will *always* come for you."

She sucked in a small sob but held on to her emotions by the tiniest of fingernails. It wouldn't take much for her to shatter.

"Hey, man!" The angry demand came across from me. I wanted to drive my thumbs into his fucking eyeballs. "I'm filing a formal protest against your company when we land." Fucking Chris Alistair the fucking Third. There was every possibility either me or him wouldn't make it to Lake Worth alive. And he was too big a pussy to even think about taking me.

"For doin' what? Savin' your sorry ass? I can see how that could get me in trouble. Especially if you're as big a pain in your old man's ass as you're starting to become in mine, but also because you weren't my problem or my job. Holly is the only person I was authorized to spring. I'm beginning to think it might be best to remedy that mistake right now."

"You left that whole village with no way to get food or supplies! If they die, it's on you. And I'll tell every reporter I come across that you committed genocide."

"Do you have any fuckin' idea what you're talkin' about?" Razor plopped down in a seat on the other side of Holly putting her solidly between our wall of protection.

Alistair gave Razor a withering look. "I know exactly what I'm talking about," he snapped. "It's the only road in or out of that village! How are they supposed to get supplies without that road?"

Razor chuckled. "Fuuuuck. Did you know they made 'em this stupid, Jax?"

"I mean, I've heard stories." I shrugged like it was really no big deal. "Not sure I believed 'em. Till now."

"Son, the villagers that close to the Amazon want nothing more than to be left alone. They couldn't care less if people show up with stuff they've never heard they needed. They distrust the few things that could make their lives better. No. Those trails you call roads are made by the cartel. If you went into this situation and didn't bother to find out, you really are fuckin' stupid."

Razor waited until Alistair finally dropped his gaze before speaking to me. "Got you guys a small space with a little privacy if you want to look her over. Make sure she's not injured and in too much shock to feel it."

"If anyone gets a private room here, it's me, you asshole." Alistair piped up again. "*I'm* the important one here. I don't care what you say, I know you were sent to find me. Not her. She's nobody! You're supposed to do what I say!"

"Hate to tell you, bro," I took over before Razor lost his cool. I could practically see steam coming out the other man's ears. I felt pretty much the same way, but Razor was bigger than me and his punch was harder than my punch. "But real life don't work that way. No one knows you guys were missing. The only way your father knows now is if your body man got a message off to him, and my boss ain't sayin' nothin' if he did. Nothin' gets by Cain. No matter how recent the development. So you're on your own. No one knows you're in trouble. Nobody is sending you help. Nobody." The threat wasn't even thinly veiled. Razor was ready to do his worst, and I was right behind him.

"Of course they knew! They sent me help! You're here, aren't you?"

"Yep," I continued. "Because *her* family hadn't been able to speak with her in several hours, and I wasn't willing to wait another two or three hours they'd agreed upon before finding out where *she* was. Like I told you in Columbia. You're only here because it was of no benefit to her at the time for me to leave you behind. I don't give a good Goddamn who your daddy is."

"OK." Razor stood. "That's our cue to leave before I have to explain to our boss how a senator's son accidentally smashed his face and fell out of the plane on the way home." He wasn't joking. The only question was which one of us would follow through first. Looked like it would be a tight race.

The room Razor took us to wasn't much. Just a small conference type room someone had furnished with a cot in addition to a desk. There wasn't room for more than two large men or maybe three small women, so adding the cot to the room made it tight. On the desk was a basin of water and some washcloths. On the cot was a change of clothing for both of us and a couple of blankets and pillows. Other than these added luxuries, the whole plane was spartan. 'Cause, you know, military cargo and troop transport. The Hilton, it was not.

"It's not much, but we can wash the worst of the mud and grime off us, change clothes, and get a little rest. Got another five hours before we get home. I don't know about you, but I'm beat." I wanted her to understand I wasn't leaving her here by herself, but didn't want to be obnoxious about it. She might not want to admit it to anyone, including herself, but I know her well enough she needed me with her right now.

"Yeah." She picked at her clothing. She was smeared in mud, but I thought I could help her get the worst of it off. The trick was to take charge and do what needed doing without seeming like I was taking charge. That was the quickest way to get Holly to completely withdraw and push me away, and there was no way I was letting that happen. She sighed and looked over her shoulder. "Thanks for coming after me, Jax. I owe you one."

"I told you, Maddog. I'll always come for you. No questions asked. I will always be there." I tried to use the road name she and Blade had come up with to help her be strong for a little bit longer, but I knew she was done. She'd had all she could take.

Tears that had slowed now flowed freely again, but Holly still held on to her control. She was trying to fight me when she didn't really want to.

She put a washcloth in the basin and left it there. Then she pulled off her tank and stepped out of her shorts. Her shoes and socks followed, and she stood facing away from me in nothing but her bra and panties.

"I'd appreciate it if you'd help me wash the grime off my back. I'm tired and sore and I can't reach or see everywhere I need to get."

"Well, that went much easier than I thought it would." I gave her what I hope was an amused smile when I was more relieved than I was prepared to admit she needed my help.

"I can't very well have the road name Maddog if I'm too big a pussy to admit to someone I trust I need help when I do, now can I?"

I chuckled softly before leaning in and kissing her temple. The more I gave her little kisses like that, the more I had my lips on her skin in even the most platonic of kisses, the more I wanted to taste her lips, to slip my tongue into her mouth and taste her until she was whimpering with need in my arms. Unfortunately, now wasn't the time. Didn't mean I wasn't going to have the pleasure of holding her. I was going to wrap her up in my arms while she slept and keep the nightmares at bay. Because I knew from experience, the second she closed her eyes the nightmares would definitely come.

"Nope. If you're gonna have a name like Maddog, you have a certain reputation to maintain.

I'm proud of you for livin' up to your name, baby."

That got a genuine snort of laughter from her. Then she chuckled. It didn't last long, though. As I started washing her back, her chuckles turned to quiet sobs. I got the worst of the dirt and mud, then helped her put on the T-shirt Razor left for her. I reached under the shirt and unfastened her bra and helped her thread her arms through the straps and her sleeves. Holly didn't protest once.

I almost helped her into the soft cotton pants without having her remove her underwear, but I knew she had to be uncomfortable. They hadn't exactly been wallowing in mud, but it looked like she'd landed in a puddle at some point. So, without saying anything or making a big deal out of it, I faced her away from me and pulled her panties over her hips and let them pool at her feet. I used the cloth to wash her hip where she was starting to bruise. She must have landed on that side because she had dried mud from there to the top of her thigh. She winced once but didn't move or say anything. She didn't balk at my care of her, or the fact that I'd just removed her underwear without her permission.

When I wrapped my arms around her and held the pants in front of her, she took the material and stuck her feet into the holes. With a muffled groan of pain, she paused and gripped my wrist to steady herself. I didn't waste time or ask if she wanted my help. I pulled them up her hips and tied the drawstring in a bow at her belly button.

I did my best to keep my touch as clinical as I could. The very last thing I wanted was for her to feel like I was taking advantage of her vulnerable state of mind. I turned her to face me before I picked her up. She wrapped her legs around my waist, and I sat on the cot.

I reached for one of the blankets lying beside us and draped it over her before pivoting a quarter turn on my ass and resting my legs on the cot so I could fully recline with Holly draped over me. She lay her head on my chest and continued to cry softly until she finally drifted off to sleep with me rubbing her back in a gentle caress.

As I lay there holding her, another band of pressure released from my chest. Not only that, but a deep satisfaction filled me at having her in my arms like this. Wrath was right. I had loved Holly from the moment I saw her. It had taken time to develop into the love I felt for her now, but it had been there from the start. I had to figure out a way to keep her from pulling away from me, because now that I knew what it was like to have this woman sleeping so trustingly in my arms, I knew there was no way I could ever let her go.

Chapter Four

Holly

Raised voices penetrated my sleep fogged brain. I was alone, but my head rested on a surprisingly comfortable pillow and there was a blanket draped over me. The room was lit by only a couple of small markers at the base of the wall, like safety lights or something.

One of the voices was Chris. It took a couple of minutes, but once my head cleared somewhat I could make out what he was saying.

"We've been treated like dogs on this trip home," he snarled. "I demand you let me in there to get some rest. We'll all be going back to Rodadero to finish what we started, and I have to be ready." Yep. That was definitely Chris. Pompous, selfish asshole. And who in their right mind would turn around and go back into that hell? I knew I wasn't going. Fuck that shit.

I sat up on the cot and groaned. The walls must have been paper-thin, because Chris heard me.

"See? She's awake. Make her go back and sit with the others while I take a power nap. You can come get me when we're ready to land."

"Jesus Christ." I swore under my breath. "What a fuckin' pussy."

I didn't have on shoes, but a thick pair of socks were on my feet. I was dressed in a T-shirt that was a size or two too big and some soft, cotton pants. The pants fit loosely but weren't overly big on me. It took me a second to remember how I'd gotten changed. When I did, I sucked in a breath at the memory.

Jax had washed me off and helped me change. I'd told him to help, and he'd been so careful with me. I remember crying myself to sleep while lying on his chest. He'd held me in a protective embrace, rubbing his chin over the top of my head gently. I hadn't exactly had a restful sleep, but I doubt I'd have slept at all if not for Jax.

With an irritated sigh, I stood and jerked the door open. "There you go, Sir Whines-A-Lot. Get your beauty sleep. Looks like you need it." I shoved past the bastard and back to the passenger seats. Which… yeah. Military transport. Not exactly Air Force One, but the fucking prick should be glad we were on the aircraft at all. We could be fucking dead.

I sat next to the other women with us. The only people in our group I knew were Andrea and Chris. Chris could go fuck himself, but Andrea was the whole reason I was here. Even though this had been a clusterfuck of epic proportions, I was glad I'd been here because I knew Andrea needed someone, and it was obvious Chris didn't give a damn.

Andrea looked up at me when I sat next to her, then immediately looked down at her lap. "You told me not to do this." Her admission was soft. "This never would have happened if we'd stayed home."

"It would still have happened. Just not to us. Everyone else here would likely be dead or wishing they were." That's when I realized that the only men on the trip had been Chris and his bodyguard, and two other men, both of whom were killed in the attack. I think in the back of my mind I knew there were more women than men on this trip, but I'd been focused on other things.

"Chris says you're all going back to Rodadero."

Andrea gave me a funny look. "He said what?"

"Yeah. Before he demanded to have the room Jax let me use to clean up. He said he needed to rest before you guys headed back once we landed. Sounded like it was going to be a pretty quick turnaround." I was fishing. From the expression on Andrea's face, this was news to her.

"I'm not going back." Andrea shook her head violently. "He can't make me this time, either."

"Make you?" That surprised me. "I thought you wanted to go."

"I didn't want to go, but he said if I wanted to be with him, I needed to get used to international travel and charity work."

"He seriously told you that?" One of the other girls sitting near us questioned Andrea. "Those exact words?"

Andrea swallowed as comprehension washed over her. "He did."

"Me too."

"Me too."

"Fucker."

All the women on the plane other than me seemed to have been sold the same song and dance. And the motherfucker had been so cool and smooth, he'd managed to make it from South Carolina all the way to Rodadero, Columbia with every single one of them and no one knew the secrets he was keeping.

"What about you, Holly?" Andrea looked ashamed, but like she really wanted the answer to that question.

"You mean, did I betray you and try to take your boyfriend?"

She ducked her gaze then, her shoulders hunching. "I'm sorry I asked that question, Holly," she said softly. "I didn't mean it like that. Honestly." She took in a shuddering breath. "OK, that's not exactly true. I did mean it like that. But I swear, I've never thought you'd do that kind of thing. It never crossed my mind before this very moment."

"Relax, Andrea. I understand. You thought you had something real with Chris, and everyone else said he played them too. You're emotionally raw and still scared after everything. Wondering how I fit in is natural." I tried to give her a smile, but the very last thing I felt like doing was smiling. "I'm here because I knew something was up with Chris but couldn't put my finger on it. That's why I tried to talk you out of going on this trip."

"I should have listened to you." Andrea was crying now.

I waved her off. "The heart wants what the heart wants. What I can't figure out is what he planned to gain from taking all his girlfriends to Columbia. Together. *Or* why he welcomed me with open arms when I wasn't in his… err… circle." I almost said harem but knew it would only insult and alienate the women here. They were victims. Not polygamists. And Chris had played them like a fucking master. Which likely meant he'd done something like this before.

That's when Andrea started crying softly. I put my arm around her, trying to console her. She shook her head and pushed away from me, crying all the harder. "This is all my fault."

"Of course it's not your fault, Andrea. How could you know we'd be attacked like that? Besides, Chris has done this before. Whatever *this* is. You weren't looking for it. I knew something was off, but never imagined he had a dozen girls he was stringing along. But had I been as close to the situation as you were, I probably wouldn't have noticed either. He's a pro at manipulating women. Man needs to be castrated."

Instead of helping, my words seemed to make

Andrea cry harder. "You don't understand!" she wailed. "Stop being nice to me! I'm a horrible human being and don't deserve anyone to be nice to me, least of all you, Holly!"

"What?" My internal radar started going off, telling me to leave it alone. Unfortunately, I've always been too curious for my own good, even knowing that curiosity killed the cat. "Why would you say that? You're my best friend. I'm always going to have your back and, though I'm a first-class bitch and never nice to anyone, I'll never be horrible to you. Especially not now."

That seemed to make her cry even harder. She fell against me, her arms going around my neck in a tight embrace. I tried to comfort her, but now I was on guard.

One of the other girls sneered. "She's upset she knows she's caught." This girl had been sitting quietly in the corner, but she seemed to have had all she could take.

"Caught?" I glared at the other woman. "What the hell are you talking about?"

"She's the reason most of us are here." This came from another woman who sat huddled in the corner, her feet on the seat with her knees drawn up to her chest. "It's probably why Chris keeps trying to get off on his own, too."

Still sobbing, Andrea clung to me like her life depended on it. I was stunned and wasn't sure exactly what to say, but I knew I needed to hear it all, no matter how much I didn't want to.

"What's going on?" Jax approached us, a wary look on his face. His gaze landed on me first. Checking on me? Then he took in everyone and frowned. "What happened?"

None of the other women said anything. Even the two who had engaged earlier looked away, obviously not trusting Jax. Andrea continued to cling to me and sniffle, but stopped her loud weeping.

"I don't know," I said softly. "But maybe you better check on Chris."

Jax gave me a long, assessing look, then turned and headed back the way he'd come. Not long after, there was a banging on the door to the room Chris had taken over after I left.

"Open up, Alistair." I was relieved to hear Jax actively checking the situation. He might be an asshole, but Jax and I had a connection. It was like we were drawn to each other. No matter how many times I told him to fuck off, the annoying asshole was always there when I needed him. And me? No matter how many times I told him to fuck off… yeah. I always welcomed him with open arms. Eagerly.

"Andrea, please tell me what's going on." I turned and gripped her slim shoulders gently, pulling her away from me so I could get a good look at her face. When I did, I felt an overwhelming rage start to simmer in my mind. Despite all the weeping and wailing, Andrea's eyes were completely dry. Her makeup was as perfect as always.

I gasped, standing abruptly and taking two steps backward, away from the woman I'd called my best friend since grade school. I looked at the other women. The ones who'd spoken out, especially, gave Andrea looks of scorn, all but rolling their eyes. How had I not seen these looks before? Had they been there since the beginning of the trip? Had I missed some really strong anger there?

"I'm curious." The bold woman looked from me to Andrea a couple of times. "You hated Chris. You obviously didn't want him for a lover or partner, so why did you come with us?"

"I thought he was up to something. That he'd hurt Andrea. I came to have her back."

"Uh-huh. So she didn't encourage you to join us?"

"Well, yeah. She did. When I asked her not to go, she said I should come with her. That way I could see she was fine, and I'd get to help some really disadvantaged people. She knows I like to participate in projects that help people in poor communities. She said these people were about as poor as it got."

"She introduced most of us to Chris." The other woman picked up the explanation. "I thought it was odd there were so many people going when I'd thought it was going to be me and Chris alone. It wasn't until after we landed in Rodadero I started putting it together that my relationship with Chris wasn't everything I thought it was."

"I can't prove it and I have no idea how to explain it," the first woman interjected, "but I'd almost bet she and Chris set up that ambush. At least, they both knew it was coming before it happened."

"Razor, get that motherfucker out here before you really do have to explain to Cain how this bastard decided to jump out of the plane." Jax sounded angrier than I'd ever heard him.

"Shit," I muttered. I turned and headed toward Jax and the other guys. I thought I should probably stay with the women to offer as much support as I could. After all, we'd all gone through something horrific and come out traumatized, but physically unharmed. At least, most of us had. Besides, I knew that, wherever this conversation was headed, I needed to divert it for a little while. Like for at least a week. I needed time to heal both mentally and physically. Though I hadn't been hurt too badly, I was still going to be pretty Goddamned sore.

"Jax? What is it?" I went to his side. He put out an arm to keep me from getting near the door, but tucked me in behind him, holding me to him with one arm, urging me to press myself against his back.

"Motherfucker's locked himself in and refuses to open the door. Do you know what's goin' on?"

"Not sure. At least some of the girls think he might have been responsible for the attack on us."

He started, looking over his shoulder at me before turning around. "That's a pretty serious accusation."

"I know. And it might be all an attempt to get even with him, but something isn't right. Andrea was only pretending to cry a while ago. And the women who are talking for the group say Andrea introduced most of them to Chris. She actively pushed for them all to go on this trip. She pushed me too. Just passively."

"OK," Jax said, nodding his head. "Assuming they're right and he had something to do with the attack. What does he gain?"

I shrugged. "Bust in the fucking door and ask the bastard."

Razor grinned. "I always liked you, Holly. This is just one of many reasons why."

Jax bared his teeth at Razor and pulled me into his arms. "Mine. Don't even look at her."

Razor chuckled. "Lock her down if you want to keep her, man. She has enough of a vicious streak to make the perfect old lady."

"She knows I'm keepin' her. Had her property cut made when I made prospect."

"Uh, hello? I'm right here." I shoved away from

Jax, but he refused to let me go. I wasn't as torn up about it as I should have been. "Don't talk about me like you think I can't hear you."

"Wouldn't think of it, Maddog." Razor winked at me, and it was hard to keep the grin off my face, but I managed. Barely.

"I know you have no reason to suspect Chris had anything to do with the attack. Aside from being a shitty human being, I can't figure out how hurting everyone he brought on a private jet, including a congressional security detail, benefits him in any way. All I'm saying is, maybe Shotgun or someone should look into the trip. See if they can find any breadcrumbs leading off in a tangent."

"Do you want to call Shotgun? Tell him what you suspect and give him some details?" Jax spoke softly. Neither man continued to pound on the door to the room where Chris was hiding. It wasn't like he could go anywhere. He'd probably try to call someone if some kind of deal had gone south, or to have his daddy's lawyers meet us at the airport. But, unluckily for him, we weren't going to the airport.

"Yeah. I need to let my mom and dad know I'm OK, too."

"Wrath's been in constant contact with us since we left, so he knows." Jax stroked my cheek and smiled down at me. "But I know it'll be much better to hear your voice."

"I'd offer you the use of the conference room, but it seems to have been requisitioned by Senator Alistair's office." Razor's dry humor was almost welcome. I fought another grin.

"Well, I voted for the other guy," I quipped. "So unless the senator actually *did* hire ExFil to come get his son, tell that rat bastard he needs to sit out here with the women he played. If you give the green light, there's at least one of them who'd gladly change him from a rooster to a hen."

"Noted." Razor nodded to Jax. "You want to do the honors, or do you want me to?"

"I got this." Jax took one step forward and kicked the door to the small room so hard, the whole thing splintered off its hinges. The room wasn't supposed to be secure or anything, so the doors were pretty flimsy. I had no doubt the effect was what Jax was going for. If so, it sounded like Chris was suitably impressed if his screams were any indication.

"Now," Razor boomed, stepping in the doorway, his massive shoulders so wide he had to turn sideways. "Time to buckle in for landing." Razor snagged him by the arm, jerking Chris's cell phone out of his hand as he did. He glanced at the screen before putting the phone to his ear. He listened for a brief moment before speaking. "Sorry. Your son's a little busy right now. I'll have him call you back after we land." Razor ended the call and tossed the phone to Jax. "Might need this later."

"Hey! Gimme back my fucking phone!"

"What are you talking about?" Jax said, looking at him all innocent-like. "I didn't see no phone." He lifted his chain at Razor. "You seen one?"

Razor grinned. "Nope. Now, come on. Let's go sit over here. There's a nice seat waiting for you in the middle of some really beautiful women."

Chapter Five

Jax

"I've seen some stupid motherfuckers in my time, but this guy takes the fuckin' cake." I was watching Shotgun go through the files on Alistair's phone while we were still in the air. Holly had called Celeste and Wrath, both of whom had said nothing other than how happy they were that she was OK. They hadn't mentioned how worried they were or how stupid it had been of her to take off like she did, and I breathed a small sigh of relief. After that, she and Shotgun had discussed what she'd found.

Holly had gone to sit in the crew section while Shotgun and I looked this over. Shotgun because he was the Black Reign MC tech guy. Me because I wanted the information first, Goddamnit. If Wrath got this before me, he'd murder the man the second he stepped off the aircraft. Shotgun said the plane's sat connection was secure and not as slow as I might think, but he wanted to take more than a couple of hours to analyze the phone data. Working on this now might not speed things up, but it didn't hurt to try. We were less than an hour out, but we continued to comb through what we could. The more questions *and* answers we had before we had to interrogate the man directly, the better.

"Surely to God neither him nor the senator could be this fucking stupid. There's got to be a simple explanation." Shotgun sounded as perplexed as I felt. Thing was, I absolutely could believe this guy was that stupid.

"I mean, no one ever accused anyone in Washington of being smart. Right?"

"Humm… You have a point there. OK. So, if we

assume they *are* that stupid, is there any possibility we've interpreted this wrong? I mean, maybe the phrase, 'get top dollar for the bitches' could mean almost anything." Shotgun actually said that with a straight face.

"I want you, Eden, and anyone else you want to have eyes on it, to make sure this is legit, not some blackmail scheme or political entrapment or whatever bullshit they do in Washington to get and hold power. I want concrete proof, Shotgun."

The other man raised an eyebrow. "You givin' me orders, pup?"

"I'm lead in the field on this one, so yeah. I'm givin' you fuckin' orders." I kept my gaze leveled on Shotgun until the man burst out laughing.

"You're so full of shit. And a dumbass." Shotgun looked genuinely amused, not like he was calling me out for not showing respect for my elders. Which reminded me, I needed to apologize to him for that very thing. And phrase it that exact way. Should be fun. "You were trying to stare me down, bro."

When I continued to stare at him, he cracked up again. "Over a video call! Which means you're lookin' at my eyes, but you're really lookin' into the screen. Not the camera."

"I don't know how Eden puts up with you, man. Now I'm thinkin' you're the one who's stupid."

The other man grinned at me. "In all seriousness, Jax. Don't kill the fucker. In fact, stay as far away from him as possible. Let Razor babysit."

"You afraid I'd kill him?"

"Absolutely that's what I'm afraid of. Not that I care overmuch, but El Diablo will. You know he takes killin' seriously. And if these guys really are guilty of human trafficking, El Diablo gets to set and carry out their punishment."

"I can be as creative and diabolical as El Diablo." I winced. Because yeah, I sounded sulky.

"Not sure I'd bet on you there, Jax. Just get Holly as far away from that guy as possible."

I started to tell him I could absolutely get behind that plan when there was a bloodcurdling scream. Followed by several battle cries.

"The fuck was that?" Shotgun's eyes were wide. You comin' in hot?"

I hurried out of the little room to the main part of the plane and to where the women had been sitting in a group. Razor leaned against the bulkhead in front of the seating separating the passenger section from the crew section. In one of the seats, Chris Alistair was tied with his hands behind his back and his legs tied at the knees, spreading them as far apart as they'd go in his chair.

"Nothing." I shrugged. "The girls are having a, err, therapy session. Yeah. Therapy session."

"Great." Shotgun's dry tone and the roll of his eyes nearly made me grin. But I honestly didn't feel like it at the moment. And yeah. I knew the other man was trying to take the edge off my anger. "I'll let El Diablo know you guys are bring home a half-dead senator's son."

"You're assuming he'll be only half dead."

"Point." Shotgun gave me a little wave before ending the call.

I wasn't sure how much I trusted myself to be anywhere near Alistair at the moment, but I had to get Holly and make sure she was ready to face everyone when we landed. No doubt her mother and father would have some words. Wrath and Celeste would give Holly time to process, but I was feeling more than a bit protective of her.

With a shrug I went forward to the crew section. Fuck that little prick, Alistair. If the girls castrated him, so much the better. There were usually soldiers at the monitor banks, but this mission had been extraction only. This close to home, Mechanic kept up with the flight instrumentation and Razor would be back in the cockpit before they got ready to land.

Holly sat in one of the console stools. She was spinning around and round. Whenever she slowed, she'd push off with the workstation and start spinning again. I'd seen her do this same thing all the time at the bar in the compound. It always meant she was stressed about something. When she was little, it had been her cancer. Having childhood leukemia meant she'd grown up used to needles and medications and chemo treatments…

Part of the reason she'd caught my interest was because, when she first came to Black Reign, she'd given Wrath what-for when he and Celeste had been going through a rough patch after they'd first gotten together. The door to Celeste and Holly's room hadn't been fully closed, and I heard Holly's shrill little voice in the hallway. She'd said, "Don't you hurt my mommy again, or I'll get Blade to do surgery on you. He said if it hurt when I woke up, it would hurt even worse if he hadn't put the needle with the medicine in my arm to make me sleep." I'd only been a teenager, but even I could tell the child meant it, and she was fully confident Blade would do exactly what she described. That show of protection for her mother told me how much she loved Celeste, and how brave she was to stand up to a man as big and scary as Wrath. She'd been all of about four at the time, and already hell on wheels.

I was reluctant to say anything to break her concentration. She'd used to do this for hours. She said it was comforting. I didn't have to start the conversation, though. Holly did it all on her own, after she'd thought through what she wanted to say. It was her way.

"Turns out, Andrea wasn't as great a friend as I thought." She gave a self-deprecating snort but looked anything but amused. She kept twirling on the stool.

"Some people are shit, baby. Don't know what to tell you there."

"The whole reason I came on this stupid trip was to protect her." She stopped spinning, her hands gripping the workstation desk tightly. "I never guessed she might have her own agenda." She turned her head to meet my gaze then. "Did she know about the attack, Jax?"

"Lookin' that way, baby. Unless me and Shotgun are both wrong, it looks like she was eyeball deep in this shit. And believe me, it's shit. I'd say the senator and Chris are both lookin' at hard prison time, but this is the kind of stuff that gets people killed. Prison or not."

"Yeah. Not that I expect anyone to go to prison." She leveled me with a look. Yeah. This girl was definitely aware of how "Uncle El" dealt with problems like the Alistairs.

"You gonna be good with that?"

"With Chris? Yep. I won't lose a moment's sleep over that motherfucker."

"But you're upset over Andrea."

"She's been my friend for a long time. Even though I know in my heart she's a horrible person, I need to know the why of it. Maybe she was threatened. In which case, it's still not all right. But I'd rather she threw *me* under the bus than someone who didn't have people who cared about them and were willing to put a sophisticated GPS tracker in my phone and my watch, then send an expensive paramilitary plane to come get them."

"Dear Lord." I sighed, rolling my eyes. "Holly, it is not OK for you to wade into danger. That's what you have me for. Me and every man in the fuckin' club. You tell us, and we take the danger."

"I didn't know, Jax," she whispered, turning away from me. "I had a feeling, but that's it. I couldn't send in the cavalry based on a feeling. Besides, she's my best friend. I gave her my misgivings and she didn't share them. I was trying to protect her without causing problems for her."

"Hey. Look at me." She shook her head, but I stepped closer and gripped her chin gently and turned her head toward me. "Did you give me gray hairs with this stunt? Yeah. An abundance of them. I have a feeling it will always be like that with you. You were trying to protect a friend. While I wish you'd've gone to me or Wrath, I'm proud of you for protecting those you love. Just promise me that next time you'll come to me. OK?"

"I suppose I owe you that much. More, even. So, yeah. I'll make that promise."

I grinned. "Good." Then I brushed my lips over hers in a tender caress. It wasn't an aggressive or intense kiss, but the sensation nearly brought me to my fucking knees. Holly was perfectly still beneath me. She was sitting on a raised stool, but I still towered over her. She didn't resist, but didn't participate for several seconds.

As I was about to pull back and reassess the situation, Holly sighed and surrendered to me. Her hands went to my sides, and she pulled me closer to her. I framed her face with my hands and deepened the kiss, lapping at the seam of her lips until she opened her mouth to let me inside.

The taste of her was intoxicating, the scent of her hair, the feeling of her body against mine. My heart pounded in my chest, a quick staccato rhythm. I pulled away reluctantly but needed to make sure she was good with my kiss. I hadn't exactly asked her, though I knew Holly wasn't the type of woman to sit passively while a man assaulted her. Not even me. Especially not me.

Her eyes fluttered open, wide with surprise and what I hoped was desire. Her breathing came in shallow pants, her cheeks flushed with a rosy hue. The sight of her -- tousled hair, swollen lips, and bright eyes -- nearly undid me. With all the self-control I could muster, I stepped back slightly.

"That was, uh," she stuttered, searching for the right words. "Unexpected."

"Is it?" I smiled at her, my hand still caressing her cheek.

A small crease formed on her forehead as she tried to process what had just happened. She narrowed her gaze in concentration. When she looked up, she framed my face in her hands much like I had hers and leaned in to kiss me.

This time, our tongues danced together, exploring each other in a slow, rhythmic waltz. It was a sweet longing and surrender, of promises and a possession so acute, I had to keep myself from growling. The last thing I wanted to do was scare her.

Her hands threaded into my thick hair, gripping the strands in an almost spasming hold. She returned the kiss with equal passion and longing. I could almost believe maybe she felt the same way about me I felt about her. Did she? Could she see me as something other than an annoying, overprotective older brother? Because I stopped seeing her as my little sister years ago.

When I pulled back this time, Holly grunted her displeasure. I looked down into her upturned face to see her flushed cheeks and nearly glazed eyes. She seemed dazed, as if she couldn't quite believe what had happened but wasn't willing for it to end. At least, that's what I hoped she was feeling. God knew I was.

"Jax." She sighed my name, her eyes still wide and shocked. There was also what looked like a wildness blossoming inside her. I could see it plain as the nose on my face. One second she was simply dazed, the next she was locked on me. Like the prey had now become the predator. And, wouldn't you know it, that show of aggression made me hard as fuck.

Chapter Six

Holly

I knew I didn't want my first time with Jax to be like this. Not only did I want it to last longer than five minutes, but my dad would kill him and Jax wouldn't lift a finger to defend himself. That didn't stop me from imagining what it would be like. Jax at my back. Taking me like he'd die if he didn't. I wasn't ready for that, and now definitely wasn't the time…

"Get that look off your face, girl. Your body can't cash that kind of check." Jax stared down at me, a stern look on his face. Unfortunately, I saw the primal interest in his eyes.

"Why? You're thinking the same thing."

"Yep. But if I show that kind of disrespect to you, your mother would never forgive me." He gave me a sheepish grin. "And your father would kill me."

"Who says it's disrespectful when it's what I want?" I put my chin up. The thought wasn't as embarrassing as it probably should have been.

"Your dad says it's disrespectful when, A, it's our first time together, and B, when I haven't given you a property patch yet. Not saying I always agree with him on that, but with regard to you?" He chuckled and shook his head. "His opinion is the only one that counts."

I opened my mouth to argue, then realized how stupid it would sound. "You know, you're right. Not sure why I even thought about arguing the point."

"Good. Because once we get home, you and I need to have a conversation. Then, what you and me do willingly, in the privacy of our own home, ain't none of anybody's Goddamned business."

There was no way to stop the smile from curling

my lips when I felt like anything other than smiling. Anger. Sadness. Pain. Even grief. Jax had always had a way of making me smile even through all the chemo treatments and tests after my leukemia was in remission. If he couldn't make me laugh or smile, he pissed me off. Well, until he figured out it was easier to piss me off sometimes. When he did that, I toughed it out to spite him. It was over before I knew it.

"There's my girl. My little Holly Sweetness." Jax pulled me closer, wrapping me up in his arms tightly. There was no way for me to not snuggle into him. There were very, very few times in my life when I let him hold me like this. All of it revolved around being sick in one way or another. Only when I was at my very end did I allow it, and during those times, Jax was the only one I wanted.

"Did you know how much I needed you? When I was sick, I mean." I spoke softly, barely able to get the words out at all. "Sometimes."

"Yeah, baby. I didn't really understand it back then, and it was different than it is now, but yeah. I knew."

I trembled in his arms but clung so tightly I was afraid he'd call me out on how shaky I was. Then, to my utter horror, tears started to leak from my eyes in steady streams. I wanted to let him hold me, to use him as a human shield to hide me from the rest of the world like I used to when I was small. Jax deserved better than me using him, though. I wasn't going to sound like a wuss when I confessed my feelings though.

"Jax." I pushed back slightly. I still clung to his shirt, but I had to look at him when I said this. I needed to know his true feelings so I'd know how much trouble I was in. "I'm only going to say this once, so consider yourself warned." I took a breath. "I can't… pretend with you. I can't do casual. I can't even have any kind of romantic relationship with you, then lose you. I'm probably already too far gone because when I think about being scared, or in trouble, or in pain, the only person I've ever wanted to be with me is you."

He grinned, then opened his mouth, probably to tell me something like all he'd ever wanted was to be my rock to lean on or some equally sappy bullshit, but I cut him off. "I'm not even sure I could leave you now and walk away for good without leaving a huge piece of my heart behind. So you've got this one chance. We've known each other long enough to know if we can spend our lives together. Don't make a commitment if you don't think you can honor it. If you can't, put a fuckin' screeching halt to this… whatever it is, between us because if you decide a week from now or a month from now or a year from now that you want one of the club girls, I'll fuck you one last time. The second you come, when you let your guard down, I will fuckin' stab you in the kidney. Both kidneys if you don't make me come first." There. That sounded tough enough for the road name Maddog.

Jax blinked down at me in surprise. Then he grinned. "That's good to know." He pulled me back to him, squeezing me tight. "You've got nothin' to worry about, Holly Sweetness."

"That's the second time you've called me that. Only Uncle El calls me that."

"Have you noticed he does that with all our women? He gives each of them an endearment for a nickname."

"Yeah. I figured it was his way of showing affection."

Jax nodded. "In a way, I suppose. But, more

importantly, it's his way of reminding us how precious our women are to us all. I learned that lesson well the first time I sat with you after a chemo treatment when you were five."

"You were nearly an adult. Why were you spending so much time with me when you should have been out drinking and getting laid?"

That got a bark of laughter from Jax, real merriment dancing in his eyes. "God, Holly. Don't ever fuckin' change."

"I'm just sayin'! Why did you give up so much of your time to stay with me? Especially when I was so awful to you." I kind of felt bad about that. "Still am awful to you."

"It's your love language." Jax gave me a big smile. "And I'm not too proud to admit I like goading you. Besides, when you fought me, it kept you too busy to cry."

I wasn't sure exactly how I expected Jax to respond, but this wasn't it. My first instinct was to scowl at him but it didn't last, and the tears came even harder. Jax closed his arms around me, surrounding me with… him. He murmured softly to me, rubbing my back occasionally with one big palm.

"I thought you were angry with me." I blurted out my worries without thinking. "Before. When you found us during the fight."

"Why would you think that, baby?" He didn't loosen his hold or even let me pull away. Instead, he tightened his hold on me and actually lifted me. I let out a soft whimper but wrapped my legs around him. He carried us back to that small room. The crew area was beyond the half wall, a long aisle separating left and right with canvas chairs along the walls. I caught sight of Chris and Andrea. Chris was in pain, and

Andrea looked scared. Her gaze met mine and she started "crying" again. Probably with no messy tears and snot like before. Thankfully, the moment didn't last and Jax kicked the broken door so that it blocked most of the opening, separating us from the chaos of my life on the outside.

"I… Because…" God, I hated feeling this fragile! I'd been doing OK until I saw Andrea again. She'd utterly played me. I still didn't know exactly what the plan had been, and wasn't sure I wanted to. It made me doubt my judgment. Specifically, it made me wonder why a man like Jax would want someone like me long term. And I told him the stark truth. I couldn't have him only to lose him. Losing him would destroy my heart.

"Honey, I can't understand why you'd think I was angry if you don't tell me what made you feel that way."

"You didn't seem to… You pushed me away and…"

"Christ, honey," He sat on the cot, his back to the wall, urging me to straddle his hips. He still held me close, like he didn't want to let me go.

"I know you were trying to protect me, looking for more of those fuckers, but it still felt like a rejection, so it's not you. It's me."

"Baby, your feelings matter. Especially after what you just went through."

"Jax, my whole life has been about my feelings. Mom tried so hard to make sure I had everything I wanted, especially when I was sick. Then she met Wrath and we got Grandmama and Pop Pops and everyone doted on me. I'm not too proud to admit I was a spoiled brat. This whole trip has been about what I wanted. I was so busy trying to prove to myself

I could do anything I wanted, I never stopped to consider how everyone I loved would feel if something happened to me. My bruised feelings are my own problem. You did exactly what you had to do, and I'll never be able to thank you enough." I was babbling now, but once I started, I wasn't able to stop. "I feel so selfish, Jax! I'm so fuckin' sorry!" And there went the tears and snot.

Jax held me tight. I thought he whispered softly to me, trying to take as much of my pain as I'd give him, but I wasn't sure. It didn't really matter. His voice was comforting, like it had been all my life. He let me get everything out, never hurrying me or telling me I had to get myself under control. Like always, Jax was incredibly patient with me.

When all I had left in me was a few hiccups and sniffles, Jax brushed my hair away from my face and urged me to look up at him. "This is what we need to talk about, baby." He gave me a smile before leaning in to give me a gentle kiss. He brushed my cheek, then my lip before kissing me once more. "I am angry with you. I'm angry with you for not trusting me enough to tell me why you had to go. I'd have come with you if you'd told me the second you knew you were going. I'd have found a way home sooner. Even not knowing, I was on my way home to go with you, baby. But, more than anything, I'm angry with myself for not making you understand you could always count on me to have your back. No matter what."

"Do you promise?"

"On my life, Holly Sweetness. On my fuckin' life."

Chapter Seven

Jax

Mechanic landed the big Osprey in the courtyard of the Black Reign MC compound. We were met by every patched member and old lady who were in the compound. Wrath and Fury were the first two on the aircraft.

"What the fuck happened, Jax?" My dad, Fury, wasn't angry, just genuinely curious. "You and Holly good?"

"We're not hurt, sir."

My dad gave me an impatient look. "You don't have to be so formal with me."

"No, sir. But If I practice with you, maybe I won't forget my manners with Wrath." I tried to keep the grin from my face but failed miserably.

"Good plan, pup." Wrath huffed out an irritated grunt but slapped me on the shoulder good-naturedly. "Being your father-in-law is gonna be so much fun. Especially since I'm gonna insist you call me *sir*. All the fuckin' time." The big bastard grinned but looked like he was only half joking. "Now, where's my daughter?"

I jerked my head toward the shut door. "We had some… developments."

"Yeah." Fury looked past us where the other women and Alistair were. The women had beat the shit outta the man for the better part of an hour. He was somewhat the worse for wear but I doubt he'd be complaining about how he got beat up by a bunch of women for a variety of infractions, not the least of which looked like trafficking. He wasn't the kind of man to appreciate a strong woman, or any woman at all really. Especially if she fought back. "Heard you rolled up on an attack. How many killed?"

I shrugged. "Not exactly sure. Some of the women didn't even realize they were all together. I'm tellin' you, this kid did a real good number on all of them."

"Holly too?" Wrath was all business now.

"Yes, but not in the same way. And it wasn't Alistair who played her. It was Andrea."

Wrath's gaze narrowed and he let his gaze track to the other women in the back. I saw the moment his gaze locked on Andrea. It was a predator's stare, the kind you saw right before he nabbed his prey. "I'll be right back."

I snagged the other man's arm and stepped in front of him. "Not now, Wrath. Talk to Holly first. Reassure her you're not angry with her. Coddle her for a while, then we'll deal with this. Andrea and Alistair aren't going anywhere."

"Where's my Holly Sweetness?" El Diablo and his wife, Jezebel, hurried up the ramp in back of the aircraft, the anger and worry in El Diablo's voice echoing inside the aircraft. Mechanic hadn't unlocked the back hatch immediately after landing to make sure Chris Alistair didn't get out of the aircraft with one of the women, hoping we'd leave him alone and not risk hurting an innocent. We wouldn't, but we'd also never let him leave this place until we knew exactly what part he'd played and doled out a punishment to fit the crime. We just happened to believe the best defense was a good offense. Keeping Alistair contained meant he couldn't hurt anyone else in the compound. Of course, in the shape he was currently in, I doubted he was able to do much.

The fact El Diablo hadn't entered at the forward hatch of the aircraft with Wrath and Fury meant he intended to go in from the aft cargo hatch. Any question as to whether or not Shotgun had kept our president up to date on the information he was getting from Alistair's phone was answered as he passed the man in question. As El Diablo approached Chris Alistair, he lashed out, crushing Alistair's nose with the heel of his hand in one hard, vicious strike. Unfortunately, he didn't knock the man out with the blow.

Alistair screamed, covering his nose with his hands. Blood poured through his fingers and dripped onto his lap. All the women hurried down the ramp except Andrea. She was closer to the front of the aircraft, a couple seats up from Alistair. She had her eye on El Diablo -- who didn't spare her even a dirty look -- and completely overlooked Jezebel. I doubted it was a mistake Andrea would make again. I could have told her she was fucked either way. Jezebel was more bloodthirsty than El Diablo, and she had no qualms about hitting a woman. As was proved when she landed a hard, open-handed slap to Andrea as Jezebel passed her. Andrea whimpered, but didn't say anything in her own defense. Which was probably a good thing, since anyone could see Jezebel wasn't in the mood for it.

Holly chose that moment to open the door. She gave Andrea only a passing glance before looking away. I saw the pain in her eyes. No doubt everyone else could see it too. She gave El Diablo a small smile before going to Wrath. "I'm so sorry to have worried everyone."

Wrath didn't hesitate to enfold her in his arms. Celeste shoved her way onto the plane at the front where her husband and my father had boarded, then she hugged Holly from behind. Effectively, Wrath and Celeste surrounded Holly with their love where no one could get to her or hurt her anymore. All three of them stood there, clinging to each other. Wrath didn't even try to hide the moisture shining in his eyes.

"Your mother was worried, honey. We're both really glad you're back home safe and sound."

"*Mom* was worried, huh?" Holly chuckled through her tears.

"Yeah. She was." Wrath sounded gruff as usual. If his voice was a little scratchy… well. It was dusty where the Osprey kicked up dirt when we landed.

"Tough guys don't worry?" She was obviously trying to put her father at ease, but I knew Wrath could hear the distress in her voice because he squeezed her tighter.

"Yeah. Tough guys worry too, kiddo. At least this one does. You, your mother, and your sisters are my entire world. I know you're not supposed to have favorite children, but you've got a special place in my heart no one else can touch, Holly." Wrath cleared his throat. "Might have been because you were sick when I met you, but I'm pretty sure it was more the way you busted my balls for hurtin' your mom's feelings. Even at four years old, you didn't let me get away with shit. Your sisters think I'm always right and never question anything I do, but you always keep me honest."

That got a startled laugh from both Holly and Celeste. "You're so full of shit," Celeste said through a watery smile.

"What? They do! Just ask them. They never tell me I'm wrong or that I'm too overprotective, or that they want to date boys or some shit. They are my precious angels, and they love me as much as I love them."

"No doubt about that last part, Daddy." Holly smiled up at her dad. It was a genuine smile, even though there was still a world of pain in her eyes. She was enjoying this brief respite from the dumpster fire this day had been. "They manage you," Holly said, patting Wrath on the chest in commiseration. "That way they can do whatever they want, and you don't even realize they're not where they're supposed to be."

"They do not." Wrath sounded scandalized, even gave Holly a fierce scowl like she'd affronted his dadhood or something.

"Hate to break it to you, honey," Celeste chimed in. "But she's right. I tried to tell you early on, but you wouldn't listen."

Wrath narrowed his gaze, looking from one of them to the other. Several times. Slowly, his face morphed from irritated, to confused, to stunned realization. "Well, I'll be Goddamned."

"Yep." Celeste urged Holly closer to Wrath and steered them toward the front of the plane. Obviously, she didn't want any issue with Andrea or Alistair and likely knew exactly what Wrath knew. I was sure Wrath was very aware of what his wife was doing. In fact, I'd bet that whole conversation had been staged to lead her in the direction her parents wanted her to go, both physically and mentally. Keep her distracted and she'd be less likely to panic. Just like when she was a kid.

I let Celeste lead Holly away, knowing I needed to meet with El Diablo and Shotgun to decide what was going to happen next. Wrath stayed. Probably because he wasn't sitting by and let everyone else punish the people who'd hurt his daughter. Everything inside me told me to follow Holly, but I knew she'd be safe with her mother until I could get this straightened out. Hell, she probably needed time with her mother to get a better perspective on… well, many things. But most of all, me. Above all, I had to have the blessing of her mother and father to make my claim valid. That was going to take them being certain I was who Holly wanted.

"What the fuck do you think you're doing?" El Diablo marched toward me, a look of utter fury on his face. Wrath closed in on the other side of me. Same look.

"El Diablo…" My dad, Fury, stepped between me and our president. I think it was pure instinct on his part and, even though I trusted El Diablo with my life, and, more importantly, Holly's life. If he and Wrath were getting ready to throw me a beating, I wanted to know what I'd done to screw up. You know. So I didn't make the same fuckup again.

"What'd I do?" I was a grown-ass man in my thirties, but I felt like a green prospect under El Diablo's displeasure.

"Get your ass inside the clubhouse and get my Holly Sweetness settled, asshole," he snapped, using Holly's nickname for me, likely on purpose. El Diablo could certainly come up with more creative derogatory names to call me than asshole.

"I wanted to check in with you and Shotgun first. Once I shut myself in a room with Holly, I don't intend to leave it until we have a plan firmly in place for the two of us. She has more grieving to do, and I intend to let her get it all out. No matter how long it takes. She knows I won't be long." Now that I knew what the problem was, I was totally throwing both him and Wrath under the bus. "Unlike some people on this aircraft, I've been as straightforward with my woman as I can be about my activities and why and how long I intend on being away from her. Only misunderstanding we've had was in me not recognizing how my feelings for her changed over the years. She didn't realize I no longer saw her as a kid sister, and I didn't explain because I wasn't sure she was ready."

El Diablo glared at me for long moments. "Show-off." Was it possible for him to sound equal parts disgruntled and proud?

"Yeah. Agreed." Wrath gave me a sheepish grin as he scrubbed the back of his neck. "I'd tell you not to tell Celeste what happened, but I know you well enough to know that's a futile request."

I chuckled. "Hey. I may be an asshole, but I'm not a dumbass. I learned from your and El Diablo's mistakes. Mainly because I make enough of my own without repeating someone else's. Your secret's safe with me. You know. Unless I need leverage." There was no way to keep the grin off my face.

"That's my boy." Fury clapped me on the shoulder, sharing a proud smile with me. I'd only gotten to know my dad over the last eight or so years but I kinda felt like this one moment was when me and my dad finally came together as father and son.

He met my gaze. I was fairly certain I saw a sheen of tears in his eyes. I grinned. "Rotor dust can be a bitch when it gets into your eyes, old man."

"Fuckin' allergies," Fury grumbled, but still smiled at me like the proud father I'd been determined to make him when I first came here to live with him after my mother died.

"Sure, allergies." I smirked back at him. The banter was a welcome relief from the tension of the past few hours. It wouldn't last long, but I needed the break before going into this meeting with the officers of my club. We all shared a quick chuckle before sobering.

I sighed, knowing this was gonna be messy. I was simultaneously looking forward to the carnage about to ensue next, and dreading coming back to Holly with blood on my hands. I knew she'd be OK with it, but I still didn't like it. "Nothing like this shit should ever fuckin' touch her." The muttered comment came out before I could censor it.

Turning back to El Diablo, I scrubbed a hand over my face, suddenly wearier than I could ever remember being. "So, what now?"

El Diablo flashed a small grin, his dark eyes burning into mine, and I knew whatever he and Shotgun found left him little doubt how to continue. "First things first -- we need to figure out what the hell Alistair's game is. How deep does this betrayal go?"

"And does his father know about it?" I was remembering the conversation Chris Alistair had had earlier. "Little punk called his old man about halfway through the flight home. I figured he'd called to complain so his daddy could ruin our lives and shit. Could have been something more to it."

I half expected everyone to tell me I was crazy, but they all looked deadly serious. "Did Holly say anything about it?"

"No. I don't think she suspected anything like this. All she knew was that she had a bad feeling about Chris and Andrea wouldn't listen to her. So, she made herself her best friend's protector."

"Why was she there?" Wrath stroked his short beard in agitation. "Why did she insist on going on this trip in the first Goddamned place? Then not tell me or her mother? I'm upset she ran off on her own and tried to hide it from me, but I'm more upset that she didn't come to me if she thought something was off with this guy."

"Already talked with her about that." Even though I knew Wrath would rather chew off his own arm than say anything to intentionally hurt Holly's feelings, I was feeling super protective of her at the moment. A combination of her running away from me straight into danger and the newness of our romantic relationship. And I can't believe I even thought the word *romantic*. That alone could get my man card revoked. "She said all she had was a feeling and that she didn't want to call out the big guns until she knew for sure there was an actual problem."

"Sounds like Holly." Wrath met my gaze.

"And before you ask, I've already made sure she knows to bring things like that to one of us in the future. I'll go a step further and tell her to keep going to someone in the club until she gets someone to listen and help her investigate until she's satisfied she has the answers she's looking for."

Fury smirked, lifting his chin at me. "Always knew you were smarter'n this lot."

El Diablo clapped me on the shoulder. "He's always been perfect for our little Holly Sweetness." He glanced back over his shoulder. "Rycks and Warlock have secured a, shall we say, safe area for these two." He indicated Chris and Andrea.

"My… father… will ruin… you." Chris Alistair was beaten and bloodied. I'm pretty sure his testicles were singing a very sad song. More than one of the women had been slightly disgruntled at how he'd played them.

"Senator Christopher Alistair the Second won't be interested in fighting me for anyone. Even his own son." El Diablo's mocking chuckle let me know exactly what was going to happen to Christopher Alistair the Third.

Alistair smirked -- or tried to. He wasn't in shape to spar with anyone. Verbally or physically. "My dad will do anything to protect me."

"He won't protect you from this. Not if he wants to continue his cushy life as a United States Senator." El Diablo gave the man a false sympathetic look. "I'm afraid having his son disappear on a relief mission to Columbia plays far better in the news than having him imprisoned for human trafficking."

"Just because I have a few girlfriends doesn't mean I was trafficking them." There was still the ghost of a smile on his lips. "Besides, I'm sure this will all have disappeared by the time my dad gets here. He'll take me home and yell at me a little, then I'll have to behave for a few months."

"Hmm..." Fury raised an eyebrow. "Maybe bring Archangel in to question him? Sounds like there's a pattern of bad behavior here."

El Diablo waved him off. "Archangel will be especially valuable in questioning Andrea, but there's really no need for him to talk with this one. Unless Shotgun finds something compelling on his phone to explain this to my satisfaction, there's nothing he could say to justify what we've found so far." He shrugged. "We'll give it a few days. See if Shotgun and Eden find anything that tells them the phone data was manufactured in any way. Until then, we'll see to it Mr. Alistair here has the best accommodations."

"You're bluffing." Alistair looked from El Diablo to me and back. I hadn't said anything to the motherfucker, so I had no idea why he was looking at me.

"About what?" El Diablo's crisp British accent made him seem more civilized than he actually was, but that was all part of the mystique that was El

Diablo.

"You can't keep me here. I have rights." He was sounding stronger now. Probably because there was just that inkling of doubt. El Diablo was good at this kind of warfare. Mental torture. There was no doubt Alistair was guilty. El Diablo wanted to ferret out everyone Alistair knew to be involved in the supply chain. Once he did, he'd destroy them all. I wasn't being dramatic, either.

"All evidence to the contrary." El Diablo smiled brightly. "I can honestly say that I'm not sure I've ever looked forward to an interrogation more." The bastard sounded cheerful.

Samson and Tank walked up the ramp, both of them looking grim. "Got a place all picked out for 'em." Tank and Samson were both big motherfuckers. If nothing else, their sheer size was a deterrent against shenanigans. Samson spoke for both of them since he was the vice president for Black Reign.

"Ah, good." El Diablo rubbed his hands together in glee. "You and Tank see Mr. Alistair to his new accommodations. Me and my lovely wife will escort Miss Andrea."

"I'm not going anywhere with you," Andrea spat out.

Jezebel grinned. "Sure you are. Only question is, will you be coming conscious or unconscious?"

Andrea shook her head, looking at each of us, her gaze resting on me. "You can't let them do this to me. I'm Holly's best friend."

"Why do women always think those big, pleading, doe eyes will get them anything they want?" I frowned at Andrea. "You're not Holly's friend, Andrea. You lost the right to claim that protection when you helped your boyfriend hurt her."

"But I didn't mean for anything to happen."

"You didn't mean..." I took a step toward Andrea. Woman or not, I was about to beat the shit outta her.

Jezebel stepped between me and Andrea. I thought she might have pushed me back or warned me to not hit the woman. Instead, she lashed out herself, landing another open-handed slap across Andrea's face. "Now." Jezebel smiled down at the other woman like they were having a pleasant conversation. "You're going to come with me. We're going to have a talk. It's not going to be pleasant and you're not going to enjoy it. But you will give me what I want, or I'll see to it what was going to happen to Holly, happens to you."

"You can't do that!" Andrea looked more than a little scared but still defiant. "You're lying to get me to cooperate."

"Oh, you're going to cooperate." Jezebel practically purred her words. "The only question is how long it takes to break you. Now personally, I'm looking forward to the task. I'm not sure you're going to feel the same way. Oh!" Jezebel grinned as though she had a big surprise and had almost forgotten to tell the other woman. "Shotgun found out the cartel leader you promised your... merchandise... to put out a capture order on you and your lovely boyfriend. They'd like to know what happened. Also, there was something about showing the greedy Americans what happens when they cross *La Familia Rosa*."

Andrea paled and shook her head, fear etched in every line on her face. "Do you know what they'll do to me?"

"Yep. Absolutely. You might want to consider what they'll do to you, too, baby girl." Jezebel grabbed Andrea's upper arm and forced her to her feet.

"Because what they will do is a bit tepid compared to what I'm gettin' ready to do." She gave Andrea a wicked smile. "You think about all the horrible things you imagine they would have done to you and multiply by... oh, say five. Ten, if you piss me off further." Jezebel's expression hardened, and I began to understand now why she and El Diablo were so perfect together. "No one messes with my family and gets a happy ending. Every person inside these walls is my immediate family. My brothers and sisters. My children. My husband. The people in the city around us are my extended family. You're in deep shit for what you did to young women and children in the community. For what you did to Holly, the rest of your life will be miserable and way too long, and if you don't understand what that means, you soon will. When the miserable part starts."

Andrea sobbed loudly as Jezebel dragged her off the plane with a handful of the other woman's hair to a waiting Explorer. Hardcase was driving while Iron was in the passenger side. He got out and opened the back door for Jezebel who, instead of going around to the other side and getting in, shoved Andrea over and pushed her way inside the vehicle next to Andrea.

El Diablo's lips thinned into a hard line. "My lovely Jezebel is feeling a bit vicious this afternoon." After several seconds as he seemed to think about something, a slow, eager smile spread across his face. "I love it when she gets vicious."

"And that's my cue to get my jump kit ready." Fury turned and headed to the door. "Go see to Holly, Jax. I'll call you when I'm ready to leave for the interrogation. You can ride with me and Noelle." Fury was the club doctor. During intense interrogations, he was called on to keep their subject alive. Sometimes it worked, others not. Fury told me once the theory was, if they didn't need to be taken apart, El Diablo wouldn't take them apart. I hadn't really understood what he'd meant back then. I believed a person needed to think for themselves and not blindly follow orders. Now, I realized no one in Black Reign MC was blindly following El Diablo. They trusted their president to do the right thing because he'd proven time and time again he wanted what was best for the members of Black Reign. Not just the club in general, but the individual men, women, and children within the compound walls. They trusted him to say someone needed to be tortured because he'd earned their trust. So yeah. Dad was going to be OK with what was about to happen. I was too.

But first, I needed to go to Holly. El Diablo was also right that I didn't need to spend any more time away from her than strictly necessary. Now, it wasn't necessary.

Even given the gravity of everything that had happened in the last twenty-four hours, there was a lightness in my soul. Holly… was mine. She always had been. I just hadn't grown into my feelings and neither had she. She was right. We knew way more than enough about each other to make a definitive decision about our future together. And I knew without a doubt there was no future for me without Holly in it.

Chapter Eight

Holly

Mom took me to her and Dad's house in the big compound that was Black Reign MC. I'm not really sure why they wanted to be called a motorcycle club other than that Uncle El, as I'd called him since I was four, liked to pretend to be normal. I suppose being known as an MC was better than being thought of as a bunch of rich people doing shady shit. While the latter might be more easily overlooked, I always had the feeling El Diablo liked looking the part of a leader of rough and rowdy bikers. He was essentially thumbing his nose at conventionality and inviting law enforcement to keep an eye on the club. Probably because he liked watching them try to puzzle out what the fuck was going on and not being able to figure it out. The truth was, Black Reign MC had more money and resources at their disposal than some small countries. All thanks to El Diablo.

Wrath, my father, was also District Attorney for Palm Beach County. As such, there was no way anyone was touching Black Reign from a legal standpoint. My mother met Vincent "Wrath" Black when I was four. I didn't know the whole story, but the end result was my mother didn't have to work two or three jobs to pay for my medical care. Didn't mean I hadn't given him shit. Even as a young kid I was full of piss and vinegar. Mostly, I think I'd wanted to see how far I could push him. The answer was pretty Goddamned far.

When he and my mother married, he'd adopted me the same day. Being a big-shot lawyer tended to pave the way, I guess. That *and* having access to a really good computer guy. I'd never known my biological father. As far back as I could remember, it was always Wrath. He was the only father I'd ever known, and he'd been a great one. My little sisters had him wrapped around their fingers as much as I did, but they were sneaky about it. I never cared if he knew what I was doing or not. He'd proven to be incredibly patient and caring with me, my sisters, and of course, my mother. *Especially* my mother. The only time he and I had ever had words was when I was a smart-mouthed teenager and I'd said something to hurt my mother's feelings. I got it now. Sometimes, a woman needed her man to have her back, even with her own children.

Mom shut the door behind us, and I let her lead me to the bathroom. My father hadn't followed us home yet, but I knew he'd be here soon. Probably with Jax right behind him.

"I'm so sorry, Mom," I said as a tear tracked down my cheek. "I know how much you and Dad love me and knew you would worry. I don't know why I plowed on without even talking to you guys about what was going on."

"Honey, Jax explained it. And I get it, baby. I do. What I hate is that I didn't make you feel like you could come to me or your father about stuff like this. We'll always have your back and take your concerns seriously. Wrath would have been happy to check into this guy for you. I hope you know that."

"I do. But I also know Dad. He'd have sent an army with me, but only as far as the nearest black site he knew of to interrogate and torture Chris. Then they'd have packed me and Andrea up and carted us home." I winced as I said Andrea's name and a fresh flood of tears slid from my eyes.

"I'm so sorry, sweetheart."

"No." I was firm in my denial. "Don't feel sorry for me about Andrea. She played me. I was blinded by my loyalty to her and never once considered she was doing something shady with Chris." I shook my head. "I don't even know for sure either of them was doing anything. I mean, we suspected, and I know Jax got Chris's phone data to Shotgun, but everything else is just speculation right now."

"We can talk about this after you get a shower. I know you're a grown woman and I'm not trying to baby you, Holly, but I'd feel better if I was in here with you in case you fall." Mom gave me a small, unsure smile, and I knew she needed this. She was right that I didn't want my mother to be in the bathroom with me while I showered, but having company in my bathroom was a small price to pay to ease my mother's worry. God knew she'd worried enough about me over the years.

"Thanks, Mom. It's probably best to have someone close. I'm dirty, hurt, and exhausted. Not taking a shower isn't even an option, and a bath would be gross."

"I love you, baby." She was tearful but smiling. "I'm so glad you weren't seriously hurt. You're my world."

"I love you too, Mom." I looked at the floor and took a breath. "Are you..." I looked back up at her, needing to see her immediate reaction to my question. "Will you be OK with me and Jax being together?"

I needn't have worried. Mom had always liked Jax. Especially when she'd seen him interact with me when I was so sick. "Holly, I've known since you were in your teens you'd claim that man for your own. I hated it when you were that young, but he kept you at arm's length. Probably for that very same reason. He was a man. You were a teenager. Jax is many things, but he's not a creep. He was never anything but appropriate with his care of you. He's had my respect for a very long time, Holly. So yeah. I'm going to be fine with it." When my mother genuinely smiled, there was nothing more beautiful. She'd always been that way. It wasn't so much her looks as her inner light. My mother had walked through hell and back when I was sick. She'd done anything she had to, to make sure I had the medical care I needed.

"It's important to me that you approve. Dad too. I… Sometimes, I think with my heart too much. Living in the moment is something I guess is ingrained in me after being so sick as a kid. I never subscribed to the mentality that if a guy picked on you, then he liked you. But when Jax picked on me, it was never malicious or hurtful. He was trying to get a rise out of me. Looking back, I know it was his way of distracting me. He'd do it over and over until I cried."

Mom gasped, a look of horror on her face. "He did what?"

"No! Mom! It's not like that!" I took Mom's hand in mine and gripped it hard. "Jax knew that, once I started crying, it was time to stop picking at me because I'd gone past the point of any kind of distraction being able to hold me together. He knew that, when I stopped fighting him, I was ready to be held. And that's what he did."

I was afraid Mom might not believe me or accept my explanation, but my description was accurate. And it was exactly how it had to be. I'd never have surrendered to Jax. I couldn't let him beat me. Jax knew what I could accept. He and Fury and Noelle had been the ones to teach me that even strong fighters get tired. Your muscles need a brief rest period after intense contraction when working hard. Your mind was the same way. Both needed a brief rest occasionally, and sometimes my body quit before my mind could. He called the times when he had to hold me "end of round two" since there were typically three rounds in an MMA fight. Noelle had been a fighter and Fury her trainer. Jax learned it from them, and held me to it the best way he could.

Instead of not believing me, my mother nodded and looked thoughtful. "I think I understand a lot of things more clearly now. And why during the worst of it, the only person you wanted was Jax."

"I'm surprised you figured it out. Instead of telling you I wanted him, I'd make up something horrible he'd done to me earlier." I smiled at the memory. It was a dark, miserable time in my life, but my relationship with Jax had been forged in those fires. And the fires had been so very hot.

"And I'd go tell your father to make him come apologize to you." She grinned, wiping a tear from her cheek. "You demanded I get your father to bring Jax to apologize that first time when I asked you what you wanted to happen. After that, I knew what to do."

"I've loved him my entire life, Mom. That love evolved over time as I matured, but I can't imagine my life without him in it."

"You don't have to convince me, honey. To be honest, Jax is the only man I could ever see me or Vincent giving our blessing to. If he's your choice, he's earned our blessing many times over. As long as he treats you right and takes care of you, I'll never say a bad word against him."

I couldn't help but chuckle. "Mom, he brought an Osprey and a paramilitary unit to my rescue. I'm not sure it's possible for anyone to take better care of me than Jax."

"Fair point."

I took my time in the shower while Mom chatted lightly with me. It was exactly what I needed. Her voice had always soothed me. She had a way of knowing the perfect amount of conversation and when it was time to keep it light or when we could discuss harder realities. By the time I'd washed myself thoroughly and let the hot water pound on some of my sore muscles, I was so tired I was practically asleep on my feet.

I'd never been able to have long hair as a child. Thankfully, after I'd gone into remission my hair had grown back nice and healthy. Once it had, I'd refused to cut my hair again. Now I was rethinking that decision. It was long and thick. Without help from a blow dryer, it would take hours to fully dry. I wrapped a towel around my head. I'd figure it out later. Right now, I wanted to find Jax. I also had to talk to my dad before I left, but I needed Jax more and more with each breath.

Mom helped me into a pair of athletic shorts and an oversized T-shirt before we left the bathroom. The second I stepped into the living room, I automatically looked for Jax.

He was sitting on the couch with my dad. Both men were deep in soft conversation. When they spotted us, they both stood. Wrath went to my mom and put his arm around her while Jax came to me.

Instead of pulling me into his arms, he steadied me at arm's length before bending to pick up a shallow box. He opened it and urged me to pick up the contents.

"My property cut?"

"Yeah, sweetheart. If you'll have me."

"You know I will, Jax." I threw myself at him, needing to be in his arms. I lost the towel, but it didn't seem to matter. Jax hugged me, wet hair and all. When I finally let him go, he helped me into my cut before lifting me into his arms. I put my legs around his waist and clung to him. I knew there were things that needed saying, especially with my dad, but I couldn't right now. It was obvious Wrath and Jax had worked it out since Dad didn't voice his objections. I'd trust everything was fine.

"Razor's gonna take us to the little house in the middle of the property. It's not far from you guys and was just finished. El Diablo said to take it if we wanted. Thought we could try it out. See if Holly likes it."

"I like you, pup," Dad said, leveling a look at Jax. "But you only get one shot at this. You break her heart, I cut yours out with a rusty knife."

Jax gave my dad a solemn nod. "On my life, Wrath. I'll protect her heart, body, and soul."

"Dad?"

"Yeah, baby." He stroked the back of my head, and I looked up from where my face had been pressed against Jax's neck.

"I'm sorry I left without telling you anything. I'm so sorry." I needed Dad to understand I knew I'd fucked up.

"We'll talk about it later. I'm not mad. I promise. I'm just happy you're home safe. If Jax ain't good to you, you come get me and I'll take care of everything." He kissed my temple. "You'll always be my baby girl, Holly. Nothing will ever change that, or how much I love you. We're good, you and me. I'm sure you've already talked with your mother, so you two are good, too." It was about as much of a reprimand as my dad was capable of giving me, and I almost grinned.

"We did," I whispered. "I love you, Daddy."

"I love you too, Maddog." He smiled at me. It was yet another piece of my past that had shaped who I was. For years after I'd come here and settled in with all the people here, I'd refused to answer to anything other than Maddog. I'm sure a therapist would have loads of fun with that little tidbit. I was sure I did it because "Maddog" wasn't afraid of anything. Holly was afraid of everything.

Jax carried me to the waiting Bronco in the driveway. Razor drove us to the little house Jax had described. It was only four houses down the small block, but there was no way I was up to walking that distance and Jax knew it, bless him.

Once inside, he took me to the bedroom and sat on the bed, settling me between his legs. I was confused at first, but then he picked up a brush on the nightstand and began working it through my hair. I rested my chin on my knees and let the soothing strokes of the brush lull me into a space between asleep and awake when all I cared about was the next stroke of the brush.

The next thing I knew, Jax had laid me on the bed and wrapped himself around me. My hair lay in a long braid over my shoulder and Jax's arm was solidly around my waist.

"Jax?"

"I'm right here, baby. Ain't goin' nowhere. Get some sleep and I'll keep you safe. I'll still be here when you wake up." The last thing I felt was his lips on my neck as he whispered. "I love you, little Holly. I love you."

Chapter Nine

Jax

Holly slept like the dead. After a couple hours, I had to move to a chair I'd pulled up beside the bed so she could see me if she woke and I could hold her hand if she needed me to. I wanted to hold her hand whether she was awake or not, but Wrath was blowing up my phone with information they were getting out of the girl. Alistair, the prick, wasn't talking. Didn't matter much if he talked or not. Apparently, his phone, and a private server he thought was impenetrable, had a wealth of information on them. None of it good for Chris Alistair the Third.

I'd just finished reading a text when Holly moaned and rolled over on her side, facing me. Her eyes opened and I reached for her hand.

"Hey, baby. Sore?"

She gave me a sleepy smile. "A little."

"Fury sent something for pain if you need it. Not too strong, but it'll help you sleep."

"No." Holly gripped my hand. "We need to talk first. Probably should have already." Those clear blue eyes of hers could drown a man. Especially when she looked at him like she was looking at me now. There was no guile, no hedging. Holly was exactly as I saw her now. Sure, she could be brash and sarcastic, but I knew it was how she protected herself. When things were going wonderful in her life, she was like this all that time. When things got rough, she shored up her defenses and concentrated on surviving. Likely due to the leukemia she'd had as a child.

"We'll talk about whatever you want to talk about, whenever you want to talk about it."

She smiled. "Are you always going to give in to

my demands?"

I couldn't suppress my chuckle. "Probably. I'll make sure I'm there when the fireworks start, and stand between you and whatever I have to until you're ready to leave."

"That's such a 'you' thing to say, Jax." She focused on my hand, threading her fingers through mine. "Are you and my dad OK?"

"We are, baby. Don't worry about your dad. He and I can work out our own problems, but he's going to allow me to make you my old lady."

"I mean, you gave me a property cut and everything. It's a little late, I suppose."

"Never too late for a daddy to protect his little girl, but Wrath knows I'll take care of you."

Moisture leaked from her eyes, though she smiled through her tears. "You've always taken care of me." With slow, deliberate movements, she raised her hand to my face, stroking my short beard. "I've loved you my entire life, Jax." Her voice was barely a thread of sound, almost like she was talking to herself. "I know I haven't always acted like it. I'm sorry for telling Mom and Dad you were mean to me when I was little. That wasn't very nice of me."

"Baby, don't apologize for that. Never for that. It was the only way you could get one of them to come get me." I chuckled softly, bringing her fingers to my lips where they were still laced with mine. I kissed her knuckles gently, letting my mouth linger on her skin. When I spoke, it was with her fingers still against my lips. "I admit the first time startled me. Especially when I opened the door to a scowling Wrath. He took a swing at me before telling me what was going on. Once he did, I knew what was wrong."

"Were you even out of your teens?"

"Not that time. But I was eighteen. Barely. It's why he took a swing at me. I was legal and he knew I knew better than to hurt your feelings."

"And I told him you had. And he believed me."

"Of course, he was gonna believe you. It's why you told him I'd been an asshole. You told him you wanted me to come apologize and that's what he was makin' me do."

"Then you let me berate you for a solid hour. I think I hit you more than once."

"Yeah, baby. You did. I took it proudly because once you tired yourself out, you crawled up in my lap and went to sleep with me holding you." I stroked a lock of hair off her forehead. "That's one of my favorite memories. The first time you showed me you trusted me and that I was able to take away at least some of your pain and frustration."

Holly sat up and moved to the edge of the bed before crawling up into my lap. She wrapped her arms around me and cried against my neck. I held her and let her cry. The sooner she got out all her pent-up negative emotions, the better she'd feel. And we could get about the business of us.

When she finally stopped crying, Holly showed no signs of being ready to let me go. I was content to simply hold her. Wrath still shot off the occasional text, but as I'd told him when I stopped answering my phone, Holly was awake and needed my full attention. If he called, I'd know it was urgent. Otherwise, I was going to ignore everything but Holly.

"So, what now?" She played with the front of my T-shirt, picking at the neckline and brushing her fingers over the material and my chest.

"You mean, what now for us?" I shrugged, leaning down to kiss her forehead just to feel the silky-smooth texture of her skin against my lips. "We live happily ever after."

She pulled back, meeting my gaze with an exasperated one of her own. "Nothing is ever that simple, Jax."

"It is with us. Sure, there are a couple things that need ironing out, but I'm pretty sure our major problems are going to disappear. After that, you and I get busy figuring out what makes you happiest."

"Me? What about you? Despite our history, I don't want you to be miserable."

That got a bark of laughter out of me. "I never thought you wanted me miserable, Holly. You needed a way to vent your anger and frustration. You chose me. I accepted the challenge willingly."

"But you didn't know I didn't mean all the stuff I said." The tears were starting again. I hated seeing her cry. Especially about our past.

"I knew. Call it intuition. Or wishful thinking." I chuckled.

"You couldn't have known I didn't mean it, because I didn't know I didn't mean it!" There was a little fire in her eyes now. That spark of temper was the thing that made me relax. Holly was ready to start fighting again.

"All I knew was I needed to make you better. Since there was nothing I could do to cure your illness, I knew I'd do the only other thing I could. Be there for you when you needed to lash out. You couldn't do it with your parents, and certainly not the McDonalds. You had parents and other people who loved you, and all kinds of bikers in this compound who'd kill anyone you needed killed. You even had a doctor doing everything in his power to make sure you were with us for a very long time to come. What you didn't have was a person you felt safe to release all the pent-up anger and frustration inside you. I knew exactly what I was signing up for, baby."

"I don't deserve you, Jax." Her chin trembled with emotion.

"Yeah you do, baby. You deserve way more than I can give you, but there is no one on this earth who will be solely focused on you and seeing to your happiness."

"You know, the leukemia came back once. Blade said he got on top of it because he monitors my markers aggressively. Says it's better to do a blood test more frequently and get a negative result than to not test enough and get a positive result months later."

"I remember." As if she had to remind me. "I was on pins and needles for months, afraid to leave your side."

"What? You weren't there until I got sick from the chemo." She sounded equal parts pissed, hurt, and resigned.

"Oh, no, honey. I sat outside your door every waking moment. The only time I left was when Wrath and Fury made me sleep. The women even made me a plate of food every time they brought you something. Then Wrath told them to stop. He told Lyric the only way to get me to leave was to not feed me. Then I'd either man up and come inside and sit with you, or go get my own food. At which time he'd simply lock me out."

"That sounds like my dad."

"Yeah, but it wouldn't have mattered. I'd have sat outside your window. You kept it open in the evening, and I could sit and listen. I'd be there if you cried out in the night."

"So that's how you got into my room."

I grinned. "Yeah. I know it's kind of creepy, but I didn't look at it that way. I was protecting you. Even if it was from nightmares. Or pain."

"It's not creepy." She cupped the side of my face. "I think it's wonderful. Thank you so much for always being in my life when I needed you, Jax."

"Hardest thing I ever did was leave for the service. In the back of my mind, I was always on edge. If you needed me and I wasn't there, I'd never have forgiven myself. The only reason I did it was because I wanted to work for ExFil. It provided a stable income for me and made El Diablo happy. I had to do my time like everyone else."

She sucked in a breath. "So, me leaving on this trip was a special kind of hell for you."

"Not really. I mean, yeah. I was upset you left before I could get to you, to go with you, and impatient to shake those losers and find you, but I knew I was coming after you and I was on my way."

"I should have known you'd come after me. I mean, I did, I just wasn't sure how I was going to let you know where I was. When my phone started blowing up with calls every little bit, I knew they were giving me time to answer before they activated the satellite GPS in my watch. After that, I knew whoever they sent, you'd be with them."

"That's my girl." I pulled her closer. "Now. Any objections to me kissing you? Because I really need another taste of you."

The smile she gave me was so fucking beautiful, if I'd been standing I'd have fallen to my knees and wept. "I'd like that very much. I need you, too."

Chapter Ten

Holly

I tried to kiss a boy a couple of times. Hated every single thing about it. Tried to have sex once, too. Nope. I'd barely gotten the guy alone with me before I backed out. Nothing felt right. I didn't like the feel of his touch on my skin or the way his lips were wet. Kissing felt… slimy. Icky. I hated it. Then Jax went and kissed me on the plane. His kiss had been nothing like I'd experienced before, and everything I'd always longed for. This kiss was even better.

His lips were firm yet tender, his touch gentle yet commanding. The mere press of his mouth against mine elicited a fire within me, as though he was the key to igniting my very soul. I wanted to believe love and romance like my mom and dad had wasn't a fluke. Hadn't I seen it in the other members of Black Reign and their women? Kissing Jax felt as though all the love songs and cheesy romance novels suddenly made sense.

He was patient and understanding, letting me explore the contours of his lips with mine at my own pace. His hands roamed my back in soothing circles, as though reassuring me and encouraging me to keep going. His body was molded against mine in a comforting embrace which felt like home. Of course, Mom and Dad had given me a loving place to live and protected me as much as possible, but Jax was different. He was mine. And I was his.

Jax pulled away slightly, creating a distance that allowed me to catch my breath. My eyes fluttered open to meet his gaze. His hazel eyes were molten with affection, reflecting an intensity that made my heart skip a beat. His thumb grazed gently across my lower lip, coaxing me to open. When I did, he slipped the tip of his thumb into my mouth. I closed my lips around the digit, sucking gently.

Jax looked me straight in the eyes, searching mine the same as I searched his gaze for some kind of clue to what he was thinking. "Just so you know, this only goes as far as you want. There's no expectation on my part. Tonight is all about you. What you want. What you need. I'm going to give you everything. And you're going to tell me what you desire most for us right now." He removed his thumb, and I wanted to chase it down and suck some more. I have no idea why that simple act was so erotic, but there it was.

"I want you, Jax. I want to make love with you." The words were out before I could censor them or maybe phrase it differently. I was certain no self-respecting biker would ever "make love." But it was what I wanted. This time. I needed him to guide me, and I needed to be able to understand what was happening.

I wasn't sure if I expected him to scoff at me or be amused. I could be naive enough to think he would even want to make love to me. What I got was a slow, wicked smile. "Oh yeah, baby. I can definitely do that. I'm going to take my time and prove to you I'm the only man you'll ever need."

"Yes. That's what I want."

Jax slid his fingers through my hair to cup the back of my head as he lowered his lips to mine again. This time the kiss started off slow and careful, like he was feeling me out or maybe giving me time to adjust to the sensations. I slid my hands up his chest and around his neck.

With his fingers tangled in my hair, Jax angled my head where he wanted me while his other arm tightened around me, holding me close. Goose bumps erupted over my skin and I shivered. I'd always loved being in Jax's arms. This was altogether different, though. This time, I was really his. His woman. I found his strength exciting, and even a little daunting. I knew he hadn't been a saint -- he was twelve years older than me -- so there was no doubt he was the experienced one in this relationship. While I wanted to claw out the eyes of every single woman he'd been with, I couldn't fault him for it when I'd been too young for him to even consider being with. At the same time, I wanted to thumb my nose at the lot of them. They might have had him in the middle of his life, but I'd had him first and now I had him last.

Slowly, as if sensing my comfort with his touch, Jax intensified the kiss. His teeth grazed my lips enough to make me gasp. His tongue swept inside my mouth to dance with mine. Small sighs filled the air as I settled into his embrace and simply let Jax have me. I'd trust him to guide me, and I'd be everything he needed.

I shifted so that I could wrap my legs around him. As turned on as I'd gotten just from his kiss, my clit felt like it was being licked by fire every time I rubbed over his jeans. I might never have had sex, but I knew how to pleasure myself and often did. What I was feeling now had nothing to do with physical stimulation and everything to do with the man doing the stimulating.

He stood and planted a knee on the mattress, laying us both down so that he pinned me. I loved his weight on top of me, his body resting between my legs. I tilted my hips, trying to get some more friction on my clit and Jax grinned down at me.

"Is my girl greedy?"

"For you?" I tried to flash him a grin, but my words came out as breathless as I felt. I wasn't in a smiling mood. I was nearly desperate to come. "Always."

"Good. Because I doubt I'll ever get enough of you, Holly."

"You'll always be with me?"

"Always, baby. Nothing could make me leave you. Nothing." I could see in his eyes and expression he meant what he said. Thing was, Jax had seen me at my worst already. If he still wanted me, I was all in, and I wasn't asking him if he was sure because then I'd have to decide what I'd do if he changed his mind.

"Good. Now, show me what to do." It was as much of an order as I was capable of. I was pretty sure it was more of a plea than a demand.

"With pleasure."

Jax kissed me again. This time his hands touched the skin of my waist and slid up my sides until I arched my back and whimpered into his mouth. He pushed up slightly, grabbed a fistful of his shirt between his shoulders, and pulled it over his head. Then he slid my shirt from my body in a slow, gentle caress.

My nipples were pebbled, and hard, aching points. I arched again, hoping he'd mash his chest to mine so I could rub my nipples over his muscles. Instead, he wrapped an arm around my back and lowered his head to take one breast into his mouth and suck.

I screamed at the foreign contact. I'd always imagined how this would feel, but the experience far outweighed the fantasy. I tightened my legs around Jax, afraid he'd leave. Or, worse, not give me the friction I needed over my clit. That might be grounds for a beating.

Jax's warm laughter vibrated through my chest. "I know you need friction on your clit, baby. And I'll give it to you. Just not yet."

"Oh, God!" I should have been horrified that I'd said that comment out loud, but my brain was scrambled. I shivered and jerked when his fingers caught my nipple between them and gently squeezed and twisted while his tongue flicked magic over the other. "Oh, God! Jax!"

"That's it, honey. Scream my name. Let me know who you belong to."

"Only you, Jax," my voice came out breathy and desperate as his teeth grazed my nipple. He chuckled against my skin, sending shivers down my spine. "I belong to you."

Lifting his head, he grinned at me with those wickedly beautiful eyes of his. "I'll never tire of hearing that," he murmured, pressing a firm kiss to my collarbone. "And so you know and understand, I belong to you, too."

That made me smile, and a satisfying contentment began to bloom inside my chest. This was where I was meant to be all along. It took time to make the journey. Now that I was here, I wasn't letting a moment pass by without appreciating what I'd found.

Jax moved his hands down to the waist of my shorts, his fingers caressing my skin over my hips and upper thighs as he slid them off. He sat up to pull them over my feet and toss them to the floor before lying back on top of me once again. A wave of nervous anticipation washed over me. I'd been exposed in front of him before, but not like this.

My illness had left scars from surgeries and chemo ports. But knowing there were scars on my body and actually seeing them were two different things. What if he… didn't want the reminder?

"Honey, whatever you're thinking, stop." Jax didn't sound angry or impatient. In fact, he smiled at me as he stroked my hair. My breasts were mashed against his chest now, like I'd wanted a few moments ago, but the thought he might not like what he saw when he looked at my naked body, no matter how briefly, had me doubting myself. And him.

"I'm sorry." I was afraid the tears were gonna start again and did my best to blink them back.

"Why are you sorry." It was phrased as a demand instead of a question. An order to be obeyed.

"I have scars. You know. From the cancer."

"Battle scars. Yep." He gave me a look that said, "And?"

"It was hard. What we went through. And I include you in that because you were the one I always clung to. You saw the very worst of it all. As much or more than my mother sometimes. You were barely an adult. I'm sure you don't want the reminder of it every time you see me."

Jax looked at me for a long time. I thought maybe I'd broken the mood, but I could feel his erection through his jeans. He was still hard and didn't seem to be flagging. "That's not it." His confident tone grated on my ears. I hated it when he pulled that superior act. Like he knew me better than I knew myself.

"Is so." I stuck my chin up defiantly.

Jax chuckled softly, that tender expression still on his face even though he was still as intense as ever. "OK, so let me rephrase. That's not all it is."

"Have I ever told you how annoying you are?" My irritation might have been more convincing if I hadn't been clinging to his arms.

"Every chance you get." He gave me another brief but tender kiss. "Now, tell me what else is bothering you."

I closed my eyes, taking a breath before meeting his gaze once more. "My cancer already came back once. Blade said there was a possibility it could recur again. Could you go through all that again with me? Because, if you can't, you need to tell me now."

It was Jax's turn to sigh. I could almost feel the disappointment radiating from him. "Honey. I'm sorry I haven't made it clear to you. I guess I thought you'd know. No matter what happens, I'm always going to be with you. If you get sick again, I'll be with you every step of the way. Face it, Holly. You're stuck with me. As long as I'm alive. You're stuck with me."

He held my gaze, really staring at me. I could see the truth in his eyes. "You really would, wouldn't you?" I know I sounded a bit starstruck, but honestly. Jax was my hero, as well as my only love.

"Yes. I really would."

"Also, I don't want to have kids." I couldn't stop myself from blurting that out. He needed to know this, though. It affected his future as much as it did mine.

"Sweetheart, if you don't want to have kids, I'm good with that. Could you tell me why? It's your body and with everything you've already been through I could understand if that's why you made your decision."

"Partly, but not really. It's the specter of the cancer coming back. I know that there are studies showing pregnancy hormones can sometimes stimulate cancer growth or even revive dormant cancer cells that didn't completely die. I don't want to die, Jax. While it's selfish on my part, I also don't want to leave my child without his mother. I'm not sure I could do chemo knowing I was pregnant, and I don't think I'd want to get an abortion. So, my options would be to do the chemo regardless of the risk to a fetus or hold off on the chemo until after the baby's born. Which would likely be a death sentence. *If* my cancer comes back. I'd rather adopt or foster. It's considerably lower risk all the way around and I could still have children." I ducked my head. "But that's all unfair to you. So I get it if you can't do this. Just tell me now."

He was silent for a moment, then he stroked my jawline tenderly. "I think you've clearly thought about your decision from several different angles. And I agree. But if you change your mind at some point, we'll get Blade to walk us through everything and help you make the decision that's best for you. I'd never risk your health -- mental or physical. And that kind of event would do both." Jax's gentle smile made my eyes mist over again. "A parent is the person who loves and raises you. Sometimes you don't find that person -- or people -- until you're an adult. So, any child I bring into my home to care for will be my child. Biological or not. Also, there's a ton of kids around the compound to spoil. You know that from growing up here."

"Why are you so reasonable?" I slapped at his chest as I yelled at him. Those blasted tears started in full force again. "You weren't supposed to agree with me!"

He gave me a genuinely puzzled look. "I wasn't? Why wouldn't I?"

"You're supposed to act like a *guy*! A guy would bitch and moan about not having offspring or an heir or whatever. If you did, it would make you seem less perfect and I could finally find a reason to back off before I lose myself completely." I was acting crazy and I knew it but, Goddamnit, I was scared!

Jax looked confused for a moment, then realization dawned on him and he rolled his eyes. "Maddog, you are not gettin' rid of me that easily. Besides, I already gave you my property patch in front of your parents. You accepted it. No take backs." He narrowed his gaze and pointed a finger at me as if daring me to defy him.

I laughed, more relieved than I'd felt in a long time. "Fine. No take backs. I don't know why I'm trying to push you away. I don't mean to." It was the truth. It was also far too late for pushing him away to do any good. I was already in love with him. The damage was done.

"You're pushing to see if you can find my boundaries. You're pushing the ones most important to you first. I can respect that. When it's all over and you finally realize I not only know exactly what I'm getting into but welcome it a thousand times over if I get to have you be mine, I'm going to remind you of this conversation. There's not a Goddamned thing I wouldn't do to keep you, Holly. Not one Goddamned thing."

"I'm holding you to that. No take backs."

He grinned. "Good. I'm holding you to it as well."

Not giving me time to continue the conversation, Jax kissed me again, building me up to where I was before things took a serious turn. Now, I wanted to feel. To learn. To pleasure. And I wanted to do it all with Jax.

With a contented sigh, I surrendered completely to him. There was no better man for me to give my virginity to. Not only would he be careful with me, but he'd make sure I enjoyed it. It wasn't in Jax to do anything else.

Chapter Eleven

Jax

Holly was breaking my heart. She actually thought her not wanting to risk getting pregnant was a deal-breaker for me. She'd soon learn that I wasn't going any-fucking-where. And just let anyone try to make me.

I stroked her skin from her neck down her collarbone and the scar from her chemo port right below it, over her breasts, down her ribcage, and to the tops of her thighs. She lay passive beneath me, only stiffening once when my fingers traced the raised area.

Leaning in, I kissed the offending spot, laving my tongue over the ridge in a tender caress. "Does it still hurt?" I didn't think so, but I was never taking a chance on accidentally hurting her.

"No." Her voice was a mere thread of sound. Her eyes were glazed and she looked almost as lust-stupid as I felt. The recent serious conversation hadn't fully left her and let her settle into the moment.

"It makes you more beautiful, you know."

That got her attention. Her eyes widened and she shook her head slightly. "I… What?"

"This scar." I traced it once again with my tongue before placing a kiss over it. "Shows how strong you are. You fought a daunting adversary. I suppose you're still fighting it. But you came out of your last battle on top. Maybe battered and bruised, but you won. So yeah. This scar, the scars on your arms from the IVs. How you consider your future carefully and know what you're willing to sacrifice and how to achieve your dreams in an alternate way."

I kissed her chin. "Baby, I hate that you went through what you did. I saw how hard it was. I witnessed how hard you fought. I hate every single bit of it. But it made you into the woman here in my arms now. I know you're strong. I know you're a fighter. I know you are capable of making anything you want happen. Even though you're one of the most capable and tough women I know, you're still willing to admit you need help. Or to put yourself in my care and trust me not to let you down."

I grinned at her and watched in satisfaction as she gasped when I gave into that smile tugging at my lips. "You have no idea how sexy that is to a guy like me." I took her lips then, kissing her harder this time. I thrust my tongue deep and she whimpered, but opened her mouth wider, tangling her tongue with mine. When I pulled back, I stared hard at her, making sure she held my gaze. "Do not ever think your scars repel me. They are badges of honor. Wear them proudly."

She nodded her head, probably on instinct. When I used that particular tone of voice, it usually sent men scattering. At least, the men I commanded in the field did. In the Black Reign compound, I was low man on the totem pole. Most of the guys still saw me as the gangly teenager trying to keep up with a defiant Holly and her hell hounds in the form of Saint Bernard dogs. She'd had a whole herd of them at one point. Then a little Holly of about nine approached El Diablo and announced he needed to get her a trainer for the dogs so the puppies could be service dogs, and that the fully trained and ready dogs should be donated to people who need them. Especially kids. I'd helped El Diablo make it a reality.

"There really is nothing in this world I wouldn't do for you, Holly." Then I qualified my meaning. "Except for leaving you. I can't give you up to another man. No one but me can appreciate you the way you should be. No one can protect you as savagely as I will."

It took her several seconds to blink away the stunned look on her face. Probably because I let my ruthless side peek out. Then it was her turn to roll her eyes. "Are you gonna talk all night or fuck me?"

I couldn't help myself. I threw my head back and laughed, rolling with her until she was on top of me, straddling my hips. "Shut up and fuck you, huh?"

"If I knew you were so chatty during sex, I'd have found something else for you to do with your mouth." Holly looked disgruntled, but also a little impatient. If there was any lingering doubt in my mind she was ready for this, that look erased it.

"You would have, hmm? And what would that be?"

"You're the one with all the experience! What do you want to do besides talk? There's got to be something."

"First of all, I want to know if you're a virgin. And before you think I won't like what you're gonna say, there is no right or wrong answer. I just don't want to hurt you."

She huffed out a breath. "I tried to have sex with a guy once, but I chickened out because it didn't feel right. But I've penetrated myself masturbating."

I smiled up at her. "Good. Now. As to my talking so much, if the situation were reversed, I'd shut you up by having you suck my cock." I raised an eyebrow. It was my turn to push her now. Not because I wanted her to suck me off, but because I wanted her to fucking tell me to eat her pussy. Now that the thought of her actually telling me to eat her pussy had entered my head, I had to hear it. Would she be demure and shy?

Blush?

"Oh, you would?" She crossed her arms over her chest, glaring at me.

"Absolutely. Only way to shut a woman up when she gets chatty during sex."

She gave me a narrow-eyed look of disapproval. "Challenge issued. Challenge accepted." She pushed off me, and back to where she'd lain before I rolled us. She spread her legs and patted her mound with one delicate hand. "Put your mouth to use down here."

"Oh, baby girl," I purred, watching her body erupt in sweat. She liked the predatory gleam I knew was reflected in my eyes. "Challenge definitely accepted. Now. Tell me. Word for word. What do you want me to do?"

I took my time moving into position above her. The sleek muscles of her thighs bunched as I wrapped my arms around them to pull them apart, so I could gaze at her pretty, bare cunt. I loved the tension gripping her, the anticipation etched across her face. It was intoxicating, and it only fueled my own lust. She wanted me. My instinct was to give her what she wanted.

"Wh-what?" Her eyes widened.

"You heard me. Tell me exactly what you want, or I'll put my mouth where *I* want it. And it might not be where *you* want it."

Again, like I knew she would, Holly stuck out her chin. Cheeks growing red, a fresh layer of sweat slickening her skin, she said exactly what I wanted her to say. "I want your mouth on my pussy."

"Fuck me…" My muttered expletive was said over her glistening lips. I had never been so hell-bent on pleasing a woman as I was for Holly right now. I loved the little bite to her voice and the willing way she did exactly what I wanted her to do, even though it was outside her comfort zone, both humbled and excited me.

Her pussy wept with need, her lips quivering as I leaned closer. I blew a light breeze over her clit and she gasped, clenching her hands into tight fists beside her. I smirked and watched as she bit her lower lip.

"Uh-uh…" I *tsked.* "None of that." I reached up and tugged her lip free of those pearly white teeth. "No holding back. You need to scream, you scream."

"But what if someone hears?"

"What if they do? You think no one here has sex?"

She gave me an impatient look. "Of course, I know they have sex!"

I grinned. "Then don't worry about it. They know we're a new couple. They know this is our house. Anyone comin' around for at least a couple months should expect to hear us havin' sex unless they fuckin' call first."

To my surprise, that got a laugh out of her. She tunneled her fingers through my hair and gripped. "Then do your best. You want me to scream, you gotta earn it."

Her bold challenge sent an electrifying thrill throughout my body, igniting all the right spots. "Oh, baby," I drawled out, "you have no idea what you've unleashed. You can bet your pretty ass I plan to earn it."

With that, I dipped my head and closed my lips around her clit in a brief, gentle suck.

I gripped her thighs with my large hands as I kissed a path up her stomach to her belly button, then back down between her legs. She squirmed under me, a frustrated whimper escaping her. She clutched the sheets beside her before her other hand slid into my hair and she pulled me where she wanted me.

I took a moment to admire the sight before me. Holly lying naked and open beneath me, ready and waiting for my touch. My kisses.

Letting my fingers trace circles on her thigh, I blew another light puff of air at her clit. Her hips jerked up involuntarily, seeking more contact. I chuckled low in my chest at her eagerness. "Patience, baby," I muttered against her skin, causing her to shiver at the sensation.

I let my tongue dart to take a long swipe from pussy to clit. Then again. Then I covered her pussy and sucked. Her scent surrounded me, filled me with a sweet intoxication. I took a moment to savor her taste. "You're laid out in front of me like a banquet for one. Woman, I'm fuckin' *starvin'*."

I growled as I covered her pussy again, licking and thrusting my tongue inside her. I sucked her lips and clit, circling my finger at her entrance but not penetrating. Not yet.

"Jax! Jax! JAX!"

She chanted my name like a mantra, her hands pulling at my hair as her hips bucked. I continued to eat her out, the taste of her driving me further and further to the edge of my own control. My cock throbbed insistently against my jeans, but for now, this was about getting her ready to take me. Holly was as inexperienced as they came. The last thing I wanted to do was stretch her before she was relaxed and eager for the burn.

"Not yet." I shook my head and pressed her hips down onto the bed with my forearm across her pelvis when she tried to grind against me. "No moving, baby. Let me do all the work."

I took another long lick, savoring her sweetness before circling her clit slowly with my tongue in ever faster circles. I could feel her muscles contracting under my touch, could see the desperate pleasure on her face as she writhed beneath me.

"God… Jax… please," she whimpered. Her fingers tugged harder on my hair and I growled in response.

"What do you want, Holly?" I asked, looking up at her as I continued to tease her clit with my tongue.

"I-I…" She shook her head and swallowed. When she opened her eyes, it was to meet my gaze without flinching. "I want to come." Bless her heart, she looked more than a little uncomfortable, but she didn't back down an inch.

"Do you?" Lick. "I don't think you're nearly desperate enough." Suck. "Maybe I should eat you out a while longer." *Lick. Suck.*

"Jax!" She screamed my name.

"Humm. Not quite there yet, but you're getting close."

Her legs tightened around my head and her back arched off the bed. "Jax! You asshole! Let me fuckin' *come*!"

"Thaaaat's more like it." I chuckled against her clit while I used two fingers to penetrate her in a shallow thrust. "You're gettin' there fast, ain't you, baby?"

When she cried out again, I slipped my fingers farther inside her, finding that sweet spot. While I circled her clit with my thumb, I lapped up her juices around my fingers. God, she was so fucking wet and hot for me!

"Ahh!" Holly's body clenched and shivered, her climax taking her over.

I gave one final lick before crawling up her body to capture her cries with my kiss. My fingers were still in her pussy between our bodies. The contractions were strong, like she was trying to suck me deeper inside her. I even still had my jeans on, but I had to taste her cries.

She gasped, as I continued to kiss her while the waves of her climax ebbed. She tasted delicious and wild, like honey and spicy, raw energy. Her body was so fucking responsive under my touch, her breaths coming in short, ragged gasps. I reveled in each small tremor against my lips, each hitch of her breath, every sign that she had surrendered to me.

"Shit, Jax." She smiled as I continued to kiss her. Her eyes were still closed and there was the most glorious euphoric expression on her beautiful face.

"I told you," I said hoarsely, trailing kisses along her throat as I withdrew my fingers from her slowly, making sure she felt me touching her. "I told you I would make you scream."

She shivered under me, her fingernails digging into my back as she caught her breath. Her eyes were glazed and unfocused when she finally looked back at me, a slow smile spreading across her flushed face. "That you did."

"Holly," I murmured against her lips, curling my fingers in her hair. "Hold on, baby. We're just gettin' started."

Her eyes were wide with need as she looked up at me. She was panting hard. I could feel my own breath hitch as I watched her chest rise and fall. Her breasts were flushed pink and sweaty. I traced a thumb lightly over a nipple and watched it tighten in response.

"You're fucking beautiful," I said hoarsely as I

unbuttoned my jeans and slid them down my hips along with my underwear. I rolled slowly until I sat on the edge of the bed, letting the garments pool at my feet on the floor. I bent over, fishing my wallet out of my pants to pull out two condoms. I tossed one to the dresser and opened the packet of the other one, tossing the empty foil next to the unopened condom on the dresser. I laid the opened latex at the head of the bed next to the pillow. I didn't expect it would be long until I needed it.

Her eyes widened farther at the sight of me. I groaned at the hungry look she gave me. "Touch me, Holly," I said gruffly. "Touch me, then get me ready to fuck you."

She nodded her head eagerly and sat up and moved next to me. Climbing off the bed, she moved in front of me, then sank to her knees. She placed her hands on my thighs before leaning in to kiss the tip of my cock.

Her lips were soft and tentative as they brushed against the swollen head of my dick, her gaze locked with mine. A jolt of heat surged through me, spreading out to ignite my entire body. My hands clenched into fists as I fought to remain still, to let her explore at her own pace.

She looked unsure for a moment, before she parted her lips and took me into her mouth. It was warm and wet and heavenly. I grunted involuntarily at the sensation, my eyes sliding shut as I tipped my head back, reveling in the feel of her tongue swirling around the tip. I was sure she got a hit of precum when her eyes widened and she sucked in a sharp breath through her nose.

"Fuck… Holly," I murmured, my voice a hoarse whisper in the silent room. I gripped her hair, the strands soft against my fingers as I guided her movements. I hadn't even realized I'd moved, but the silky strands bunched in my fist anchored me when nothing else could.

She took more of me into her mouth, sucking me deeper while her hand began to stroke my shaft. I let out a low growl of pleasure as her ministrations sent a sharp thrill shooting up my spine. She was still hesitant, but as she continued to suck and I continued to groan with every pull of her mouth, she gained more confidence. Her tongue swirled around the head of my cock again before starting a rhythmic bobbing. I groaned, throwing my head back as her mouth worked its magic.

"Christ, Holly," I managed to gasp out, my breath hitching each time she took me deeper. My fingers tightened in her hair, not to control her but to ground myself again. The pleasure was intense, overwhelming, and I knew I wouldn't last much longer if she kept up. And no fucking way I was coming down her throat the first time I was with her. I'd do that later.

My hips thrust involuntarily and she pulled back slightly, her cheeks flushing a pretty pink under my gaze. But then she moved again, taking me in her mouth once more, and I had to bite back a moan.

"Holly, stop," I bit out through clenched teeth as I gently tugged her away from me by her hair. She whimpered but eagerly got to her feet and threw herself into my arms.

"Please, Jax," she whispered. "Please. I can't wait anymore. What do you need to hear to fuck me already?"

My heart pounded in my chest at her words and a satisfied growl rumbled in my throat. Grabbing the condom from where it still lay on the corner of the bed already open. My hands were shaking ever so slightly. I hoped like fuck she didn't notice because that would be the height of embarrassment. Then again, this was my Holly. It was worth as much embarrassment as it took if it put her at ease.

"Help me put this on." The gruff order came out through the haze of need. "My fuckin' hands are shakin' too fuckin' much."

A small nervous giggle escaped her as she reached for the small latex circle. Her fingers touched mine as she took it from me, sending another jolt through me. I'm not sure I was this nervous the very first time I fucked a woman, and this was infinitely more important.

I took a deep breath, trying to steady myself as she unrolled the condom over my pulsing erection. Her touch was gentle as she pinched the tip and rolled it down my length. I was long and thick, and the lip of the condom didn't roll all the way to the base.

Holly looked up at me with wide, clear blue eyes. I gripped her upper arms and pulled her to her feet. She came to me willingly, wrapping her arms and legs around my body before kissing me again. She clung as I stood and moved us back onto the bed, lying on top of her so that, once again, she was pressed into the mattress.

"I-I'm ready, Jax," she whispered against my lips, her eyes shiny with what appeared to be a mix of excitement and fear. "Please don't make me wait any longer."

I nodded at her, placing a slow, deliberate kiss on her lips before pulling back to gaze at her. Taking a deep breath, I hooked her right leg higher over my hip, angling myself at her entrance. I could feel the heat of her pussy against my cockhead through the condom, and I had to bite back a groan.

"Sweet God," I murmured, pressing against her. Her eyes widened as she felt the head of my cock press against her entrance. I watched those beautiful blue eyes clench shut as she bit down on her bottom lip.

"No, Holly," I said softly, trailing my fingers down her thigh. "Look at me. Open those beautiful eyes and watch me as I enter you."

She nodded her head, opening her eyes to look at me. "Do it." She hissed her command, her eyes wild with need. "Do it now, Jax!"

Without another word, I pushed into her. The sound that escaped her lips was half gasp, half moan, and it was the most beautiful thing I had ever heard. The tight heat of her wrapped around me was incredible. She clung tightly to me, and I wanted to puff out my chest. This woman, this beautiful, courageous, stubborn woman wanted me.

This absolutely had to be good for her. So, slowly, with more restraint than I thought possible, I began to move inside her. Each thrust brought a new sigh or whimper from Holly, each more arousing than the last.

I pressed my forehead against hers, feeling the sweat bead there as I tried my best not to get too lost in her. Holly's fingers dug into my back, then my ass as she urged me to take her deeper, harder. She braced her feet on my calves and tried to take control of the pace and all my aspirations of holding back evaporated as I drove into her.

"Oh God," she whispered in my ear, her breath hitching. "Jax…" Her body tensed and then shuddered under mine. Her pussy squeezed my cock with relentless convulsions. Then Holly arched her back and screamed in a long, loud yell. She thrashed beneath me, bucking like a wild Mustang. It was all I could do to stay on top of her. Except for when she wrapped her legs around my hips and dug her heels into my ass.

Yeah. Game over.

My control snapped like a frayed wire. In the heat of her orgasm, my restraint crumbled. I drove into her with hard, powerful strokes. She took it all and begged for more. A surge of primal satisfaction coursed through me as I watched her come apart under me again.

"Fuck," I groaned as I felt the familiar tightening at the base of my spine. My thrusts became erratic, harder and faster as I neared my own climax. The room echoed with our mingled moans and cries, the air heavy with the scent of sex and sweat.

I was teetering on the edge, staring into the abyss. "Holly," I groaned again, feeling my release coiling tightly, ready to snap. "I'm… fucking hell. I'm comin' right… fuckin'… now!"

Her hand cupped my face and pulled me down for a kiss that was so full of passion, so full of need that it sent me spiraling over the edge right then. But Holly wasn't done with me.

"No," she gasped, her body already trembling under me in aftershocks. "Don't stop, Jax. I want more!"

"Christ, Holly…" My words were a ragged whisper, my body shuddering with the maddening climax ripping through me. Her fingers dug into my back, urging me on. "I don't… fuck… I don't wanna hurt you."

But Holly was having none of it. Her eyes flashed fiercely up at me, her nails digging harder into my skin. "You won't," she growled back at me, pulling me closer. "Make me come one more time. Please!" The whispered plea was more than I could ignore. And wouldn't have anyway. If Holly needed, I provided.

My groan echoed loudly in the room as I gave in to her demands, losing myself in her cries and the way she gave me exactly what I wanted. She screamed her pleasure and wasn't shy about telling me to move the way she wanted. I thrust into her one more time and this time there was no holding back the tidal wave that crashed over me.

As my orgasm ripped through me, a guttural shout erupted from my throat. Holly's cries mingled with mine and together our voices danced through the room until we were both finally silent and still.

I was stunned. I'd never lost my mind so completely with a woman. And, by God, it felt right.

"Did I hurt you, honey?" I could barely muster the effort to get the words out.

"No. Not at all." Holly's sweet sigh was so filled with contentment I breathed a heavy sigh of relief.

"Thank God, because I really want to do that again. Soon."

The smile she graced me with was nothing shy of glorious. Yeah. I was a goner.

Game.

Fucking.

Over.

Chapter Twelve

Holly

The next three months were the happiest of my life. Not only did Jax and Dad take care of Chris and Andrea, but I didn't have to do anything. All anyone would tell me was that I didn't have to worry about either of them anymore.

Some of the women stayed in the Black Reign compound because they had nowhere else to go. Seemed Chris had a whole thing going where he'd preyed on homeless women. Of the eight young women who'd stayed, all but one had been homeless for a few weeks when they'd met Chris. He'd given them a place to live and, after a while, convinced each of them that there was "just something about you I can't live without." Then he'd taken them all to Columbia. That's where the whole thing kind of went off the rails. I didn't know where Andrea fit in with it all, but El Diablo finally put his foot down.

"I've never denied you anything you wanted, Holly Sweetness." He tried to look contrite, but I could tell he wasn't a bit sorry to keep this from me. "But I will not budge on this. It's over. Neither of them will ever hurt you again." I tried to watch the news for any indication that Chris had gone back home, but Jax had kept me so busy having sex I decided it didn't really matter. Nothing was going to interrupt my happiness.

Until I woke up this morning. I hadn't felt bad, exactly. Just… off. Jax was already up. I remember him kissing me awake and letting me know he had some business to take care of outside the compound. I thought he said something about ExFil, which meant he wouldn't be back until later in the evening.

I glanced at the clock. It was after eleven, but I

was beat. I'd have blamed it on Jax keeping me up all night for sex, like he did most nights, but he hadn't. I'd slept through the night.

"Fuuuuck." I groaned and turned over onto my back. I shivered and groaned again. My whole body ached. And I was sweating.

A memory flashed through my mind. The day in Blade's office when he'd told me my leukemia had returned, but we'd caught it early. I'd felt just like this. Only, we'd all thought I was just sick. A cold or something.

I sat bolt upright in the bed, instantly wide awake. My heart pounded and my breath came in sharp pants. "No," I sobbed out. "Please no."

With trembling hands, I reached for my phone. I didn't even think about calling anyone but Jax. He answered on the first ring.

"Hey, Maddog. You sleep in today?" His voice was cheerful, like he was happy to hear from me and maybe a little amused that I'd slept late. He loved it when he wore me out enough to keep me in bed half the morning and normally I did too.

"Jax?" My voice was soft and shaky. It was easy to tell something was wrong.

"Honey, what's wrong?" Gone was the easygoing lover I'd grown obsessed with and in his place was my fierce protector.

"I'm sick." My voice broke on the last word.

"I'll call Blade and Doc."

"NO!" I took several deep breaths to calm myself. "I can do it. I just panicked."

"Because of the last time."

"It feels the same, Jax." I started crying then. "I don't want to do this again! Chemo sucks ass!"

"Call your mother, Holly. I'll get Blade to come

to you now. I'll be with there in an hour. Less if I can catch Cain before he leaves. And, baby?"

I took in a shuddering breath. "Yes?"

"No matter what happens, I'm gonna be right by your side. Every step of the way. You hear me?"

Closing my eyes I took another deep breath and let it out. I pictured Jax's face and let his warmth fill me. "Yes, Jax. I hear you."

"That's my girl. I'm coming. Hold it together until I get there. We'll figure this out together."

"OK. I can do that."

"I know you can. Call me back when Blade gets there. If I don't answer it means I'll be there in less than twenty minutes. If I answer, I'm still close to an hour away."

Not that I understood that, but I didn't have to. I had to know he was on the way. Which meant, I really hoped he didn't answer when I called him back.

I got up and dressed after unlocking the door for when Mom got there. She and Dad arrived five minutes later. I sat on the couch, my forearms on my knees with my phone clenched tightly in my hands. The second Mom hurried through the door, I was up on my feet and in her arms shaking and sobbing.

"It's going to be all right, honey," Mom said, though she was crying as hard as I was. "We'll figure it out and get through it together. Blade will do everything he can to help us. You know he will."

"I'm scared, Mom."

"I know, sweetheart. Me too. Me too."

I sat with my mother on the couch. She had her arms around me while we both cried silently. My dad stood guard at the door, watching for Blade to approach. Fifteen minutes later, the man in question skidded to a stop in a big, black Bronco in front of my house. He'd obviously hurried over the second Jax had called him.

I dialed Jax's number, attempting to get him on a video chat instead of a call. I needed to see his face and look into his eyes. He didn't answer so I glanced at the time. He better be here in less than twenty minutes like he said, or I was gonna kick his ass.

"What happened?" That was Blade. Dr. Donovan Muse. He was a member of Salvation's Bane MC in Palm Beach, but his office was about halfway between there and Lake Worth where Black Reign was located. He must have hurried straight over. I recognized his medical bag immediately and a fresh flood of tears started.

"I'm sick." I sounded as miserable as I felt. "Like last time."

"When did it start?" He sat next to me and reached for my face, his fingers immediately seeking the lymph nodes in my neck.

"I woke up like this. Uh, achy. I woke up in a sweat, and I have no energy. I went to bed early and slept through the night. I shouldn't be this tired."

He pulled out his stethoscope and put it in his ears before warming the bell between his hands. "Raise your shirt for me, honey. You know the drill."

I did. Thankfully I'd dressed and at least had a bra covering me.

Blade listened to my heart and lungs, then took my temperature, blood pressure, and oxygen level. "Your temperature is slightly elevated, but not horribly. Did you eat a good supper last night before bed?"

"I wasn't that hungry. I had some grapes and a banana, though. And water."

"How about during the night?"

"No." I shook my head. "I didn't wake at all until Jax told me he was leaving and wouldn't be back until this evening. Something to do with ExFil but I was too sleepy to really process much more."

"Any abnormal bleeding? Nose bleeds or anything?"

"No."

"OK." He stopped, smiling kindly at me. "You know I have to take blood, right?"

"Yes." I gave a miserable sniff. I really wanted Jax here for this. I don't know why. This wasn't anything compared to what would come next if the leukemia had returned. I met Blade's gaze. "Why would this happen now? Why?"

"First of all, sweetheart, we don't know that anything's happened. All we know for certain is that you have a slight fever and body aches. Which could be any number of things other than leukemia."

"Yes, but the last time --"

He cut me off. "The last time you'd been feeling bad for a month and a half. Let's not borrow trouble. OK?" Blade was firm but gentle. "First thing we need to do is get some testing started. Some of it I can get started now, some of it I'll have to take to my pathologist. But I promise you, in twenty-four hours, I'll have a definite diagnosis."

I nodded and was about to surrender my arm for him to draw blood when there was a deep rumble in the background that intensified to a bone-jarring roar.

I put my hands over my ears and looked at my dad. Wrath had been leaning against the wall, looking out the front storm door. Which was when the windows on the house started to rattle. It felt like I was in the middle of the biggest, hardest, rock festival in the history of the world.

"What's going on?" My mom had to yell to be heard over the horrible noise.

Wrath chuckled. At least that's what it looked like. I couldn't hear a fucking thing. He held out his hand to me, beckoning me over beside him. As I stood and made my way around the couch to the door, he pointed out the window. There, in the courtyard just beyond the houses, a huge-ass military style helicopter was slowly touching down in the grass.

"What the hell is that?" I tried to ask my dad, but he just shook his head and pointed to his ears. He couldn't hear me.

A couple minutes later, the thing settled for a brief moment, then lifted off again. The helicopter went straight up, then banked as it turned and left the way it had come. Off in the distance, I saw a lone figure jogging from the courtyard toward the house. And I'd recognize that wonderful figure anywhere. "Jax," I breathed.

"Yeah, baby girl. Looks like your boyfriend knows how to make an entrance."

"He got a ride on a freaking Black Hawk?" I wanted to lash out at Jax even though I knew it was unreasonable. But it felt like Jax had been out having fun while I was scared out of my fucking mind. On the other hand, he'd definitely made an entrance. As well as gotten here in the fastest way possible. "I guess this is why he said if he couldn't answer when I called, he'd be on the way." I sounded disgruntled when I was really happy to see Jax. I was falling back on old patterns, needing to deflect my fear by being angry at Jax.

Wrath chuckled. My dad had an odd sense of humor because I didn't see anything funny about the situation.

Dad held open the door when Jax approached. The man was focused on one thing and one thing only. *Me*. "Holly!"

The second Jax reached me, I struck, smacking at his chest. "You left me!"

He looked like I'd slapped him. "I just went to work for the day, baby. I was comin' right back."

"*Work*? You were joyriding in a freaking helicopter!"

"Honey, I bullied my boss into having a teammate bring me home ASAP. We had to file all kinds of flight plans and pull strings that didn't exist to get permission. Hell, I'm not even sure Cain got permission so much as he got some higher up somewhere to ignore the big ass military bird flying in civilian airspace." He looked panicked as he looked from me to Wrath and back.

"That's some… creative maneuvering there, boy." Wrath grinned and scrubbed the back of his neck with his hand. He shook his head and chuckled. "You hijacked a Black Hawk to come to your girl when she needed you. Color me officially impressed."

I sniffled and Jax scooped me up, sitting on the couch with me in his lap. I wrapped my arms around his neck and buried my face in his shoulder. "I'm sorry," I whispered.

"Hush." He kissed my temple and hugged me tight. "Don't apologize. You've got nothing to apologize for." He held me like that for several minutes while Blade filled him in on what was happening. I didn't pay much attention because I was too busy soaking up Jax's strength. I was going to need it to get through this.

"Listen to me, Holly." Blade pried my hand loose where I'd curled my fingers in Jax's shirt. He gripped my hand in both of his and leveled a look on me. "You're gettin' way ahead of yourself. I've got a bunch of tests to do, but, like I said, I'll have an answer for you in a day. Maybe less. Can you give me that long? Can you keep it together? You're scaring Jax. I'm not dealing with that pussy when he goes all caveman on me because I have to draw your blood." I knew it was nonsense to get so worked up, but I think I was having PTSD or something because all the memories from my childhood came rushing back.

I sniffed and wiped my nose on the back of my wrist. "He is a shade overprotective." I took in a deep breath, then let it out slowly, doing my best to drive down the panic I knew wasn't logical. Later. Once we knew what we were dealing with, then I could panic if necessary.

"That he is. Now. I know it's uncomfortable, but let's get this done so I can start testing your blood."

I nodded. "OK."

Blade took several different vials of blood and a couple nasal swabs, which I didn't understand but didn't protest. He'd just finished when his phone buzzed from his back pocket. "Good," he said as he glanced at the text. "I may have results for you quicker than expected." He smiled. "I wasn't sure she'd be available right away, but she's waiting at the office." He packed away the samples in a biohazard bag and put everything in what looked like a small lunch bag. "I'll be in touch the second I have something." That last he addressed to Jax.

Jax looked down at me. "I'll be right here. I'm not going anywhere."

Chapter Thirteen

Jax

I could see panic had Holly deep in its clutches. She was looking for something to be royally pissed at so she could deflect her fear with anger. After Blade left, Wrath and Celeste stayed and the four of us sat on the couch in silence for a long while. Celeste gripped one of Wrath's big hands in both of hers. Holly cuddled in my lap as miserable as I'd seen her since her last bout with leukemia.

"Jax," she whispered, her voice shaking with suppressed emotion. "I'm scared."

"I know, sweetheart," I whispered back, squeezing her a little tighter. "But remember what Blade said. We don't know anything yet. I'm gonna be right here with you regardless. You get me?"

She nodded miserably before tucking her face back against my chest and sitting passively. I could only imagine what was going on in her head. Scratch that. I knew at least part of what she was thinking because I was thinking it too. What if this was another relapse? How many could she have before the cancer became resistant to treatment? My reassurances didn't seem to make much of a difference for either of us.

"Why don't I make us a snack?" Celeste stood with a smile and headed to the kitchen. "Nothing fancy, just something to keep hunger at bay." The attempt at normalcy was much appreciated. I was surprised when Holly agreed without protest. She even managed to nibble on some of her sandwich before pushing it aside.

"Nervous stomach?" I murmured the question in her ear. We hadn't moved from the couch, Celeste having brought one plate with both our sandwiches and chips on it.

"I'm afraid I'll be sick if I eat too much right now."

I got it. I was tied up in knots too. I ate because I knew I'd need my strength if this didn't break our way. Again, if Holly needed, I'd provide.

As the evening wore on, Holly grew increasingly restless. Her fears chased each other in circles around her mind and I did everything I could to distract her. I could see it happening and was powerless to stop it. We watched a movie in the living room, flipping through channels until we stumbled upon an old rom com that left Holly and Celeste giggling despite the worrying. Thankfully, it was hard to hang on to a fear not right in front of you. This respite was as much a blessing as an exercise in frustration.

It was nearly dark when Blade pulled back into the driveway. Wrath was on his feet while the truck was still moving, opening the door and beckoning Blade inside.

"She's fine," Blade said as he trotted from the Bronco to the door. Thank God the man appreciated the urgency of the situation. Not so much in an acute illness sense, but how Holly and everyone who loved her were currently in a kind of limbo, unsure if we needed to prepare for the worst or laugh at our own panic.

"What do you mean, she's *fine*?" Wrath snapped at the other man. "She's anything but fine! Can't you see how stressed she is? That can't be good for her."

"Calm down, Wrath. I mean she's literally fine." Blade smiled as he moved around the couch. "You have the flu, honey." He grinned. "Influenza A, to be exact. Your white count is slightly elevated, but that can happen as a normal progression of flu. I'm still going to run several more tests on you, which will include a bone marrow aspiration." Holly whimpered, but nodded her head in understanding. "I don't want to do it because anything came back abnormal. I mean, it did, but nothing the flu wouldn't easily explain. However, since you've had one recurrence and several recent stressing events, I think it's better to be safe, and that's the most accurate early detection method. I'm also going to do some scans. But your swab came back positive for Flu A. COVID was negative. We'll know for sure if you start showing more common symptoms of the flu in the next twelve or so hours. Sore throat. Cough. Congestion. Sneezing. That sort of thing."

As he spoke, Holly covered her mouth and coughed a couple of times as if to prove his point. I kissed the top of her head. Had I been standing up, I'd probably have fallen on my ass. I actually felt lightheaded with relief.

There was a loud *THUMP,* and I whipped my head around in the direction of the noise. Wrath lay in a heap on the floor.

"Oh, goodness!" Celeste hurried to her husband who was starting to come around now that he was no longer upright. Me and Blade took out our phones and started taking pictures. "Would the two of you quit clowning around and help me get his big ass on a chair?" Celeste was never angry. I thought she might be close now.

"I got this," Blade said with a chuckle. "You keep your woman where she is."

Blade knelt beside Wrath. Instead of helping him to his feet, he snapped a small capsule under his nose and waved it a couple of times.

"Motherfucker," Wrath roared. "The fuck was that?"

"Ammonia capsule. Also known as a Howdy Cap. 'Cause, you know, you sit up and say howdy."

"You're an asshole, Blade."

"What? You were out cold!"

"I was not! Just stunned, that's all." Now Wrath looked more disgruntled than angry. "Anyway, I'm fine now." He started to get up on his own, but Celeste stopped him.

"Right," she drawled. "You're pale as a sheet. If you fall again and break your fool neck, I'm not waiting on you hand and foot. Not over stubbornness."

"Fine." Wrath stuck out a hand to Blade who pulled him to his feet. Then he eased Wrath to a chair. Celeste got him a glass of water and what looked like a couple of over-the-counter painkillers. Big fucker'd probably need it after inhaling a big ol' lung full of ammonia.

We all sat in silence for a while. Then I got the giggles. Once I started, so did Mom. Before I knew it, everyone but Dad was laughing. Blade actually wiped tears from his face.

"I don't see anything so very Goddamned funny." Of course, Dad was disgruntled.

"You fainted," Blade supplied helpfully. "Like clutched your pearls and fuckin' *fainted*."

"You're an asshole, Blade."

"Yep." He clapped Wrath on the shoulder. "Holly, I'll let you know when we can do that aspiration. I know you ain't exactly lookin' forward to it, but given the recent stressors I still think it's prudent."

"I agree. Will you promise to give me some good medicine?"

Blade leaned in and kissed the top of Holly's head. "Absolutely. Enough for a couple of days so you can stay as high as you want while you recover. Jax, you call me if she needs anything."

"I will."

"Now, Wrath. Let's get you to the truck."

"I'm fine now." He shrugged Blade off and stood still for a couple seconds while he made sure he was going to stay on his feet. Or at least, that's what I'd have been doing. Knowing Wrath, he could just as easily have been trying to figure out a way to get Holly to leave me. "Holly, come here." He held out his arms, and Holly stood and rushed to her father. He enfolded her in his larger frame and stood there holding her for a long moment. Wrath was always the cool one. His responses were measured and always in control. Just not with his daughters. "I love you, kiddo. You decide this one ain't worth the trouble and needs killin' you come tell me."

"I will, Daddy." I could see her smile and thought I might be safe. At least for a while. When Wrath finally let her go, Holly covered her mouth and coughed several times before her eyes started watering, and she instinctively looked out the window into the bright light. Then she sneezed three times. "Ohhh," she groaned.

Blade tossed me a couple of pill bottles. "Fever reducer and antivirals. May not help a lot, but it might keep her from getting really sick. Instructions are on the bottles."

"Got it."

"Fluids and rest, Holly. Fluids and rest."

"Yes, sir." She sighed and snuggled back against me while our guests let themselves out.

I wasn't willing to break the silence. As far as I was concerned, if I could get her to sit like this and doze off, so much the better.

"I'm sorry I panicked." Her voice was small, like she was ashamed of herself. Which wouldn't do at all.

"Baby, if you hadn't called me and I found about it later, I'd have blistered your ass but good. You did right to call me, and you had good reason to panic. I was there. Remember?"

"Yeah. I guess you were." Then she looked up at me, her eyes wide. "But you came to me. In a freakin' Black Hawk! Who the fuck does that?"

I laughed, leaning in to kiss her. "I do, honey. I will always do whatever I have to do to get to you. I work for and with men who would do the same thing if it was their woman so they're all gonna pitch in and pool their resources to help our women. Do you believe me now? When I say I will always be with you? No matter what?"

"Well, if I can't give the man who basically stole an attack helicopter so he could get to me half an hour faster the benefit of the doubt, who can I give it to?"

"That's my girl."

"Ohmigod!" She clapped a hand over her mouth. "Don' kisme!" Her words were muffled behind her hand, but I got the message.

"The flu wouldn't dare make me sick," I quipped. "If I want to kiss my girl, I'm gonna kiss her."

"No!" She wiggled until I let her up. "No kissing." She pointed a finger at me just before she started coughing again. Then sneezed once for good measure. "Don't like bein' sick." She pouted prettily, but I could see she felt more miserable.

"Come on. Let's get your medicine, then back to bed."

"Will you stay with me? I mean, I could lie with my back to your front, so maybe you won't get sick."

"I will definitely lie with you, honey. I'll be there

to get you fluids or medicine when you wake up. I'll hold you while you sleep."

"You won't be gone in the morning?"

If she looked unsure of herself, it was fleeting. The second I smiled at her, she relaxed, and I knew she might finally get it. "No. I'll be right with you. And if you wake up while I'm in the bathroom, I'll leave the door open."

"Eww, gross." She wrinkled her nose. "I don't want to listen to you pee." Her lips twitched a little before she managed to get the grin under control.

"I'll try to do it quietly."

She finally gave in to the giggles. Until she started coughing again. I shifted her so she wrapped her legs around my waist and stood, carrying her to the bedroom. After she'd taken her medicine and drunk a full glass of water, I helped her into clean underwear and one of my shirts before putting her to bed. I got a box of tissues for the nightstand for both of us and another full bottle of water for later.

After that, I propped a pillow behind my back and sat back with my weight against the headboard. Holly cuddled into my side with one arm draped over my waist. I put on a movie and we watched in compensable silence, laughing occasionally.

Finally, she stopped giggling and her breaths were deep and even. I looked down at her sleeping form. She was my world. My everything. The one person in my life I never wanted to be without.

"Jax?" She didn't open her eyes, and her speech was slurred like she was only half awake.

"Yeah, honey." I kissed the top of her head and spoke against her hair.

"I love you. So much."

"I love you too, Holly. My little Maddog."

She smiled. "It's a better name 'n Jax."

I chuckled, hugging her a little tighter. "Yeah, baby. Maddog is the perfect name for you."

"'Cause I'm as badass as my road name."

"You always have been, Holly. The most badass of the badasses." She smiled again, this time, leaning up to kiss along my jaw before settling back against me again. "Sleep tight, honey. Sleep tight."

Archangel (Black Reign MC 11)
A Bones MC Romance
Marteeka Karland

Sonya: I put a blow-up doll in the neighbor's holiday yard ornaments, so my father sends me to a man he thinks can help me "find my inner self" -- as in a job. Just my luck, the man he sends me to is the man I've had a crush on forever. Archangel is strong, soft-spoken, always in control, and the most perfectly made man I've ever seen. He's unflappable. I can't resist, even knowing the price I'll pay. I just hope I can slink the walk of shame back home before he knows I'm gone. That might be the only chance I have of protecting my heart.

Archangel: I don't know what Thorn was thinking when he sent his daughter to me. Sonya has plagued my every filthy fantasy since the first time she came home from college to visit friends at my club. I'd known then I needed to stay away from her. Not only am I way too old for her, but her daddy is the president of their club. Which puts me and Black Reign MC in a delicate position. Sonya running isn't a surprising. Kinda expected that. What wasn't on my Bingo card was my forgotten past catching up with me.

Chapter One

Sonya

"This might be the time we finally push him over the edge." Caroline was my best friend and partner in crime. Right now, she was looking at the man in question with a wary gaze.

"We taking bets?" I didn't look at Linnie but kept my eyes on our tormentor, Sheriff Grady Bassett. The frown he gave us said we were in big trouble. *Huge* trouble. To be fair, we often got into mischief in his county.

Sheriff Bassett didn't take us to jail this time. Instead, he marched us inside the courthouse and left our asses on a bench outside the courtroom to wait.

"Guess we get preferential treatment, huh?" Linnie wasn't as comfortable breaking the rules as I was. I was trying to help her work through her discomfort. It was clear how nervous she was now, though. We were the same age, but Linnie was a natural rule follower. I… was not.

"What about it, Lawdawg?" I addressed Sheriff Grady. "We gettin' special treatment?" Lawdawg was a play on his job as well as his actual road name. While mine and Linnie's dads were members of Salvation's Bane MC, Lawdawg was a member of a nearby MC called Black Reign. Our clubs were allies and, as such, had several functions a year together.

"Just saving everyone time and money, sweetheart. Besides, if I took you to jail for the proper processing, we'd never have gotten here before Judge Daily was done for the day. Since it's Friday, that'd mean you'd be in jail until at least Monday morning."

"Point taken," I drawled. Then I gave him a bright smile. "Anything to save the good taxpayers of

Glades County and Moore Haven a couple of bucks."

Lawdawg shook his head, frowning at first me, then Linnie. "Your daddies shoulda spanked the pair of you more often as kids."

"That's a mean thing to say." Linnie was better at pouting and being all innocent and shit than I was. She always went first.

"And vandalism isn't?" The bastard looked at us like we were still wayward children.

"We didn't vandalize anything." Linnie sat up straighter.

"You put a blow-up sex doll in the back of Santa's sleigh in Mrs. Cranston's front yard, Caroline."

"There was no permanent damage done and all anyone had to do was pull off the duct tape. And that is *not* an admission of guilt. I happened to watch as the police removed the sex doll in question from the Santa blow-up. Besides, anyone who has Christmas decorations still up deserves to have fun had at their expense." Linnie was learning. Good argument. Reference to the alleged crime without saying we did it. Point out no harm was done. "As to the residential area, there is no one in that subdivision under the age of sixty, and all their grandkids live in other states." Yep. She was getting good.

I could be mistaken but if anything, Lawdawg looked amused. "Doesn't matter. If it did, you'd be spending the weekend in jail rather than going to see Judge Dailey now."

"Come on, Lawdawg." I rolled my eyes, wanting to stomp my foot in irritation. And no. I would never call him Deputy Dawg or anything to his face. Very often. "This is horseshit and you know it. We didn't hurt anyone or scar anyone for life. Besides, someone didn't mind the sex toy being out in public too much because it was hanging half in half out of a trashcan in the neighborhood before making its way to Santa. Ain't sayin' whose house it was in front of, but the house number was 2187, and the female who put it there was yelling pretty loud at the male trying to get her to come back inside so they could 'talk'."

Lawdawg rubbed his chin, looking thoughtful. "That explains some things, believe it or not." Then he pointed an accusing finger at me. "Girls, your daddies are gonna be pissed."

"Our daddies ain't gonna find out." If my tone was clipped, fuck the bastard. He didn't like it, he could damned well take himself someplace else. And let me get the fuck outta here.

"Your daddies already know, sweetheart."

"Tattletale. Don't you know snitches get stitches?"

"I know little girls who get arrested for pranking get their asses spanked."

I snorted. "I'm twenty-one years old, so I can say with absolute authority" -- I narrowed my eyes at him --"not in this fucking lifetime, baby."

Lawdawg gave me an evil grin. "Yeah? Wait a while. Your daddy's sendin' someone to get the two of you. Should be here before we're through in court."

"Sonya's riding with me," Linnie piped up.

"Look. How long's this gonna take? We got shit to do."

"You're a brat who needs a lesson in manners, Sonya. How the fuck did Thorn raise boys who were so straight and narrow, then raise a daughter who's a hell-on-wheels wild child?"

I barked out a laugh. "My brothers? Straight and narrow? Are we even talking about the same fucking people?"

Lawdawg pointed an accusing finger at me. "You've got a mouth on you, Sonya."

"No shit, Sherlock." Sparring with Lawdawg was always fun. I think he enjoyed it as much as I did. Probably why I never managed to truly piss him off like I did most other people, though not for lack of trying. "You just now figuring that out?"

"Nope. Just was never tempted to duct tape it shut before today." He gave me a big grin like it was all the height of hilarity, but I could tell he was actually getting a bit ruffled.

My dad was president of Salvation's Bane MC in Palm Beach, Florida.

"Gee, Lawdawg, tell me how you really feel." I rolled my eyes at him and crossed one leg over the other and my arms over my chest.

"Oh, I plan on it, young lady. You're old enough to do better than this." He pointed a finger at me. "You need to grow up and act your age." He glanced from me to Linnie. "Both of you."

"It was just a bit of harmless fun! No one got hurt. We didn't make any noise and keep people up. We did it in a neighborhood with no young children around. And we didn't even break the law. At least not any important ones."

"You put a blow-up sex doll in the back of Santa's sleigh in Mr. and Mrs. Cranston's front yard."

"It was Mr. Robinson's! We watched Mrs. Robinson bring it to the trash in front of their house last night when we went for a run. She was screaming at him. He was trying to get her to go back inside and 'talk about this like civilized adults.' We saw an opportunity and we took it."

Lawdawg opened his mouth to respond but the court bailiff chose that moment to open the door to the courtroom. "Sheriff."

"Jon. He ready for us?" Lawdawg stepped aside slightly to hold the door open.

The older man looked from Lawdawg to me and back. "Christ, Grady. Again?"

Lawdawg shrugged. "Afraid so."

"Come on, then." Poor Jon sounded resigned, like this was something he had to endure every couple of weeks. Hmmm. Come to think of it, he actually *did* have to endure this every couple of weeks. My bad.

Bailiff Jon led us inside the courtroom of Judge Rupert P. Dailey. Lord knew I'd seen the inside of this place more than I should have. It was all in good fun; I never did anything dangerous or serious. This was just a fun place to pull pranks.

Judge Dailey looked up from where he'd been reading something at his desk. He sat behind the bench in the main courtroom where he presided. When he met my gaze, he started and did a double take, then frowned. "Christ, Grady. Again?"

"*Déjà vu*," I muttered.

"You two." The judge sounded tired, like he was so exhausted he couldn't manage much longer.

"Look, Judge. In our defense, anyone leaving their Christmas decorations up this long deserved to be poked fun of. It's spring, for crying out loud!"

"Not another word, young lady." The order was given by both Judge Dailey and Lawdawg. In unison. Like fucking choir boys or something. I wasn't saying that out loud, but the thought made me want to giggle.

Judge Daily and Lawdawg exchanged a look, and the judge sighed. "What sex toy did the two of you run up the flagpole this time?" I opened my mouth to answer, but Judge Dailey immediately raised his hand in a gesture to stop me from speaking and shook his head vigorously, his eyes comedically wide. "No, no, no! It doesn't matter. I don't want to know! I don't want to know!" I smirked at Lawdawg. We were totally getting a slap on the wrist. "Grady, have you made arrangements to get these young ladies home?"

"I have, Your Honor." Grady gave me the side eye before turning his full attention to the judge. "Caroline's stepmother is on her way. I'm making sure Sonya gets home."

"But --"

"And she'll go." Lawdawg spoke over me, turning his head to give me a stare promising death and destruction if I didn't shut the fuck up. Now. I did. Not because I was afraid of the big bastard, but because I was trying to learn the finer points of knowing when to keep my mouth shut. Seemed like a good time to practice. "Without. Further. Comment." He spoke through clenched teeth. Yeah. We might have broken him this time.

"Good! Can I assume whatever mischief they left behind has been… disposed of? And any mess cleaned up or fixed?"

"It has, Your Honor."

"Don't let me see you in my courtroom again, ladies. You've caused enough mischief to last several lifetimes. If I see you again, it will require some jail time for giving me a headache. Understood?"

Me and Caroline both muttered, "Yes, Your Honor," before Lawdawg took us each by the upper arm and escorted us back outside and to his waiting truck. It was emblazoned with "Sheriff" on the side and a light bar with blue and white lights on top.

"Great," I muttered. "The fucking Lawdawg mobile."

"Get in the back and stay put. Both of you." He

remotely started the vehicle before unlocking the doors for us. Of course, he put us in the back seat where we couldn't get out once the door was shut.

"What a stick in the mud." Linnie crossed her arms over her chest, indignant. But I could also see her relief. She was likely sweating over dodging a bullet with the whole jail thing.

"I'm sorry, Linnie," I said softly. "I know you're not as comfortable with breaking the rules as I am. Yet I keep dragging you into my messes."

"What? Sonya, no! You've been my best friend since the first day I met you. Sure, you push my boundaries, but we never hurt anyone or anything and it's all in good fun. Embarrassing for some, maybe, but never maliciously." She gave me a bright smile. "Besides, think how boring people's lives around here would be if not for us."

I reached out to grasp Linnie's hand. "Thanks for being such an awesome friend, Caroline."

"You're an awesome friend too, Sonya. Now, I have a serious question."

Nodding, I met and held Linnie's gaze. "Why are they separating us?"

"Exactly. They already know what we did. Why would they need to separate us?"

Lawdawg opened the door, bracing one arm on the open door, the other on the door frame. "We're separating you because you're not going to the same place."

I narrowed my eyes at him. "Do you have this truck bugged?"

"Of course. Everything inside these four doors is recorded. It's all for safety purposes. But it comes in handy when two brats think they need to get their stories straight."

"For the love of God, Grady! You already know what we did! If we're going separate places, where are we going?"

"Well, she" -- he nodded at Linnie --"is going home with her mother. Like I said."

"And me?"

This time, his smile was the smile of a man who was about to see justice served in the most satisfying way. Not gonna lie, the look made me nervous. "You're going with him." He stepped back and jerked his head to the left, indicating the straight stretch of US 27, leading from one end of town to the other.

Two blocks down, I saw a big, black Harley heading our way. Even from this distance the roar of the pipes was distinctive. And I knew the sound well. A dense trail of smoke had covered the four lanes from where one of the residences was burning a small pile of brush. Just like in the movies, the big Harley I'd known was attached to that rumble parted the haze with smoke circling behind him like a jet trail. The man sitting on the bike was just as intimidating as the machine. All the scene needed was a slow-motion sequence and it would be perfect.

Archangel. He was the most unflappable man I'd ever met. There was an eerie calm surrounding him most of the time. Sure, he laughed and had a good time like anyone else, but he was the peacemaker. The person everyone called when they didn't want El Diablo or El Segador to take up the cause. More than once, I'd heard Archangel make the statement you knew when you had a successful negotiation because neither party was completely satisfied. He didn't play favorites, and he was always fair, but the man had a giant stick up his ass the size of a telephone pole.

He crossed two lanes of traffic at the corner to

pull into the parking lot of the courthouse, not even hesitating at the light as he did. Brazen, considering where he was, and that three deputies and two city cops were sitting close by. He parked the bike in front of Lawdawg's truck before turning it off and putting down the kickstand. A long, thickly muscled leg was lifted over the seat as Archangel dismounted and walked toward the truck and Lawdawg.

I knew there was drool dripping from the corner of my mouth, but I didn't fucking care. Archangel was the most perfectly built man I'd ever had the pleasure of viewing. No matter how many times I saw him, he was still awe-inspiring. If anyone saw me, all I would have to do was point at the man and any red-blooded woman on the planet who looked would understand. He wore snug, black jeans. The material clung to his hips and thighs in all the right places. He didn't have on a shirt, but his plain leather vest covered most of his rippled torso. Which left his arms bare, and a sliver of chest and abdomen showing when he walked. Muscles and thick veins roped his arms. Tattoos peeked from his vest and crept up his arms. His salt-and-pepper hair was over his collar but artfully shaggy, and his beard was full and neatly trimmed. Mirrored aviator sunglasses rounded out his outfit. The man rocked it like the ultimate bad boy.

"Hoooooly shit. Are you seeing this?" Linnie sounded awed, and I glanced at her sharply.

"What the shit, Linnie, you whore!" I wasn't really mad. This was how we communicated.

"What?" She didn't take her gaze from Archangel and the question was more of a demand. "Tell me you weren't eye fucking him too and I'll be ashamed. Or something. OK. No, I won't be ashamed, but look me in the eyes and tell me you weren't eye fucking him. Besides, we always eye fuck him together."

"I'd love to. But I'm too busy eye fucking him to look you in the eyes and tell you I'm not eye fucking him. Because I'm eye fucking him like crazy. Also, I've changed my mind. We can't eye fuck him together anymore."

"You sure know how to pick 'em, Sonya. If you change your mind and decide he's too much work, let me know. I'll give it a shot."

"Like hell." I turned and hissed at my friend. "Mine."

"You know he's so much older than you as to not be believed, right? The man is practically ancient!"

"Red and Rosana have more of an age gap than me and Archangel."

"Right. Use their successful age gap relationship to justify your own. I'm sure it will go over with your dad as well as it would with my own father." She had a point.

"Why's he here, I wonder?"

"Don't know, Sonya, but if the look on his face is any indication, the reason can't be good."

Whatever was being said between Archangel and Lawdawg seemed to have gotten under Archangel's skin. He snatched his glasses from his face and leaned into Lawdawg's space. His lips moved, but I couldn't tell what he was saying. Mainly because Archangel had his teeth clenched. Lawdawg shrugged and jerked his head toward the truck where we sat and watched them from the back seat.

Archangel turned his head to look at the truck and us. Lawdawg spoke, gesturing with his hands a couple of times while Archangel continued to stare.

Finally, he nodded, and stepped away from

Lawdawg, moving toward the truck. Archangel came to my side and opened the door. "Come on. Out with ya." When I hesitated, he added. "Or I'll haul you out over my shoulder. Choice is yours." Though his eyes looked like he was furious, his face was relaxed and his voice was calm.

"What crawled up your ass?" The only person in the world I loved pushing more than Lawdawg was Archangel. Probably because both men were so naturally uptight yet unflappable. Anyone who followed the rules so close to the edge should feel anxious at least some of the time. Neither of these men were. Both of them stayed true to their consciences, but when the shit hit the fan, they were the calm, driving force behind fixing the fan and cleaning up the shit.

"When I'm called an hour and a half away to take a young woman in hand who's acting like a spoiled teenager, it tends to eat away at my social niceties."

"Look, you don't want my company, I'll happily catch a ride back with Linnie and Talia. I'm not sure why anyone called you to begin with. I don't belong to your club."

"No. You don't, thank God, but your daddy thinks you need a come-to-Jesus meeting about what you're gonna do with your life. I owe him one, so I got drafted."

I blinked. "Are you fucking kidding me?"

"Afraid not, Sonya. Now, come with me. We've got a long ride ahead. You can rest tonight, but tomorrow we're going to sit down and figure out your next steps in life."

"Oh really." I raised an eyebrow at him. "What if I don't want to talk with you about my future? I happen to like my life the way it is."

"And that'd be great. Except for stunts like this." When I would have continued to argue with him, Archangel snagged my upper arm and pulled me with him to his bike. His hold wasn't painful, but it was clear he wouldn't tolerate me trying to get away from him.

He took the helmet strapped down to the back of the bike and shoved it on my head. "Fasten it, then climb on behind me."

Well, the circumstances weren't ideal, but I was getting on the back of Archangel's bike. *Archangel*! My secret crush. The only person in the world who knew about my slight infatuation with the big biker was Linnie. And she was my ride-or-die chick. A vault for my secrets same as I was for hers. He had no way of knowing, but Archangel was giving me a longtime dream. And fuck, if I wasn't gonna enjoy every fucking second of it.

Chapter Two

Archangel

What the fuck was Thorn thinking, having me talk to Sonya? I didn't want to *talk* to Sonya. Not for a very long fucking time. After I'd fucked her out of my system, which could take several days, then we'd fucking talk. If Thorn knew the complexity of my affliction, he'd blow my head clean off my shoulders and I wouldn't lift a finger to stop him. Any man my age having the thoughts I was having about this girl needed to be castrated right before he was eviscerated, because it went beyond lust. Oh, yes. I wanted this girl to be fucking *mine.* It was bad enough she was the daughter of the president of another club, but I was forty-eight years old. She was twenty-one. Yeah. Not happening.

I took the state road back toward Lake Worth. There was less traffic and the way ahead wasn't always straight. Meant I needed to concentrate on something other than the woman with her arms wrapped around my waist, precariously close to my cock. Well, not really, but I imagined she was closer. Hell, I could practically feel her slide her hand down to cup my crotch. She wasn't, but I had an exceptionally vivid fucking imagination.

By the time I rolled into the Black Reign compound, my control was shot to shit and back. My cock was impossibly hard, and I had broken out in a sweat that had nothing to do with the heat and humidity of the Florida afternoon. Sonya had laughed and hollered practically the whole way home, obviously enjoying the ride. I couldn't think about her other than to make sure she didn't fucking fall off. Last thing I needed was Thorn's daughter getting hurt in my care.

I pulled in front of the main compound. It was a huge, obnoxious structure that was more like a luxury hotel. The rest of the compound consisted of several large buildings with various businesses and group housing for the club. Beyond that was a kind of subdivision with houses for the brothers with families. And still farther was open land. A lot of open land.

There was a small picnic area with a wooden deck extending into a pier over the freshwater pond to allow for fishing or swimming. There were a couple of small, furnished cabins a few of the women had started maintaining to have a place to get away from everyone occasionally. Some of the older kids used them for parties and get-togethers away from the adults. I had no doubt more than one young man or woman had lost their virginity in one of those cabins. Or on the pier. Or under the hot noonday sun or bright midnight moon. It was truly a magical place.

I'd normally bring someone to that quiet oasis for meditation and as a way to create a sense of peace before an exceptionally hard conversation. I found the tranquility helped ease one into troubled situations, helping them to focus on the problem and figure out a solution. No way I could take Sonya to the little haven. No. Fucking. Way.

Shutting down the bike, I spoke over my shoulder to Sonya, trying like shit not to let her know the effect she had on me. I knew Sonya well enough to know if I showed weakness, the woman would attack without mercy. "Off."

"Sir. Yes, sir." She snapped off a mock salute before shifting her weight on the back peg so she didn't get burned climbing off.

I gritted my teeth, sure the muscles in my jaw

bulged with tension. Thank God, Rycks met us at the door of the clubhouse. "Angel, everything good?"

"Not in any way," I muttered, taking a deep breath. "Will you please see to it Miss Sonya has a private room away from the club girls?"

Rycks raised an eyebrow but nodded. "Not a problem." He turned his gaze to Sonya and gave her a kind smile. "Welcome, Sonya. How's your father?"

"Apparently, more than a little pissed off." I glanced at her to find her smiling brightly. "I'm *supposed* to be finding something to do with my life. Archangel here is *supposed* to be helping me."

"I see." Rycks glanced back at me again. I met his gaze with a steady one of my own. The other man shook his head in confusion, so I just shrugged.

"She needs rest, and I need to prepare."

"She's not tired," Sonya interrupted. "She'd love to party with the rest of the club though."

If anything, Ryck's smile got wider. "You would."

"She would not." I turned to see Lawdawg hopping out of his truck. It was a testament to my distraction I hadn't even realized he'd pulled up.

"Christ," Sonya huffed. "I thought I left you back in Moore Haven."

"Sorry to disappoint you."

"I think I'd like to call my dad now." Sonya lifted her chin and gave me a stubborn smirk. "I'm not sure what was supposed to go on here, but you are obviously not up to the task, Archangel. So I'd like to go home now." The sweet smile was more saccharin than sugar. Little did she know she'd just waved a red flag in front of the bull.

"Challenge accepted," I snarled. "Rycks, I'm gonna need a side-by-side."

"I'll tell Mechanic. Where you takin' her?"

"To the pond. Is Lyric in the clubhouse?"

"Yep. I'll have her meet you in the common room. She'll get whatever you need."

"Now wait just a Goddamned minute." Sonya had an outraged look on her face, but something bothered me about her expression. She seemed too… calculating?

"You started it." Lawdawg grinned, looking supremely satisfied. "Now you gotta see it through."

Sonya rolled her eyes. "You really need to get that giant stick outta your ass, Lawdawg."

Rycks barked out a laugh before schooling his expression. Or rather, he tried to. "Yeah. This should be fun."

"I tell him that all the time." Eden, Lawdawg's spunky wife, wrapped her arms around his middle and hugged him from behind. "If you figure out how that works, let me know, Sonya."

"Hey, Eden! Is Bella here?" If Sonya thought Rycks and Lyric's daughter would save her, she really needed to think again.

"Doesn't matter if she is." I was done with this shit. "This doesn't involve Bella. This is between me and you."

Up to this point, I'd done everything in my power to stay away from the woman. I'd been attracted to her since she'd come back from her second semester of college. She and Caroline had spent the entire summer with Bella because she'd been in a motorcycle wreck and had been broke all to shit and back. Though I knew Sonya and Caroline were closer, the two girls had pulled Bella into their circle and the three of them were fast friends. The only reason Bella hadn't been in that mess today was because she was still recovering from the most recent surgery to her leg.

"Just because my dad doesn't like my life choices doesn't mean he can dictate to me. If my own father can't, you most certainly can't."

That was it. I ducked and put my shoulder against Sonya's abdomen and lifted her so she was draped over my shoulder.

"Hey! Put me down, you bastard!"

I swatted her ass. "Mouth shut, missy. You're in enough trouble as it is."

"I will totally carve out your balls for this, Archangel."

I ignored her. "Rycks. Is Mechanic on the way?"

"Yep. He is." The man looked too amused for my peace of mind.

"If you, Thorn, and Doc had spanked those girls when they were little, I wouldn't be in this fuckin' situation."

"Hello?" Sonya beat a fist on my back and squirmed, trying to get down. "I'm right here! I can hear you talking about me!"

I swatted her ass again. "Told you to shut it, woman. I meant it."

"Leave me outta this, Angel." Rycks put his hands up in surrender. "I personally think Thorn needs to be shook up from time to time, but I suspect he gets more of a kick outta her antics than he wants to admit. And Bella is a contained, well-behaved young woman."

"Uh-huh. Seem to remember going to get her out of more than a couple scrapes when she started college."

Rycks waved me off. "You can't count Freshmen Orientation. Those parties are supposed to be wild."

"Seem to remember Bella's roommate got her

head shaved after passing out drunk, and Bella didn't even attempt to deny it. As I remember, she told the girl she was going to do it if Bella had to help her back to the room."

"Look. To be fair, I told Bella not to let people walk all over her. She tends to lean toward the side of caution."

"Not that time."

"I'll pass on to Thorn and Doc instructions to spank their kids more often. All right?" I could tell Rycks was amused, but I wasn't feeling it. Much.

"You do that. Call and talk to him. When Thorn asked me to take this on, the man was furious."

"Furious?" For the first time, Sonya looked less than confident. I looked over my shoulder to see she had a sliver of worry in her expression. I probably liked it too much.

"Nervous now?" I raised an eyebrow at her. Hopefully, the scope of her transgressions was finally dawning on her. "Think you finally pushed your daddy too far?"

"Why are you so fucking pissy, Archangel? I didn't do anything to you." Oh, she was angry. She was also worried and lashing out. Anger was a classic response in someone who was such a force of personality, especially when someone she cared about was upset with her. Good. She needed to understand what she was facing as the consequences of her actions.

"I already told you. I got called out only to be told half my day is about to be gone and I'm being expected to sacrifice the other half -- and God only knows how many more days -- - bringing a stubborn wild child to heel."

She snorted. "Well, good fucking luck with that, hot shot. Besides, I'm not the one who called you outta bed and away from your fucking beauty sleep."

Rycks, the fucking bastard, outright guffawed. "I think maybe I understand now why you're such an ugly bastard, Angel."

"You're not helping, Rycks."

"Not trying to." The bastard was still grinning, not to mention looking entirely too smug.

We were interrupted when Mechanic pulled up in the requested side-by-side. "Someone call for a ride?" His grin was wide and all too knowing. What the fuck was up with everyone having so much fun at my expense?

"I'll take a ride back to Salvation's Bane." Sonya braced herself on my back and pushed up, looking back at Mechanic.

I swatted her butt again. "Keep it up. You're about to write a check your ass can't handle."

"I swear to God, Archangel. You smack me one more time, when I get down -- and I *will* get down -- me and you are gonna come to blows."

"You know better than to throw down that shit, Sonya." Rycks leaned over to look at the annoying woman. "He's just gonna spank your ass again."

It was my turn to laugh, only I sounded almost sinister. Or coulda sounded like I was turned on beyond belief. I was really hoping it was the former. "That ain't a spankin'," I drawled. "Trust me when I tell you she doesn't want a real spankin'."

I knew she was only going to continue to be a brat until she got her way. Right now, all she knew was she didn't want to go with me. Once we got to our destination and I gave her her own space, she'd settle. For a while anyway. Remainder of the day, we rested. Tomorrow, we talked.

Rycks helped me get her into the passenger's seat

in the side-by-side. I stalked around the other side of the vehicle to hop into the driver's seat.

"Where are you taking me?" Sonya glared at me while she adjusted her seat belt.

"The Oasis. It'll help you calm the fuck down."

"Oh no, you didn't!"

I flashed her a cocky smirk, a look that said I was in charge and found her attempts to pretend she was in charge amusing. "Yeah. I did. Get used to it, little girl."

Sonya did something unexpected then. Instead of getting even more angry or threatening me or even physically striking out at me, she gave me an assessing look. "Hmm. Might be time to see what you're really made of, Archangel."

"Always up for a challenge. Just be prepared to deal with the consequences of anything you start."

I'd meant to threaten her, but she didn't look at all intimidated. "I always am."

Something about the way she looked at me and the grave way she spoke told me Sonya was, indeed, prepared to accept whatever happened from the bomb blast she was about to create. And I had a feeling the fallout was going to be nothing short of nuclear. There was every possibility neither of us would survive.

Chapter Three

Sonya

If I dood it, I gets a whippin…

I remember watching an old cartoon where a "wascally wabbit" was contemplating doing something he knew would get him into trouble. I now knew exactly how the poor rabbit felt because I was in the same situation. And I was going to resist just as hard as the rabbit did. Which was to say, not very Goddamned much.

Archangel took us deeper into the Black Reign property, to a place I'd never been to before. Wasn't surprising since this wasn't my club, but as much time as I'd spent here with Caroline and Bella, whatever this place was must be extremely private.

It took us about fifteen minutes of driving. I knew the Black Reign compound was big, but the property must be pretty damned big. I wondered how far from the border of their area we were. I should probably be wondering what the big bastard was gonna do to me, but, honestly, I didn't care. He wasn't going to hurt me or my dad would never have given him permission for this. I was about to throw Archangel a curve ball and couldn't wait to see how he reacted.

The "Oasis," as he called it, really looked like an oasis. There was a privacy fence around the entire area, as well as three enclosed structures. Two of them looked like one-room cabins, while the other one had walls on two sides and was screened in on the others. Beyond that was a neatly kept pond. The grounds were immaculate. The place was like some fancy, exclusive spa.

"Wow." I didn't bother to hide my admiration.

"This is some place!"

"This is where I bring people to meditate and reflect. It's tranquil, and I find it helps set a relaxing mood."

There was a long silence. Very long. There was so much to unpack in Archangel's explanation I wasn't sure where to start.

After what had to be a full minute of us staring at each other, neither of us willing to give anything away, I finally found my voice. "Meditation. Reflection."

Archangel lifted his chin at a stubborn angle, daring me to say anything further.

Naturally, I did. "I wasn't aware bikers practiced meditation and reflection. Do your brothers know about this? How about the club whores? Is this some form of punishment? Because if it's punishment, I'm afraid Imm'a have ta pass."

"Keep it up. Thorn won't get the chance to spank you because I will."

"You say that like it's a threat or something." I grinned and twirled one long, curly strand of my hair.

"This might be beyond my capabilities," he muttered, scrubbing a hand over his face like he was bone weary. "Not on no sleep." He focused on me again, seeming to be trying to make a decision. Then he nodded his head once. "This cabin is yours. The only electricity is what it takes to run water. There's no cell coverage out here either. There is a small bathroom with plumbing, but the shower is barely big enough for one person." He turned to the side-by-side and picked up a large duffel bag. "Lyric packed some things. You should have everything you need in here to be comfortable, including several changes of clothing."

"OK… What exactly are you expecting to happen here?"

"I expect you to do as I tell you and to open your mind up to what you have to offer the world. To find a way you can help your club and your family. I'm going to help you find your way."

I blinked up at him. "Wow. That wasn't rehearsed *at all*."

He clenched his jaws and his fists, giving me a look that said he wanted to flay me alive. "Go to the fuckin' cabin, Sonya. Make your bed. Set up your shit the way you want it. Walk around the fucking pond. I don't give a fuck. But get some rest tonight and be ready to start at sunrise."

"Fine, Mr. Cranky Pants."

"I've locked the gate to this place. You can't get out and no one can get in. It's only the two of us until we get this done."

I tried to look put out, but inside I was rubbing my hands together with glee. "Fine. Fine. I'll just take my shit and go sit with my thumb up my ass."

"I'll have supper ready in a couple of hours. We eat and work in the shelter." He pointed to the half-enclosed building I'd noticed before. "No matter what task you've been assigned, we always eat three meals a day together. Seven, noon, and five. It's where we talk to each other and express our concerns and share our accomplishments with each other."

"This has got to be some kind of alternate universe." I know I was staring at Archangel like he'd grown a third eyeball, but I couldn't help it! "What *are* you?"

"Curious?" He arched one dark eyebrow.

"You kind of maybe sound like you might have done this a time or three. So I want to know if you're, like, some kind of New Age healer or shaman or something."

"I'm a soldier who's seen too much death and turned to philosophy. I've studied several different religious sects and methods of healing mental trauma through different meditative techniques. If you want to know why, you'll have to stay and not fight me on what I'm asking of you."

I laughed softly. "By God, you're good. Fine. I'll play your little game." More because it suited me to take my time with this. Well, for the moment anyway. "I'll be here every day. Do what you tell me to do. Mostly. And I'll try to pick up what you put down. I'll keep an open mind and all that shit. But you have to give me some kind of time frame. I have no intention of being stuck here indefinitely."

"I don't like having a time limit. Defeats the purpose."

"And I'm not signing over my life to you until you see fit to call a halt. I'll give you two days."

"A week. Minimum." His gaze was flat and cold. I'd thought I'd seen his icy exterior crack earlier, but either I was mistaken or he'd reinforced his defenses. "And I prefer two weeks."

"Four days. I'll reevaluate after that," I countered.

He nodded. "Fine. Now go get settled. I'll see you in the shelter in two hours for supper."

I found myself exhilarated as I raced to my cabin. It was only feet from the one Archangel was using. In fact, the window next to my bed faced a window in his cabin. I thought I saw him moving around, but the sun was glaring off the glass too much.

Turning away from the window, I tossed my duffel on the twin bed shoved against the wall. Lyric had packed sheets, a comforter, towels, and washcloths, as well as clothing all the way down. She'd also included a bathing suit and flip-flops as well as assorted toiletries. The cabin was spotless and cozy, even if it was small. I found I rather liked the tiny home. I found this place to be somewhere I could live comfortably. At least until I got bored. I had a feeling the next few days promised to be anything but boring.

* * *

Sonya
Two Days Later…

I was bored outta my fucking mind!

"In, and hold… Let it out." I felt like I was in a Richard Simmons video. Only without all the fun and laughs. And don't judge me for knowing who Richard Simmons is or for watching his videos. If I'm exercising, Imm'a have fun doin' it. "That's it. Good job, Sonya. Now again. Close your eyes. Listen to the breeze through the trees, the rippling of the water." His voice was oddly hypnotic, but all I heard was a sexy cadence telling me to do shit that was sexy.

"Now, take off your top and pull your tits out of your bra. That's right. Show me those pretty nipples. How they harden when the breeze tickles them."

"Oh yeah," I whimpered.

"What?" The word was nothing short of a demand.

"Hmm?" My gaze snapped to him. I tried to look all innocent and shit when I'd gotten caught red-handed daydreaming about Archangel instructing me to strip. No doubt, if he'd left me alone, I'd have gotten to the part where he fucked me. "Did you say something?" Oops.

Archangel frowned down at me. Even with both of us sitting on the grass, he was still taller than me. Or maybe it was my imagination. He was so much larger than life! Not to mention my ultimate fantasy. Besides, like I said, I was bored. "Are you even listening to me? What were you thinking about just now?"

I leveled a look at him. "Do you *really* want me to answer that question, Archangel? Because I will. Then you'll have to be the one to deal with the fallout." I raised an eyebrow at him. I wasn't bluffing either. What did I have to lose by telling him I was fantasizing about stripping for him? It wasn't like anything was going to happen, and it might get him to call off this little charade and I could go back home. Worst case, he avoided me for the rest of my life. Sure, it would be embarrassing, but Archangel would never be cruel about letting me down. He'd reject me but do it gently. Or he'd fuck me and I'd get to live out several fantasies. Which… yeah.

If I dood it, I gets a whippin'…

"You're a brat, girl. I have a feelin' you ain't gonna respond to anything short of force."

I smirked. "Probably not. You got a plan for that?"

"You're testing me." He gave me a knowing smile. A soft and tranquil smile. Like I was falling right into his plan. "Good. You need to know I'm dedicated to helping you."

"Bullshit," I sang out, smiling. It really was funny. "You don't even want to be here. You think I don't know when someone doesn't like my company?"

"Never said I didn't like your company. You're one of the most interesting people I've ever met. You simply have a problem with authority. I'm here to help you realize you don't always have to buck the system. Especially with those close to you."

"Like my mom and dad?" I shook my head. "Dad is a bit of a control freak. I get it. Unfortunately, he has a daughter as stubborn as he is, so good luck with helping me be OK with him making all my decisions for me."

"Sonya, Thorn doesn't want to make all your decisions for you. He just wants you to make better ones so you don't get into trouble."

"OK, that's a good one." I actually laughed. "My father doesn't want to make all my decisions for me? That's the very definition of what he wants! He just wants me to think his 'suggestions' are all my idea so I don't feel like he's telling me what to do."

He tilted his head. "Do you really think your father tries to manipulate you into doing what he wants?"

"Of course he does! Mom will even say I'm right. Did you even look into this whole situation before you agreed to brainwash me?" It was a barb. I couldn't help it! His horrified expression told me I'd hit my mark. I didn't really think he was brainwashing me, but the look on Archangel's face was too funny not to continue.

"Sonya, I don't want to brainwash you or convince you not to make your own decisions or anything like that. And I happen to know your father only has your best interest at heart. He loves you."

"Oh, I know he does. I love him too. Doesn't mean I'm going to change who I am to make him happy. Changing myself would make everyone miserable." When he opened his mouth to respond I interrupted him. "*Really* fucking miserable." I gave him a knowing look with raised eyebrows.

"You don't have to change who you are, honey. Just… don't put blow-up sex dolls in the middle of people's Christmas decorations."

"It's almost fucking spring! Who leaves their

Christmas decorations up this long? They were asking for something to happen. You're trying to take away all my fun." I tried to pout, but couldn't hold it. A laugh bubbled up and had to escape. To my surprise, Archangel laughed with me, real mirth shining in his eyes. It was a stunning moment. Though I'd seen him smile and laugh occasionally, this was a real, honest-to-God laugh like he was enjoying himself to the fullest. I couldn't help softening toward him. Just a little. "You should do that more often." I reached out to touch his hand which was resting on his knee where we'd been meditating. Or, as I liked to call it, sitting cross-legged with our eyes closed, being bored out of our minds.

He stiffened at my touch but didn't pull away. "Do what more often?"

"Laugh." I smiled at him. "You look loads younger when you laugh."

"And there's the brat." Archangel tried to scowl at me, but he couldn't hold it any better than I could. "You're smart, Sonya." He turned his hand over and gripped my fingers. "You could be anything you want to be. Why are you still hanging around home?"

I shrugged. "Why move away from home? I have everything I love right here. My family. My friends. I work around the clubhouse grounds and garage. You know, cooking and cleaning and shit. I do it because I like taking care of my peeps. Why change that if I'm happy? Besides, I'm doing more work than all the club girls combined. Sure, I don't fuck the guys, but I earn my keep. I don't expect to stay in the compound for free just because my dad's the president. I never have."

"He just wants to make sure you can survive on your own. You know. Away from the club."

"Why would I ever need to?" I wrinkled my nose at him. "I've seen what the world outside the club is like. And I don't mean when I was pulling those little pranks I pull in Moore Haven. People are mean at the best of times in the outside world. Inside Salvation's Bane, or even here at Black Reign, everyone respects each other. Well, except the club girls, and even they have lines they rarely cross. Besides, Dad doesn't know everything I do. I have some… hobbies."

"If you mean the clothing and toy drives you do for the local group homes and nursing homes, I know about them."

I gasped. "Have you been spying on me?" I wasn't really shocked. In fact, I was surprised Ripper, the intel officer for Salvation's Bane, hadn't discovered it sooner. He probably had -- the guy was good -- and just hadn't said anything.

"I don't know why you keep it secret, Sonya. Be proud of what you're doing. Bring more attention to your cause."

"That kinda takes the point out of it," I muttered. No. Not many people thought the way I did.

He blinked at me before narrowing his eyes in an adorably confused look. "I don't understand."

"I'm not the primary fundraiser for any of those things. I just contribute. Also, if I went around bragging, 'look what I did,' then it makes the giving about me showing the people in my world what good things I'm doing. Not about me helping kids and seniors who can't help themselves."

"I get that. From what I've seen, your usual M.O. is to find out what was raised and match it. What I don't understand is where the money comes from. Thorn would be raising hell if club money came up missing. Not because he objects to giving charitable donations, but because he's the fucking president."

"Surely you know I'd never steal anything from

anyone. Especially not from my dad's club." Now he was just pissing me off.

"Of course I know you'd never steal from your club." OK. Maybe he got to live a while longer. "Which is why I can't figure out where your money is coming from. You don't have a job or money of your own."

Or not.

"Ah. I see." I grinned. Because, finally, I *did* see. "This has less to do with me figuring out my path in life than it is about Dad wanting to know where I'm getting my funds. Which means Ripper *did* rat me out."

"I didn't say your dad was only interested in where you get funds. I didn't even say he was curious."

I sighed. "You didn't have to, Archangel. If he doesn't know what I do to get money, then he wants to know. He should have come out and asked me."

"Can't speak to that, but he does want me to help you to find, as you say, your path in life."

"If I tell you what I do, will you call this whole thing off? I'll go back home and stay out of trouble. As long as I can anyway."

"I'll take it to your dad. Ultimately, it's your decision. I can't force you to do anything. But I don't think you'll outright defy your father."

Shit. He was right. "Look, I got an Only Fans page, all right?"

"What?" He snapped out the question, his eyes going comedically wide. I had to fight to keep from laughing. The look on his face was priceless. Like if he had mind bleach, he'd use it.

"I sell pictures of my feet, Angel. Where did your mind go?" I shrugged like it was all no big deal. "Ask Ripper. He caught me when I first set it up. He said the only reason he didn't tell Dad was because there was no harm in showing my feet, but any breach of his trust in me would not only result in him ratting me out, but in my Internet and phone privileges being taken away. Since he was the tech guy, he could pull off the restrictions with ease and good luck telling Dad why Ripper had grounded me when I complained. It was quite diabolical."

"You definitely need a spanking."

"I'm twenty-one, Angel. I've got plenty of time to be an adult. I want to enjoy getting into trouble for petty shit like the aforementioned blow-up sex doll while I'm still young enough to appreciate the humor. There's plenty of time to grow up."

For some reason, he stiffened. He snatched his fingers away from mine and stood abruptly. "Yeah. Plenty of time." He backed two steps away before stopping, lifting his chin like he'd just realized he was retreating. "Take the rest of the afternoon to reflect on… uh… something. Growing up." Then the man beat feet back inside his cabin.

"Was it something I said?" I didn't get a reply to my muttered response.

Chapter Four

Archangel

I was fucked. I mean, *really* fucking fucked. When Sonya and I had carried on a normal conversation where she expressed her love of her MC life and about her relationship with her father and the rest of her family at Salvation's Bane, she'd been so animated and unfiltered. She truly meant what she said.

I also understood a little more about Thorn. He was worried about his daughter and needed to know how she was making her money without asking her and possibly insulting her by insinuating she was doing something illegal or, worse, stripping or sex shows or something else he didn't want to know his little girl was doing. No one else cared if she was making her money with some skin, but daddies were a different breed. So yeah. I got it. I'd still be calling him out on his deception later, but right now I had bigger fucking problems.

First, Sonya was more than what she presented to everyone. There was an intriguing depth to the wild child I doubt anyone other than Sonya's mother, Mariana, or possibly Caroline and Bella, had realized existed. Thorn might have a clue, but he'd never admit it. Because, despite his instructions to me on making Sonya sit down and come up with a plan for her future, Thorn never wanted his little girl to grow up and not be dependent on him. He only sent me to find out about her funds. He'd used this latest escapade to throw me to the wolves.

Second -- and this was really the more disturbing part -- somehow in the middle of the conversation between me and Sonya just now, I'd fallen in love with her. Fucking hard, too. I wasn't being dramatic either. The longer she'd talked, the more my fucking heart had opened up, needing to drink in all her brightness and energy.

I'd dedicated my life to helping El Diablo and all the members of Black Reign MC to keep from falling into complete darkness. We'd all done some pretty bad things in our past. Most of us would do them again if necessary. I had taken it as my calling to help us all keep the pieces of our souls together as much as possible. Up until now, I'd thought I'd done a decent job with my own soul. Until I let Sonya fill me with her presence. That was when I realized how many holes I had inside me. Because Sonya's light spilled out from me, from those missing parts of humanity inside me, and I began to heal.

I shut the door and leaned against the cool wood, then thumped my head against it and groaned. I'd broken out in a sweat and my heart felt like it was going to beat out of my chest, almost like a panic attack. Which was probably an accurate description of what was currently happening to me.

The one sink in the place was only a few steps away along the counter running the short length of the back wall. I managed to make it without my knees giving way, though it was a struggle. I braced one hand on the counter while I turned on the water with the other. The cool water felt good on my skin, so I splashed my face. Water sluiced from my beard and I shook my head, sending droplets flying.

"Christ," I muttered. "What the fuck am I doing?" I had to get a grip. What Sonya had said to bring me screaming back to reality was that she had plenty of time to be an adult, reminding me of her age. She was twenty-one. *Twenty-one*! I was forty-eight!

Besides the fact she was the daughter of an MC president and far outranked me, she was young enough to be my daughter. A wide age gap like ours worked for some of my brothers, but even they might blink at close to a thirty-year difference.

I needed to go apologize to Sonya for running off, but there was no way I could be near her right now. Not and keep my dick in my pants.

Just as well. If Sonya knew the effect she had on me, there'd be a war. First between her and me for dominance. Next between Black Reign and Salvation's Bane because her daddy would demand his pound of flesh for me defiling his daughter, and El Diablo would have my back to the death. I'd kept the peace for years inside the club. I could keep the peace outside as well.

The fading light seemed like a blessing. No electricity other than to keep running water meant no lights. I could meditate and calm my mind and my heart. I could get through this with my self-respect intact. Thorn would have no reason to come after me.

I pulled open the curtain so the sunlight filtering through the trees would hit the bed in the morning. A good night's sleep would help me regain perspective and maybe help me to calm down. I thought I'd fallen in love, but maybe I was wrong. Maybe it was the meaningful, fun conversation with a beautiful woman. I could have felt this way about any woman. But, given the fact my whole purpose in the club was to talk to people and look to the deeper meaning of what they're telling me, I doubted my feelings stemmed from anyone other than Sonya.

I pulled my shirt off and tossed it on my duffel before kicking off my shoes and shorts and sitting on the bed. Normally I slept naked, but it didn't feel right for some reason. I was the only person Sonya could come to for help or if she needed something. So there was a reasonable expectation she might come in on me at some point. It seemed safer not to have my dick out.

The night was warm and slightly sticky. Both windows were open to allow the breeze to move freely through the cabin. It was a calming sensation over my skin, so I didn't use the light sleeping bag I'd packed. Instead, I lay on top of the material and let the wind kiss my skin until I drifted off…

* * *

Archangel

Sweet God in heaven! I woke up to the most intense sexual need I'd ever experienced in my whole fucking life! I was about to come and I wasn't even truly awake yet. Hell, I wasn't even really sure where I fucking was.

Whoever was sucking my cock had me losing my fucking mind! I groaned and threaded my hands through the silkiest hair imaginable in a tight grip. I wanted to wrap the strands around my cock and jack off with them, but that would mean pulling out of the mouth currently swallowing me down.

It was full dark, the moon but a tiny sliver in the sky. No light gave me a clue as to my surroundings or the people in them. It would be like one of the club whores to sneak into my room and get me to fuck her, but I didn't think that was the case currently. Every time I thought I could put together what was going on, I'd hear a greedy slurp, followed by a contented sigh of pleasure. Any hope I had of holding a coherent thought vanished.

"Christ!" I thrust my hips up so my cock slid farther into that hot, wet mouth. I tightened my grip in her hair so I guided her movements. "So fuckin' good."

A feminine moan hummed around my cock, pushing me that much closer to the edge. Her soft palm gripped the base of my cock and worked the length she couldn't fit into her mouth. Which wouldn't do. I batted her hands away and pulled her down farther by her hair. She gagged, but put her hands on my thighs and held on.

"So fuckin' good!" I growled as I fucked up into her mouth.

"Mmm…" She hummed around me when I let her up. She backed off to a more comfortable depth, but a few seconds later, she gagged herself on my dick again. This time with feeling. She swallowed as she gagged, massaging the head of my cock with every movement of her throat. Saliva and thicker mucus brought on by her exertions eased her way and she continued to take me deep over and over until she had to come up for breath.

I counted backward from ten, trying to keep my control, but it was a losing battle. When I reached four, I erupted into her mouth with a loud groan. She didn't pull back, didn't protest when I shot my jizz down her throat. Instead, she swallowed with a contented hum and licked my tip before she pulled away completely.

"Come here," I growled, pulling her up my body with her hair. She let out a small cry before she giggled. There was something I needed to process. I needed to slow down. But then her lips were fused to mine and I forgot my own fucking name.

I tasted myself on her tongue every time I thrust mine into her mouth. She whimpered but rubbed herself all over my body. Like she was trying to rub her scent on me. While she did, she kissed me like she wanted to devour me. Like she owned me.

No! No one owned me. But the more this woman

kissed me, the more her lithe curves tormented me, the more I questioned my inner declaration.

With a snarl, I flipped us so that I pinned her to the bed with my heavier frame, never breaking our kiss. I pressed against her pussy where my body was situated between her legs. I still had on my boxers, but I thrust against her like I was fucking her.

The second the thought of sticking my dick in her pussy entered my head I knew it was prophetic. I was going to fuck her. It wasn't going to be gentle either.

"Get my fuckin' shorts down," I growled, fully expecting her to obey me. She did. Her cool fingers were at my hips, tunneling under the waist of my boxers. Her nails dug into my ass as she pulled me to her.

"Angel…" Her voice was a needy whisper dancing through my head.

"Fuck." I shifted my weight so I could reach between us to guide my cock to her entrance. The second the head touched her opening, she arched her back at the same time I thrust and I was inside her to the fucking hilt.

I grunted at the same time she gasped in a startled breath. I knew I needed to stop, to figure out what the fuck was going on besides the best sex of my life.

Her fingers slid from my ass to grip my hips and she stilled me. I shoved inside her once more and held still. I could control myself from taking her like a rabid dog, but I had to be inside her to do it.

A growl escaped me as I pressed my face to her neck and inhaled, needing to take her scent into me so I could keep her with me forever. I nuzzled her, coaxing her to relax again, to be that little nymphomaniac who'd swallowed me down. I needed to… *fuck her*!

"Just give me a second." Her voice was a mere whisper, but I could hear the slight tremor. "One second."

"Tell me what you need."

She turned her head and found my lips. Her kiss was like black magic. Forbidden but so much Goddamned fun. I flexed my hips and she met me. I wasn't a small man so I'd had more than one woman need to adjust, but the small hesitation gave me the time to realize something was off. Her kisses and tight little pussy were rapidly driving my returning sanity off again, but a tiny corner in the back of my mind was telling me I needed to hold still and pay way more attention to the woman in my arms.

Then she arched her hips, driving me just that little bit deeper inside her. Her pussy clamped down around my dick and she gave a surprised yelp, then screamed as her pussy milked my cock with her orgasm.

"Angel!" My name on her lips as she came was the final nail in my coffin. I wanted to hear that voice in that tone every single day for the rest of my life. Two quick thrusts later and I came. And came. *And… came…*

With one last grunt, I collapsed on top of her. Sweat coated our skin, and we were both breathing hard. I buried my face in her neck. When she tilted her head and exposed more of her skin to me, I kissed and licked her flesh tenderly in praise of her giving so freely of her body. The show of affection wasn't something I ever did but was as natural as breathing with this woman.

I rolled us to our sides, my arms still locked tightly around her. When the fog started to lift from my brain as the blood rushed from my dick back to my brain, the thing I was missing hit me like a bullet between the eyes.

"Sonya." Her name was like both a whispered prayer and a plea for mercy.

"Wow." She smiled as she breathed out the word. "You came hard."

"Fuck yeah, I came hard," I muttered as I tried to catch my breath. I hadn't meant to speak out loud but opening my big fat mouth was the very least of my problems. "What the fuck was that, Sonya?"

She gave me a dazzling smile, stretching beneath me like a contented cat. "I was bored. And you needed a good fuck." She shrugged. "Looks like we both win."

I was so stunned I couldn't say anything. This was what I'd been missing. I'd just come my brains out inside Sonya's sweet pussy. And I was ready for another round.

Sonya continued to smile. She must have felt my cock growing hard where it rested against her thigh because her eyes got wide, then she slipped her arms around my neck. "So... do you want a repeat?"

It felt like someone tossed a bucket of ice water in my face. I jerked back and practically jumped out of bed. "Holy fuckin' hell!" I shoved myself away from her and stood, pulling up my boxers in a couple of jerky motions. I gave her a pointed look meant to chastise her like the naughty little girl she'd been. And, oh, my God, I was going to hell for that thought! "No more of that!" Took everything I had not to tack "young lady" at the end.

There was a brief flash of hurt in her expression before she smirked and rested her arm on her hip as she lay on her side. "Up to you. I figure if we've still got a couple of days before we leave, we might as well do something besides sit on the ground with our eyes shut… *breathing*." She sat up and reached for her shirt, turning her body away from me as she shrugged into the garment. She gave me a little wave. "See you in the morning, Archangel." The smile she flashed was meant to be cocky and confident. Instead, I thought I saw hurt and doubt. Then she opened the door and was gone.

I closed my eyes and pinched the bridge of my nose. My cock was still leaking cum and was rapidly getting hard again. Fuck! How the fuck had I let this happen? Being half asleep was no excuse. There is no way I should have been so caught up in the pleasure I forgot where I was and who I was with. I'd told her we were locked in this place, and I'd meant it. No one came in or out without my knowledge. So, had I listened to that little feeling in the back of my brain, I'd have realized who was in my bed. The truth was, I hadn't wanted to know who was sucking my dick. Because knowing would have meant stopping her sweet mouth from taking my cum.

For the first time in a very long time, I was at a loss as to what to do. Where my instinct had been telling me to stop before, now it was telling me to go after Sonya. To keep her now that I'd made her mine. I could deal with Thorn. My problem was not knowing what she wanted. So yes. We were going to have to talk about this sooner rather than later.

I took a breath and held it, trying to locate that inner calm I'd been trying to teach Sonya about. There was no peace to be found. Not while Sonya wasn't in my arms.

I opened the door to my cabin just as the door to hers clicked shut. She hadn't slammed it or even hurried to her private space, instead taking her time and quietly shutting herself inside. I did hear the snick of the lock as I took the first step onto her porch.

"Sonya? Open up."

"I'm sorry, Archangel. Now the adrenaline's gone, I'm really tired."

"Me too. Open up." I knocked several times on the door for emphasis.

"Please, can you just let me be? I'm sorry I came to your cabin. I won't do it again." Yeah. That wasn't happening. I could definitely hear the hurt and regret in her voice and I wasn't having it.

"Open. Up." I put some force behind the command. I hoped it would get her back up. She'd deal with me better if she was angry or stubborn than she would if she was feeling vulnerable. Because now that I'd had time to replay a few of the events leading to this point, I knew she might not have been a virgin but wasn't much more than that.

I heard her heave out an exasperated sigh before unlocking and opening the door. "Are you always so fucking stubborn?" Her upturned face was a mask of indifference and annoyance, but a mask was all it was.

"Nope. I'm usually worse. Let me in."

She stepped back and gestured inside. Our cabins were the same. Other than the bed, there was a small table with two chairs and not much else. I took a seat at the table and indicated for her to do the same.

"Do you mind if I go to the bathroom first?"

I winced, but nodded. "Of course. Take your time." I had to be careful here. Really fucking careful.

She disappeared into the bathroom, and I scrubbed a hand over my face. I'd really fucked this to shit and back. I had to find a way to fix this, more for Sonya's sake than my own. I'd take whatever Thorn dished out because I could have stopped fucking her at any time. But I didn't want her getting hurt more than she already had been. She deserved a better man than me. Someone she could grow old with. While I knew I'd never look at another woman as long as I lived, she had her whole life ahead of her. The last thing she needed was a man twice her age.

The second she opened the bathroom door and took the three steps from the door to the chair, any hope I had of keeping her at arm's length vanished. Nope. Sonya was mine. The look on her face, the uncertainty and dread, made me want to kick my own ass. Not because I'd fucked her. Because I hadn't held on to her after I'd realized what the fuck was happening.

"So?" She laced her fingers tightly together in front of her on the table. "What did you want to talk about?"

Chapter Five

Sonya

What had started out as a fantastic idea had rapidly… devolved. Not only had I made a fool of myself, but I had touched Archangel without permission, which had put him in a tenuous position. Especially if my father found out. If the positions had been reversed, there was no one in either Salvation's Bane or Black Reign who wouldn't kill Archangel for taking advantage of me. I get the dynamics were different and he was both mentally -- in terms of age and life experience -- and physically my superior. He could have fought me off where I'd have been at his mercy. But the end result was still the same. I'd sat at the table with every intention of playing off the whole incident, but the truth was, what I'd done was inexcusable.

Before Archangel could say anything, I ducked my head so he couldn't see tears forming. "I'm sorry, Archangel." I whispered. "I didn't think about what would happen after. I only thought about what I wanted and that if you didn't, you'd stop me."

Archangel let out a long breath. Then he reached out to put both his big hands over mine. "Look at me, Sonya." I shook my head, but he simply reached out with one hand and tilted my chin up. "Yes." When I still refused to look at him, he brushed my lower lip with his thumb. "Give me your lovely eyes, little Sonya."

I gasped in a small breath. There was such gentleness in his voice and touch, I had to comply. But when I met his gaze, the heat and need I saw reflected my own. Sex with Archangel had surpassed my every fantasy and left me longing for so much more. Looked like he'd enjoyed himself too.

"Sonya." His voice was rough, gravelly as he stared into my eyes intently, obviously wanting me to believe whatever he was about to say next. "Whatever you think you did wrong, don't. If I'd truly wanted to stop things before they got out of hand, I could have. My inaction is on me."

His eyes were swirls of gray and green that seemed to shift with his emotions, but there was a softness in them that caught me off-guard, making my chest tighten and my breath catch. I wasn't sure exactly what he was feeling, but whatever emotion was dominant was something he embraced with his whole heart. Archangel was a hardened man with internal walls built out of concrete and steel. Yet, here he was revealing a vulnerability I was quite sure he'd rarely shown to anyone before.

"I'm sorry." I couldn't help the apology. It needed to be said.

"OK. Apology accepted." He gave me a hint of a smile. "The real problem is, you're right. You didn't think." His tone was gentle, and he didn't break eye contact with me. "What you did, Sonya… It was dangerous. Reckless even. As much as you enjoyed it, as fan-*fucking*-tastic as it was for me, we can't ignore the possible consequences."

"I understand that," I replied in a barely audible whisper. A single tear slipped and traced its way down my cheek. I was well aware of the damage that could already have been done. We hadn't used a condom, but I couldn't say I'd have done anything differently if I'd been given the opportunity. So, yeah. He was right about consequences. What kind of person did that make me?

His gaze softened, and he reached out to wipe

my tear away with his thumb, his touch tender and lingered longer than I'd have liked given he hadn't declared his undying love for me. I knew that was a laughable fantasy, but it was still my fantasy. "It's going to be okay, Sonya. But we need to clear a few things up." His voice had an intensity I found impossible to ignore.

He leaned back in his chair, giving both of us space to breathe. I watched him swallow hard, the movement of his Adam's apple jerking my heart in a painful beat. Archangel didn't seem like a man who was at loss of words, yet here he was struggling to find the right ones. And even though I wanted him to speak, to clarify the muddled mess in my mind, I also dreaded his next words because they might shatter me completely.

"Sonya." The word came out barely audible, as if caught in his throat. "What happened between us… it can't happen again."

I'd known he was going to say something like this. He wasn't wrong. Hearing him voice it, though, was a punch to my gut. I stood slowly and moved to the window in front of the counter running along half the back wall. I braced my hands on the flat surface and took a deep breath. I was very much afraid I might cry if I didn't get a grip on myself. I wasn't sure what hurt more, his words or the fact he was right.

After a moment, I felt Archangel move in behind me. His body caged me in, his hands on either side of me where I stood with my back against the counter, which surprised me. He was telling me that us having sex had been wrong, but now he was all up in my space? I gritted my teeth against the urge to lean back against him. I still had some pride.

"Sonya." His voice was rich with emotion when

he finally spoke again. He pressed his body against me. I sucked in a breath. I could feel the heat coming off of him. How was I supposed to resist this attraction when he was clearly baiting me?

"I don't mean to hurt you." His voice faded away like a summer breeze before he could finish, leaving behind an emptiness that echoed the hollow feeling inside me.

I turned to face him then, preparing to meet those gray eyes of his with an unconcerned look. "You didn't." I smiled up at him. "You're right. I shouldn't have touched you without your permission."

"Honey, I don't care about that." He was looking at me intently now. His brows drew together as he continued to stare at me. Then Archangel shivered slightly, his eyes narrowing. His jaw clenched. Very slowly, he leaned back away from me. He didn't take his hands from the counter or his gaze away from mine. "Fuck me," he whispered. The next thing I knew, Archangel was kissing me like his life depended on it. And I surrendered to him.

The feel of his lips against mine was like nothing I'd ever known. They were firm and demanding, yet tempered. There was something far more intimate in Archangel's kisses that left me with no room to think about anything else but the taste of him and the way he made me feel. His hand slid up my spine and into my hair, holding me still as he plundered my mouth like he was starving for me. I knew I was starving for him. I'd had a taste before and wanted so much more.

He pulled away abruptly. Breathing heavily, he stared down at me. "I can't do this. Not with you." He shoved away and walked out of the cabin, leaving me standing there, shaking and lost. OK, that comment hurt. Not with me?

I followed him out the door, fully expecting to have to hurry to catch him before he got inside his own cabin. Surprisingly, he stood just outside on the tiny porch, bracing himself against the railing with his hands. He was obviously struggling with something, but I had my own thoughts to worry about. Like I'd let this man take me to unmanageable heights and wasn't willing to never experience sex with him again.

"What does that mean?" I demanded, moving around to see as much of his face as I could. I needed to see his expression clearly. "Not with me."

"It means I'm not fucking you. Not again." If I were guessing -- and I totally was because Archangel was good at covering his emotions -- I'd say he totally wanted to fuck me again.

"Well, that's unfortunate." I tried to sound light and airy, like none of this actually mattered to me. "I was hoping to find out more about your path of philosophy. But if you're giving up already, I must be more than you're used to handling." It was a calculated risk, baiting Archangel, but I threw out my line and waited to see if I'd made a fool out of myself or hooked me a whale. Or a shark.

"Don't do that." He growled. "Don't use your fucking wit to try and manipulate me."

I held my hands up in surrender. "Fine. So, who's up for a movie and some popcorn?" I grinned, needing to back off and come at him from a different angle. This was a very bad idea. A very bad idea. But I had this sickness. Once I started something, I had to finish. Call it morbid curiosity. I wasn't sure where this road was going to lead, but I was hauling ass down it as hard as I could go.

Archangel gave me a threatening look, actually going so far as to point a finger at me. He opened his mouth to say something but promptly closed it again. His gaze swept me from head to toe, his nostrils flaring. "Did you put on underwear?"

The question caught me off guard, but this was my opening. If he ended this little therapy session, I'd never get another chance to be with him because he'd never put himself in a situation where I'd have the chance. Then my lips tugged upward and I couldn't stop the words that I uttered next. "Why would I have done that?"

"Christ, woman!" Archangel lunged for me, fisting his hand in my hair. His kiss was brutal, his tongue darting between my lips to claim what he refused to admit he wanted. The intensity of it left me breathless, as if he was trying to consume the very air I breathed.

He pressed his body against mine, pushing me back against the door of the cabin. His cock hardened against my belly and a wave of satisfaction washed through me. Archangel might have been saying one thing, but his body was telling a very different story. No doubt he wasn't happy with himself or the situation, but he was going to fuck me again. I just had to keep pushing and not let up for an instant.

I wound my arms around his neck, pulling him closer. His hand tightened in my hair as he thrust his tongue deeper, tasting every part of my mouth. As quickly as he'd started kissing me he broke away, panting heavily. He pulled back just enough to look at me, his gray eyes dark and filled with a torrent of emotion I wasn't sure he understood. Granted, I was no expert, but I swore Archangel looked like he was both completely lost and right where he wanted to be.

I thought he'd pull back again, maybe leave me here for the night, which I couldn't allow, but he stared down into my face for long moments. His grip tightened in my hair, and he pulled me up to meet his lips again. His other arm tightened around my back, clamping me to him like an iron band. He lifted me and I locked my ankles around his waist as he got us inside and to the bed.

Archangel shoved me down on the bed, taking in every inch of my body with a hunger that both terrified and thrilled me. He stripped out of his clothes, his movements brutal and swift. I held my breath as he crawled back on top of me, his cock hard and leaking pre-cum against my stomach. He leaned in, his forehead resting against mine. "You make me feel things I shouldn't."

"You make me feel things I can't get enough of. I want more." My hand slid over the muscled expanse of his back, trailing down until I cupped his ass with both hands. He groaned and kissed me again, grinding his cock against my bare pussy.

"Get your fuckin' shirt off, woman." His snarl made me shiver and cry out. I obeyed as fast as I could, shrugging out of the T-shirt. He helped before tossing the garment to the floor and lying fully on top of me.

All that delicious muscle pressed me into the mattress again. I had almost made myself believe I'd imagined how good it felt to have Archangel in such a dominant position over me. I was at his mercy. At the moment, he looked like he had none.

I shifted my hips and Archangel slid inside me with his next thrust. When he did, he jerked like I'd slapped him, a glaze seeming to go over his eyes. Something like euphoria glimmered in his eyes before he slid them shut and groaned.

He held himself deep inside me, letting out his breath slowly as he rested his forehead against mine.

"Fuck..." Archangel breathed the word like a prayer. Then he moved inside me, starting out slow but getting faster and harder with each stroke. I welcomed him with a moan, tightening my legs around him to hold him close. Archangel drove inside me, his hips slamming against mine in an almost violent rhythm. The breath slammed out of me as he rode me. He nudged my head to the side and latched on to my neck, sucking. Leaving his mark.

My heart rejoiced even as my head tried to tell me to slow down and take this for what it was. Scratching an itch. Hooking up. Sure, I'd push him for all I was worth. I'd push until he pushed back. But I knew it would eventually end.

Chapter Six

Archangel

I was drowning in her, losing myself completely in the feel of Sonya's body beneath mine, surrounding my cock. I knew this was wrong on every level, but I couldn't seem to stop myself from taking what she was so freely offering. What I so desperately craved.

With every thrust into her tight, wet heat, I fell deeper under her spell. This wild, infuriating, beautiful woman had me completely enthralled. I wanted to possess her, own her, make her mine in every way.

Sonya moaned and arched beneath me, her nails raking down my back. The sting only spurred me on, making me fuck her harder. Faster. I felt like I was possessed, chasing my release, chasing that sublime connection with her. The only thing I knew would give me relief, would calm my raging mind and body, was… her. Sonya. I'd been obsessed with her without really acknowledging my feelings and this is where it landed me. Balls-deep inside the woman of my dreams, knowing no good could come of this.

"Angel," she gasped, her head thrashing on the pillow. "Oh, God! Yes!"

"That's it, baby." I growled my praise for her, sounding like some fucking caveman. I'd be lying if I said I wasn't proud of the way I made her lose control. I loved that she clung to me, that she urged me on. I knew I'd pleasured her before and was doing so again. The question was, could I please her enough for her to want to stay with me? To give me a chance to work this out between our clubs. And her daddy. "Come on my cock, Sonya. Milk my cum and take it deep in that sweet pussy." She did.

I was so fucked, beyond comprehension or

salvation. With every thrust, every quiver, every shudder of Sonya's tight little body beneath mine, I fell deeper under her spell. I knew this had to stop, but I'd be Goddamned if I could remember why. I didn't want to stop, and she didn't seem like she wanted to either. I wanted to consume her. Possess her. I had a driving, dominating need to make her mine in every way possible. Including with my property patch, which was totally fucking insane. Not only was Sonya way the fuck too young for me, I wasn't nearly good enough for her.

None of it stopped me from fucking her now. I was really going to have to come up with a way to explain this to Thorn. Preferably without losing any important body parts. Was I scared of Thorn? No. I simply had too much respect for the man to not take whatever punishment he thought best to deal out with regard to a dirty old man fucking his daughter when he was supposed to be mentoring her.

My hips pistoned forcefully as I drove into her welcoming heat again and again. She clung to me, nails digging into my shoulders, legs locked around my waist. Her moans and cries spurred me on, inflaming my lust to impossible heights.

How the fuck had I lived my entire life without this? Sex had never been like this. I'd never imagined sex *could* be like this!

I nipped and sucked at the tender skin of her neck, overcome by the primal urge to mark her as mine. *Mine*. The word echoed in my brain. Yeah. I wanted Sonya to be mine. Hell, she *was* mine. I just had to figure out how to make it permanent without spooking her. Because I had no illusions the girl wanted me actually in her life. She wanted the rough, hard fuck of a biker. As I saw it, my job was now to make her so addicted to the sex that she was willing to take me on. Yeah. I could do that.

A plan to make her addicted to sex firmly in my mind, I focused entirely on making Sonya come as hard as possible. The instant and immense relief that fell over me was like a warm blanket in the cold of winter. Pleasure Sonya well and she'd never want to leave me. Yeah. It's a hard life.

She screamed, her pussy squeezing my cock in a forceful massage as she milked my cum from my dick. Denying her wasn't even a question. I came, planting my seed deep inside her hot pussy. Both of us shouted our releases, the sounds echoing through the tiny cabin as we came together in a powerful climax.

I collapsed on top of her, my weight pinning her down. We lay there, both breathing hard as the sweat dried. Sonya ran her fingers through my hair, and I lost myself in the feeling. She kissed my jaw and chin, sighing softly before settling beneath me. I knew how she felt. I wanted to praise her for giving herself to me so completely and selflessly, but I wasn't sure how to express everything I was feeling. Hell, I wasn't sure exactly what I was feeling, which was damned embarrassing. It was my job to take care of everyone's feelings because I was the level-headed one. The one who had a Zen-like calm. Now, I was anything but calm.

I wanted to love on her some more. To cuddle and kiss and show her I could be sensitive to her needs. Unfortunately, all I could do was pull her to me. I couldn't do much more than simply breathe. Not after coming my brains out more than once. My body had other ideas. I was spent, tired as hell. I let myself be pulled down, cuddled against her warm body and fell asleep with the scent of Sonya enveloping me like a warm blanket. And I slept like the dead.

* * *

Archangel

For the second time today, I woke up unsure of where I was. Shit like this never happened to me. I was always aware of my surroundings. I groaned, reaching for… something. I opened my eyes and recognized the tiny cabin… and it all came back to me in a rush.

Sonya. The woman who'd haunted me. The soul-shattering sex. And she was not in my bed where she was supposed to be.

I sat up with a groan. "I'm definitely gettin' too old for this shit." I found my pants and slung them on. My shoes followed. I couldn't find my shirt and said fuck it. Clothes weren't important. Finding Sonya was.

She wasn't in the other cabin, or out by the pond. Which was when I noticed the front gate wasn't closed all the way. Immediately, I patted down my pockets for my keys. Not there. I hurried to the gate, knowing what I was going to find.

"That beautiful little bitch." In the padlock on the gate, my keys were looped over the lock while the hook was open and hanging in the ring that would latch the gate. I had to chuckle. It wasn't funny, either. I couldn't remember the last time I'd slept so soundly I missed someone moving literally right under my nose. The woman had completely worn me out and I was not sorry. Not even a little bit. Thorn could try to kill me if that's what he wanted to do, but I'd fucked Sonya and loved every blistering second of it.

I took in a deep breath, the morning air warm and fresh, puffing my chest out. Yeah. Sonya had screamed my name. Several times. I'd satisfied her too. She'd clung to me and begged for more until she'd finally gone limp in my arms. So yeah. I was damned proud of myself.

I hurried back to my cabin and found a clean shirt, then went in search of my wayward charge. She hadn't taken the side by side, which surprised me. Likely she was hoping to slip by security and outside the compound without anyone knowing. She should have known better. Ripper didn't miss anything. I took the vehicle she'd neglected and headed to the main part of the compound. Even if she didn't head there straight away, she'd end up there before she could leave.

A few minutes later, I skidded to a stop in front of the main clubhouse. I hopped out and went inside, looking for Sonya. She wasn't in the immediate area, but there were other places she could be.

"Ripper? You here?" Ripper's office was just off the common room. If he was in the clubhouse, he'd be in his office.

"Yep. That you, Angel?" Ripper leaned back in his chair so he could look out the door. "Though you were with Sonya at the Oasis?"

"I was. She stole my keys and gave me the slip."

Ripper, the bastard, thought that was the height of hilarity. "Fuck me," he chuckled. "She's her father's daughter. Girl's fuckin' smart."

"Yep. Can you see if she's still on the property?"

"She's on the property. I got an alarm from your privacy gate when she opened it. She's finally realized she's going to have to go to the main gate to get outta here. Either that or she knows you'll be onto her soon and figured speed over stealth." He nodded out the door. "If you head to the gate now, she'll be about ten minutes behind you."

"Thanks, man. I owe you one."

"Nah. Just bring the hellion back and spank her ass."

I nearly stumbled. I did choke, but didn't stop to catch my breath. Instead, I ignored Ripper's laughter and hurried to the main gate. Sure enough, ten minutes later, Sonya hurried in my direction.

Chapter Seven

Sonya

Fuck. Yeah. I'd run straight to Archangel. To be fair, I hadn't planned on bailing and hadn't been able to get an idea of my surroundings or the layout of the whole compound. And Black Reign MC had a seriously large compound area.

He leaned against the gate, one foot hooked on the bottom rung and an elbow resting on the top. The smug bastard looked bored. Unconcerned, even. While me? Yeah. My stupid insides were fluttering like freaking fairies had taken up residence.

Three other men hung out at the gate, obviously on guard duty. Their vests labeled them as prospects, but I didn't know them.

"Hey, Angel!" I waved and smiled brightly when I really wanted to punt him in the balls and dart out the gate before he could recover.

"Hey yourself, little runaway. Pretty sure this is not where I left you." He raised an eyebrow, daring me to contradict him.

"Yeah? Where, exactly, did you leave me?" If he wanted to play hardball, we'd play hardball.

The bastard didn't even flinch. "Beside me, in my bed." His gaze didn't waver from mine and he didn't speak quietly, but I was too busy gaping like a fish to form any kind of witty reply. Also, it was hard not to notice how the prospects all perked up and crept closer, obviously listening intently to the conversation now. "Uh-huh." He grinned when I said nothing. "That's what I thought. Come on, Sonya. Back to bed with you."

"I can't believe you said that!" Not what I needed to say, but that's what came out.

"Oh? In that case, what lesson did you learn from our encounter?"

"That you're a bastard?" I smiled sweetly at him.

"Not to bait me. You might find you're the bait."

"You realize what you said is on the way to Salvation's Bane right this second. Right?"

"You mean, good news travels fast?" Archangel didn't look the least bit concerned.

"You're happy about that?" I know I looked like I thought he was insane. *Because the man was totally insane*!

"Your dad would have found out sooner or later." He shrugged. "Might as well start as I mean to go on. I'll never lie to him about you. I respect you both too much for that."

"And what, exactly, is he finding out? That we slept together?"

"All of it, Sonya. And I wouldn't keep our relationship from him."

"Are you stupid or something?" I couldn't believe this shit. "My dad will kill you, Archangel. *Dead*. No further questions necessary."

"No, he won't." How could he look so smug at a time like this? And why wasn't I panicking about my dad finding out about me and Archangel like I let on I was? Probably because I knew I was the only person in the world who could stop Thorn from doing anything he Goddamned well pleased. Well, me and Mom. So if I told him not to kill Archangel, he wouldn't.

"You think not?" I gave him a skeptical look. "How do you figure that? And exactly what kind of relationship you gonna tell him we have? That we're fuck buddies? Yeah. I see that going over reeeeally well."

"Because --" He crossed to me and threw an arm

around my shoulder, and guided me back toward the clubhouse. "You're going to be my old lady."

Of all the reasons I'd expected Archangel to name, me being his old lady wasn't even in the top fifty.

We'd taken several steps before I could finally find my voice. "You really have lost your Goddamned mind." I stopped moving away from the gate and freedom, planting my feet on the asphalt as best I could. Of course, Archangel tried to make me continue, but he didn't force the issue when I refused. "What makes you think I want to be your old lady?" I totally wanted to be his old lady and that was the shit of it! He was going to break my fucking heart!

Archangel raised an eyebrow at me. "Don't you? You came to my bed, Sonya. You initiated this between us. And I know you felt what I felt -- this isn't just physical attraction or a casual fling. There's something deeper here."

"That's not the point!" I sputtered. "You can't just decide something like that without even asking me." I swallowed hard, unable to deny the truth in his words. There was definitely more than just lust between us. At least, there was for me. Knowing Archangel, he saw this as his way of taking responsibility for his actions.

He shrugged. "I'm asking you now. Be my old lady, Sonya."

I gaped at him. "That's not asking! That's telling!"

"Fine." He grinned slightly before taking a step closer, never looking away from me. God, I loved having his full attention. I was in so much trouble. "Sonya, will you be my old lady?"

My heart was racing. Part of me wanted to snag

what he was offering and hold on for dear life. The other, more realistic part knew this was the wrong thing to do.

"I'm sorry, Archangel," I said softly. "I'll tell Dad it was my doing, but you don't love me. And I…" I swallowed. "I d-don't love you." Emotion was clogging my throat because the lie burned like acid.

Archangel's eyes narrowed as he studied my face intently. "You're lying," he said softly. I opened my mouth to protest but he cut me off. "Don't. I can see it in your eyes, Sonya. You feel what's between us just as strongly as I do."

"It doesn't matter," I whispered, fighting back tears. "This can't work. You know that."

He stepped closer, cupping my face in his large hands. "I know there are obstacles. I've been tellin' myself that for several days now. But it's been a long Goddamned time since…" He trailed off. Something like anger and hurt flashed on his face before his expression smoothed over. He took a step back, giving me some space, clearing his throat. "Never mind. Come on. Let's get back to the clubhouse. We can get your things, and I'll take you back to Salvation's Bane."

"NO!" I yelled, stepping away from him. I took a breath and spoke again, this time more softly. "No. I've got Linnie coming to pick me up." As if on cue, I heard her little Mustang rumbling as it pulled up to the gate. "See?" I smiled and waved.

"Wait!" Archangel lunged for me, grabbing my arm and pulling me to him. "You have my number programmed in your phone. Use it, woman." His gruff tone was as rough as his voice. Then he kissed me until my head spun.

I was so startled I forgot I wasn't going to kiss him anymore… and kissed some more. God, I was going to miss sex with him! I knew to the depth of my soul I'd never find pleasure like he'd shown me ever again. He was still the man of my dreams and probably always would be.

He caressed my cheek as he ended the kiss with one last sweep of his tongue and press of his lips to mine. I stared up at him and I knew my emotions were clear in my eyes. Archangel would know how I felt. Would he pity me? The young woman who had a hopeless crush on him?

I shook myself and backed away from him a couple of steps. "I'm sorry, Archangel. About everything. I took liberties I shouldn't have."

"You were curious. I could have stopped you at any time."

"Yes," I whispered. "I suppose you could." This was so much harder than I thought it would be. And I knew leaving him was going to hurt, which is why I'd snuck off on him in the first Goddamned place.

"Promise me you'll call me if you need me, Sonya." His gaze was steady on my face, his expression relaxed. This was his serene mask. I'd always seen it, but I'd gotten to know that look very well over the last few days. It meant he'd put up a wall between us. Though I was the one leaving, I found the distance, both physical and emotional, was an ache I wasn't sure I could overcome. Also, I found I hated that fucking mask.

"Yeah," I said, giving him a smile that was as fake as his was. "I will." No way would I ever call him.

He sighed. "Sonya, promise me." That was his stern voice. The one that said I better do what he told me to do.

"Fine, Archangel. I promise." I had to get outta here before I did something unforgivable. Like throw myself in his arms and accept his request that I be his old lady. Or cry. I started to go again, but somehow, I ended up in his arms, clinging to him like my life depended on it. He hugged me just as hard and those stupid fucking tears tried to prick my eyes again.

I'd just loosened my grip when another car whipped through the gate ahead of Linnie's Mustang, side-swiping the driver's side, and headed straight for me and Archangel. His arms tightened around me and he whipped around to put himself between me and the approaching vehicle. I heard the screech of tires and the scent of burning rubber hit me in the breeze as the little red sports car skidded to a halt.

One of the prospects at the gate pulled a gun as he ran toward us. The other prospect was with Linnie. Shouts came from the clubhouse as everyone inside hurried outside to contain the threat.

The engine was shut off. The doors opened upward at an angle. I didn't recognize the emblem on the front, but I was guessing it was something Italian and very expensive.

"Colm! What do you think you're doing? This your new little bitch?"

I gasped and my focus went immediately to Archangel. Or, rather, Colm. Of course, I'd known Archangel was his road name, but that's all he'd ever been to me. I'd never even wondered what his real name was. Not because I didn't want to know about his past or anything. It was just a name. No matter what name he was given at birth, he was still the same man.

"Gloria?" Archangel still had his arms around me. If anything, he held me tighter since the driver had revealed herself.

"Don't act so surprised to see me."

"Now isn't the time, Gloria." Archangel's face hardened. For the first time since I'd met him, Archangel looked just as deadly as every other member of his club or mine.

"Why? Because you've not sent your little whore on her way yet?" I stiffened and a stab of hurt sliced through my belly. I tried to push away but Archangel still refused to let me go. I knew what he was doing. By retaining his hold on me, he knew I'd wait passively until he either let me go or this Gloria left. Though I loved pulling pranks, I didn't like true confrontation. The shit that went down in Moore Haven was just that. Shit. All in good fun. This was a whole different ball of wax.

"Call her names again, and I'll forget our history, Gloria. She's off limits."

Gloria gave a delicate snort and stepped away from the vehicle. The woman was as sexy as the car. Long, loosely spiraling golden hair, a killer figure that spoke of both hard work in the gym and not a little bit of plastic surgery. She wore skintight leather pants and a formfitting leopard print halter top that showed her cleavage to perfection, and six-inch pumps that matched her pants. Her makeup was flawless, and she carried herself like someone used to being obeyed. She was older than me and had history with Archangel before he was Archangel. So where did that leave me?

Gloria waved her hand dismissively. "Whatever. Say goodbye so we can talk, Colm."

I looked up at Archangel. He'd already taken up for me. He was holding me so possessively and protectively I knew he was going to tell her to go to hell.

But he was silent, staring at me. When he spoke, something inside me died. "Maybe it's best if you go,

Sonya."

"Angel?"

"Linnie is waiting for you. I'll have Red and Rosanna fix her car. If they can't make it better than it was when it was new, I'll get her another one."

"I don't care about the damned car, Angel! What's going on? Who is this?"

Archangel winced and, once again, for a very brief moment, I saw what he was feeling. Regret. Longing. Resignation. Anger. Pain. I reached out and touched his face, wanting to take away his pain.

"Go on. I'll talk to you later." He gave me what I thought was supposed to be a reassuring smile, but it was anything but comforting.

"No. Tell me who she is, Angel."

He looked down at me and I could see that whatever he was about to say was going to kill something inside me. I wanted to tell him never mind. I didn't want to know who she was. But he'd already taken a breath to speak.

"Gloria is… my wife."

Chapter Eight

Archangel

I stood there and watched the dimming light in Sonya's eyes flicker, then die. She jerked as if I'd slapped her. I might as well have.

"Your... *wife*?"

"There's more to our past relationship than just us being legally married, honey."

"Don't 'honey' me!" To my utter horror, Sonya's eyes filled with tears, but she blinked them back heroically. The girl had backbone, but I could see what this was costing her. She tilted her head back in a stubborn tilt. Her chin quivered as she struggled to hold on to her emotions. "You want to honey someone, honey her." She pointed an accusing finger at Gloria.

"Sonya, please." I tried to frame her face in my hands, but she batted me away and stepped back a couple of steps. "I swear to you, I wasn't trying to keep this from you. I'll explain everything."

"What's to explain?" Now her voice wavered and she winced, sticking her chin up defiantly. The tears overflowed then, but she still stood her ground. "She's either your wife or she's not. Which is it? Ex-wife? Explain this to me, Angel." She winced again and gave a humorless laugh. "That's an oxymoron," she muttered through her tears. Because two more of the vile things slid from her eyes for her to bat away angrily.

"I hooked up with her in Vegas right before I left for special training in the service. I was drunk, and she was hunting for someone like me. I'm still not exactly sure how she managed it, but when I woke up the next morning, we were in bed together and I was informed I'd gotten married."

"Why not get it annulled?"

"I was going to, but she spun me a story about an abusive family and being told she was being married off to a man she'd never met so her father could have a business tie to him. I had no family and no reason to think I'd be coming back alive. I figured with the money she'd get in death benefits, not to mention a portion of my pay, she could leave and go wherever she wanted. Then my death would have counted for something, and someone would remember me when I was gone."

She still looked hurt, but I could see she was at least considering what I'd said. "You made it back, though. When was this?"

"Fifteen years ago, honey. We wrote a few letters to each other. She sent a few care packages, and we talked a couple of times the first year. Then I went deep undercover and couldn't talk to her for two years. When they'd recruited me for that mission, the primary requirement was that the operative not be married or have children they were responsible for. There were three of us chosen. Not for our skills, but because we had no close family ties. No one we had to keep in touch with or would miss back home and not be able to give a hundred percent. I caught hell from command when I had to make arrangements for the paperwork to be filed so she could get benefits. If they could have replaced me, they would have court-martialed me for that stunt. But I figured if I was going to give my life for my country, the least the people who'd demanded my sacrifice should help me to make someone else's life a little better, and I didn't flinch."

"Sounds like you," she muttered, toeing a pebble on the pavement.

"It was seven years before I spoke with her after

that. And it was only to let her know I'd made it back to the States if she wanted a divorce or whatever."

"I take it she didn't want a divorce?" Sonya glanced from me to Gloria and back. Gloria was busy flirting with one of the prospects. The man was trying his best to ignore her, but Gloria was nothing if not persistent. I was literally living proof she always got her way.

"Actually, no. She did want one. She was supposed to meet me for lunch to sign a standard divorce agreement. Once she said she wanted the divorce, I went to a lawyer to do the paperwork. I gave her half my benefits and kept her as my beneficiary in the event I was KIA. It was very much in her favor. I was career military and spent all my time on bases or overseas because I was special forces. Until I met El Diablo, my life was the military. I had nothing and no one else. Never needed or wanted anyone else. Kept things simple."

"Except you had a wife you barely knew." Sonya sounded equal parts understanding yet bitter, as if she were resigned to the fact she'd lost me before she'd ever had me. Which could not be further from the fucking truth. "So why aren't you divorced, then?"

"Because I never showed up." Gloria was headed toward us with purpose. Her hips swayed with an erotic twist that made a man wonder what she could do to him if she were on top during sex. Her breasts were high and firm and barely bounced at all when she moved. There was no denying she was a beautiful woman, but she did absolutely nothing for me.

Sonya stiffened and backed away from me another step, eying us both warily. That's when Linnie came up beside Sonya and took her hand in solidarity.

"Why wouldn't you meet him after you'd said

you wanted the divorce? Was he lying? Did you really not want it?" Sonya gripped Linnie's hand in a white-knuckled grip. I could see sweat beading her upper lip and brow and she was trembling.

Gloria waved her hand like it was all no big deal. "My boyfriend took me on a trip to the Maldives. Besides, it wasn't that important. I figured I could worry about it later."

"Sounds like it was pretty serious between the two of you. Why wouldn't you want to have your divorce final in case you decided to marry the other guy?"

"Why would I want to marry the guy? You marry a man rich enough to afford a private resort room in the Maldives at fifty thousand dollars a night and all you get is a prenup saying you get nothing from him in the event you divorce unless it was a gift. However, if you're the girlfriend, you get all the benefits of his money and get to negotiate your personal allowance in addition to all the trips and clothes and basic necessities of being on the arm of a billionaire." She gave me a superior smirk. "I had Colm's pay coming to an account I never touched. Compared to the money I got from Jasper, it wasn't much, but it let me have a personal stash. I saved every penny of my allowance I could so I'd be OK if we broke up. Getting a divorce was last on my list of things occupying my time because it wasn't strictly necessary."

"Then why bother meeting with him at all?"

"Why not? I probably would have if Jasper hadn't sprung the trip on me. After that, I forgot about it."

"We haven't spoken since, Sonya," I said. "By that time I'd taken up with El Diablo, so when I called her about a divorce, I told her about Black Reign and that she could find me here. I'm assuming that's how she found me?" I raised an eyebrow at Gloria.

She shrugged. "Yes. I'd have come sooner if I'd known this wasn't an ordinary motorcycle club clubhouse." She looked over the emasculate grounds with appreciation. "Who did you say owned this place?"

"No one you need to worry about, Gloria. If you'll please wait in your car, I'll take you inside when I'm ready."

"I don't have all day, Colm."

"Gloria, go wait by the car." I was losing patience. More, I was starting to panic. Caroline was tugging Sonya away from me back toward her car. "Sonya, please stop." I tried to keep my voice as calm and tender as I could when I spoke to Sonya. "Talk to me."

"Why didn't you try to find her again?"

"What was the use? I had the papers. I'd given her a way to contact me. And I was gone most of the time with either my unit or something for El Diablo. We were married, but had spent exactly one night together that I didn't remember. That was it, Sonya. She was a passing acquaintance with a legal tie to me, but it didn't really matter because no one else did. You and I are too new for me to have worked out everything, but me and Gloria would have been one of the first things I took care of. Shotgun would have taken care of it like he did with Warlock when Warlock's mother had married him and Hope without his knowledge. I would have explained all this to you right out of the gate if I'd had the chance."

Sonya still looked uncertain, but I thought she might believe me. She still glanced at Gloria with more than a little resentment in her eyes. "Look, I'm not saying I don't believe you, but this is something I need to think about."

"Of course. Just promise me you'll let me see you tomorrow."

"You're going to be busy tomorrow, Colm." Gloria buffed her fingernails on the collar of her halter. "Your little girlfriend will have to wait a few days."

"Tomorrow," I said again, never taking my gaze from Sonya. "And you know I do not break my promises."

She nodded, then sighed. "Yeah. OK. You can call or text, I guess." She sounded so defeated I wanted to throttle Gloria, then take Sonya back to the Oasis and make love to her for the rest of the week. Sure, it was a fast turnaround for me, but I was a believer in listening to my instincts. I knew beyond any doubt, Sonya was meant to be mine.

"I'll call you tonight after Gloria leaves. If you're still awake, I can come get you. Otherwise, I'll call you first thing in the morning. I'll call until you answer and tell me you're ready, then I'll come get you. Both instances will involve talking with your father, too."

"Don't get upset when he doesn't show up, sweetie," Gloria said, looking down her nose at Sonya. "Because he won't."

"That's it." I'd had enough. "Prospect!" I yelled at the two men manning the gate. Normally I'd call them by name, but I needed them to know I meant business and they better not give me any fucking lip. "Escort Gloria outside the compound. Do not let her back in, no matter what she or anyone else says."

"Colm! No! I'm telling you, you need to listen to me."

"I'll listen to you when I get Sonya taken care of

and not one second before. You don't get to order me around."

"You're my husband. You have to do what I say!"

I finally understood why she'd targeted a drunk military man. Because no man who was sober would have spent more than ten minutes in her company, let alone married her skank ass, and a military man would mean he was away from her most of the time, which meant he might not insist on a divorce the second she opened her fucking mouth. That might have been a stretch, but I was betting it was close to the truth. And I still had no idea why she'd targeted me in the first fucking place.

"That's not how it works, Gloria. I was never the easy-going man you met in Vegas. You met the face I put on in public. No one tells me what to do. For any reason." Then I lifted my chin to indicate Sonya. "Except her. For Sonya, I'll do anything. *Kill anybody.* So keep that in mind when you're throwing around your little attitude. I'm not warning you again."

"Fine, Colm." I suspected Gloria kept calling me by my given name to remind Sonya she'd known me far longer. It was something the club girls did all the damned time once they found out our real names. "But don't say I didn't warn you." She hiked her thumb over her shoulder, giving me a little sneer. "I'll just wait by my car." The look she gave me as she rolled her eyes was one of supreme irritation.

When she was gone, I reached for Sonya again, but she retreated once more. "Not yet, Angel," she whispered. "I need to have a clear head. To think without being reminded of what I'd be giving up."

"Whatever is going on with Gloria, I'll help if I can and make it go away. In return, she'll agree to the divorce. I've done as much as she'd allow me to do, which was make sure she had money. Shotgun can get Wrath to write it up for a simple dissolution of marriage. No one pays anyone anything. No one gets anything. But I will keep you involved every step of the way. I will always keep my promises to you, Sonya. I will be over either tonight or first thing in the morning."

She searched my face for whatever she needed to find for a long time. When she finally nodded, I was able to breathe again. "OK. I can do that. But, Angel?"

"Yeah, baby."

"Please don't try to play me. I know you could. But my dad will see straight through you, and he will kill you. I'd rather you just tell me straight and let me decide what I'm comfortable with than to find out later you were stringing me along as your dirty little secret."

"Never, baby. You have me. I'm yours. I have every intention of making it official both in the club and with the law."

"I'll reserve judgment, then. If what you said was true, I think I can understand. It was just bad luck she turned up before you could explain the situation and make it right. I know it's not fair to doubt you since we only just… you know." She cleared her throat and tucked a lock of hair behind her ear. "But I'm going to get Ripper to look into this. Given the circumstances, I'm not going to apologize until after he tells me what he found."

"Honey, you don't have to apologize. Never for protecting yourself." I turned my head to look at Caroline. "Linnie, are you OK to take Sonya home or do you need me to get Red to drop the two of you off back at Bane?"

"No. I think the car's drivable. She scuffed the

whole side and took the mirror off, but it's fine."

"I'll talk to Red about fixing it. Will you stay with Sonya when you get home?"

"Of course."

Caroline's gaze darted back to Gloria where she stood resting against the hood of her Maserati. I had no idea what the woman wanted, but I absolutely would not let her take up more of my time than strictly necessary. I wasn't losing Sonya now that I'd claimed her.

"Keep her away from Sonya." Caroline was normally sweet and kind to everyone. But I could see more of Doc in her than she'd admit to. Her father was the same way. Kind and caring until someone pissed him off.

"You have my word."

I wanted to pull Sonya into my arms and tell her I'd make everything all right, but I couldn't. The fact was, I'd slept with Sonya. She might have forced the issue, but I hadn't wanted to stop.

I *was* married. I wasn't lying when I told Sonya I hadn't thought about Gloria in years. I'd had no reason to. She was a one-night stand, or would have been if not for the whole Vegas wedding thing. I knew absolutely nothing about the person she was and had no desire to know.

"Good." Caroline gave me a crisp nod before tugging Sonya to the car.

Sonya kept looking back at me like she was afraid she'd never see me again. Or maybe, if she did see me, like nothing would ever be the same again. I didn't take my eyes from the little Mustang until Caroline had them out of sight.

When I turned my gaze to Gloria, I let her see a glimpse of the man she'd tricked into marrying her. I stalked toward her. I could only imagine what I looked like. I was pissed. Good and fucking pissed.

Whatever happened next wasn't going to be pleasant.

Chapter Nine

Sonya

I wasn't nearly satisfied with Archangel's explanation. Seemed like he had played it stupid, and Archangel was most decidedly not stupid. I didn't think he was lying, but I needed more. I needed to know how anyone could let something like this go for so long. I'd been ready to leave to spare myself pain; now I wanted to stay because I was in *so much* pain. Maybe that made me a glutton for punishment, but I'd been infatuated with Archangel, literally, for years. I'd known I was too far gone to stay away from him after we'd had sex, but I'd hoped to pull back slightly and sort of regroup.

"Talk to me, Sonya." Linnie drove down the highway between Lake Worth and Palm Beach. She was taking every back road known to man, likely trying to draw out the drive as long as I needed her to.

I shook my head, swallowing back the lump of emotion stuck in my throat. I couldn't break down before I was safely inside my room at the clubhouse. I turned my head to try to express to Linnie I just wanted to go home, but the tears started coming and when I opened my mouth to speak, the only thing out of my mouth was a sob of despair.

After that, things were a little fuzzy. I cried so hard my head ached. It was hard to keep from screaming, but I wouldn't have done that to Linnie. Instead, I turned my face toward the window and hunched in on myself. Linnie would get me somewhere safe and likely call in reinforcements.

I'd somewhat calmed down when we pulled into the parking lot of a hotel. She snagged her phone and my backpack from the back seat. "Ripper got us a suite.

Two bedrooms. Two baths. Let's get you inside, and I'll go get some necessities and food. Pizza good?"

That was Linnie. She'd take care of everything. It was what she did. She might be less adventurous than me, but she was the fixer of our trio while Bella was the one trying to keep me and Caroline out of trouble.

I nodded numbly, allowing Linnie to guide me into the hotel and up to our suite. Linnie opened the door with her phone and, once inside, she guided me to the couch. She was gone for a moment but returned with a blanket and set it on the couch beside me.

"Let me help you get your shoes off." She knelt and helped with my shoes and socks. I tugged up my knees and turned to lie with my back against the couch, curled up in a ball. Linnie draped the light blanket over me and sat on her knees in front of the couch. She brushed my hair gently from my face when it fell forward. "I'm so sorry, Sonya." There were tears in Linnie's eyes. She knew how much I was hurting because she knew how big a crush I had on Archangel.

"I didn't even know his name." It was an inane thing to say, but it was all I could come up with at the moment. My voice wavered and tears spilled from my eyes to streak down my cheeks and my temples where I lay on the couch.

"I know. Bella is on the way. I'm going to get some stuff. Do you want me to wait for Bella to get here?"

"No. Actually, why didn't we go home?"

Linnie smiled, leaning in to kiss my forehead affectionately. "Because you'd hate it if anyone saw you cry. And I don't think you're quite ready for Thorn to kill Archangel yet."

"I'm so glad to have you as my friend, Caroline."

She smiled at me. "I'm glad you're my friend too,

Sonya. We take care of each other."

I nodded. "We'll always take care of each other."

"Yes. We will. Always." She stood and leaned in to kiss the top of my head. "I'll be back. Bella has the key on her phone so she can let herself in. "Pizza and beer?"

I managed a half-hearted smile. "Sounds perfect."

As soon as the door clicked shut behind Linnie, my tears started flowing again. I had a small window of time to get this out before my best friends surrounded me and we set about helping me dull the pain. I clutched the blanket tightly around myself as I let the grief envelop me.

How could I have been so stupid? Of course, a man like Archangel would already be taken. I should have known better than to throw myself at him. He was quiet, but so much larger than life it was hard not to focus on him the second he entered a room. Now, I'd gone and really fallen for him, only to have my heart crushed. Hadn't I given myself this talk already? Like, before I'd gone and fucked him? I'd been right. But no number of pep talks could have prepared me for him telling me he had a wife.

Once the harsh sobbing was finished and the immediate storm had passed, I pushed off the blanket and stood, heading to the bathroom. I washed my face and used the bathroom before washing my hands. When had I ever let myself feel this way over someone else's actions? Not only that, but Archangel was right. He hadn't had the opportunity to tell me because there'd been no reason. You know. Until there was.

Of course, my leaving had also contributed to the problem. So I got it. Didn't mean I was going to stop Ripper from digging up all the dirt he could. It was time to test Archangel's word not to lie to me. I wanted the information going into that conversation ahead of time.

My phone chimed from where Linnie had put it by the couch. I picked it up and looked.

Archangel: *Can I come to you now?*

In a way, the early contact from Archangel immediately telling myself I needed to go into any conversation with Angel from a strong position told me I was making the right decision. And, God knew, it had been a very long time since I'd made the right decision. I knew what wrong decisions felt like.

Me: *I'm not ready. You're going to have to give me a couple of days.*

Archangel: *I'll check with you every 12 hours.*

Me: *Why don't I message you?*

Archangel: *Tried that once. This is where I ended up.*

He had me there.

Me: *Forget I asked that. Once a day will be fine.*

Archangel: *Every 12 hours.*

Archangel: *You don't have to answer every time. I'd appreciate it if you answered at least once a day though.*

Me: *That's fair.*

Archangel: *I will always answer if you reach out to me, Sonya. Do it.*

As I set my phone back on the table, the tears started again. This time, it was a slow, steady trickle instead of the all-consuming grief I'd experienced before. I reached for tissue by the lamp and blew my nose and tossed the tissue in the trash can by the couch.

The whirr of the electronic lock signaled Bella's entrance. She gave me a consoling smile as she shut the door behind her.

"Hey, Sonya." She hurried to me, setting down a

backpack beside the couch before giving me a hug. "I'm so sorry."

"Nothing to be sorry for. Just… piss-poor timing on everyone's part." I tried to give her a small smile, but I don't think I managed very well.

"Caroline said you hadn't told her what happened. Only called her to come get you so you could sneak out. She said you weren't upset when you called her, so what happened?"

I filled Bella in while we waited on Linnie to get back. She said she'd talk to Ripper, but I wanted to talk to him too. I also hoped Linnie told Ripper to keep this one close to the vest. I wasn't ready for my mother and father to know about any of this.

"Holy shit." Bella's eyes were wide with shock. "Holy shit! That's insane!"

"Right?"

She reached over and took my hand in hers. "It's going to be OK, Sonya. We'll figure out what to do. If we need to prank Archangel, we can do that. I'm sure we can find something appropriately embarrassing."

Her comment got a genuine laugh from me. "Thanks, Bella. I don't know what I'd do without you and Linnie."

"You'll never have to find out. We're your ride or die chicks."

The door lock whirred again, and Caroline came in with two huge pizza boxes and dragging a cooler behind her.

"Good God, Linnie!" Bella jumped up and ran to our friend. She snagged the pizzas while Caroline continued with the cooler. "You could have told me to meet you in the lobby."

"I was good."

The normal conversation helped pull me out of

the fog of hurt, and I knew I'd be OK. My friends would always help me when I was down. We were a team.

"I'm so fuckin' lucky to have you guys." I gave them a watery smile. "You're the best."

"Come here, Sonya." Linnie pulled me and Bella into a three-way hug. I let their love fill the holes in my heart. I recognized part of my heart would belong to Archangel for a long time to come, but these two women would be with me.

"You know," Bella said when we finally broke away and started dishing out the pizza. "If what he told you was true, Archangel and Gloria's marriage didn't sound like a real marriage but more of a paperwork technicality."

"Yeah," I mumbled around a mouth full of pizza. "I've decided I'm not talking to Angel until I get some facts from Ripper's investigation. Did you ask him, Linnie?"

She nodded. "I told him everything I heard and some of what you filled in for me that I'd missed before I got there. He says he'll have some questions for you, and to call him when you've had a chance to rest."

"It shouldn't have hurt, but it did," I whispered, setting down my slice and popping the top on a beer. I took a long pull before setting it down with a gasp. "I've had a crush on him forever. Then this happened."

"OK, so fill in the rest of the gaps, Sonya." Linnie took another bite, wiping her mouth. "What is 'this'?"

I let my head fall back on my shoulders to look at the ceiling. "Well…"

"Yeah?" Linnie wasn't going to let this go. I wasn't exactly sure how I was going to say this, even to my best friends in the world.

With a sigh, I sat up and closed my eyes. "I slept with Archangel."

I opened my eyes, needing to see their reactions. Both of them stared at me blankly, like they didn't understand what I'd just said. They glanced at each other briefly before Bella cleared her throat.

"Um, by slept with, you mean..." She let the sentence hang, obviously wanting me to fill in the blank so they didn't hurt or embarrass me. Yeah. I loved these girls!

"I fucked him, Bella. And, sweet baby Jesus in the manger, he fucked me too."

There was a beat of silence before both of them dissolved into giggles. And just like that, we were all laughing until my tears were tears of joy. No matter what happened next in my life, I'd always have these two. They'd have my back, and I'd have theirs.

Then I had a thought. I got up and snagged my phone before grabbing another slice of pizza and taking a huge bite off the end. I wiped my fingers, then picked my phone back up and drafted a text.

"Sending you guys something to proofread." I grinned as I hit send. Both their phones dinged simultaneously. As they read, Bella's eyes got wider and she made an "O" with her mouth, while Linnie's face split in a grin until she was laughing nearly as hard as she had been before.

"Oh, Lord..." Bella's face was a delicate shade of pink, but she was fighting a grin. "You realize if this works out like we all hope it will, you're gonna get the biggest spanking in the history of spankings. Right?"

I shrugged. "Maybe. Besides, I've not decided if I still want him or not."

Bella did smile then. "That's my girl!" She held out her fist for a bump and I obliged.

"I made a couple of minor adjustments and sent it to everyone in Bane and Reign I had phone numbers for, with a note to pass it on to everyone but the club whores." Linnie beamed. "Pure genius, Sonya. Pure fucking genius."

Chapter Ten

Archangel

"You've got a lot of nerve coming here, Gloria." I'd never wanted to hit a woman in my life more than I wanted to hit the woman in front of me.

"I'm your wife, Colm." She waved off my words like they were of no concern to her. Figured. "I have every right to be where you are."

"Bullshit. What do you want? Why are you here?"

She stuck her chin up in a stubborn mien, but as I studied her, I could see she was mostly bluster and bravado. Underneath, the woman was uneasy. I held her gaze, never letting up. Then she huffed out a breath. "Fine. I need a place to stay."

I just stared at her, unsure if I'd heard her correctly. She was going to have to explain, and I wasn't asking her for the courtesy. I took a threatening step closer, and her eyes widened. It was easy to see the exact moment she realized she'd underestimated me, this club, and the entire fucking situation. Her unflappable demeanor shattered.

"No, wait!" She stumbled backward in those ridiculously high heels. She fell against the hood of her Maserati. "I'm sorry! I'm sorry!"

"Just a suggestion, Gloria. When you trick someone into marrying you, you should really find out what kind of person you're scamming. I gave you a pass in Vegas. I felt sorry for you and had no reason to think I'd be coming home alive. Not to mention killing someone right before you deploy to a place you're likely to get killed is just really bad karma."

"I'm sorry, OK?" She tried the pretty pout, but it did nothing to soften anything inside me. Especially after watching Sonya riding away from me as hard as that fucking Mustang would go. "I was in a bad financial spot. I overheard you and your buddies talking and seized the opportunity."

"What opportunity? Why *did* you trick me into marrying you? You were never going to get rich. Hell, I don't even remember fucking you. Did we even do that?" I was getting increasingly agitated. Mostly at my younger self.

She shrugged like it was really no big fucking deal. "I needed the money. Once I got myself out of my tight spot, I realized I had a nice little nest egg, so I saved the rest. Mainly because I didn't need it anymore, but also because I felt bad about tricking you out of it. As to the fucking part, Colm, you were really way too fucking drunk to fuck, if you know what I mean." She gave me an angry, embarrassed look. Did I have to reference our hooking up on what she'd made our wedding night? Not at all. Didn't mean I wasn't going to continue this confrontation. Just because I did my best to keep the peace didn't mean I wouldn't be passive aggressive.

"You could have contacted me anytime and given back the money, as well as freed me from a marriage neither of us wanted."

"Who said I didn't want it?" She looked almost as outraged as she had when I'd asked her if we'd fucked. "A strong man to protect and look out for me?" She gave me what she probably thought was a seductive smile. "I came back hoping you'd be my husband in truth as well as name." Gloria reached out and slid her hands up my chest over my T-shirt and tried to wrap her arms around my neck. I grabbed her wrists -- hard -- and shoved her back into her car. She had to grasp the mirror to keep from falling and, because she'd already swiped Caroline's Mustang with the driver's side, the mirror fell off and Gloria landed on her knees on the pavement.

She sucked in a pained breath, and it took everything in me not to go to her immediately. The poor prospect wasn't so disciplined. He lunged for her and helped her to her feet.

"You all right, ma'am?"

"No, I'm not all right!" she snapped, reaching for him to help her up. Of course, the guy did.

Ben was barely more than a kid. He'd been taken in at Black Reign when he was sixteen or seventeen and had begun prospecting immediately. More for him and his street brothers who'd been taken in with him to feel like they were contributing than for any real desire for them to patch in. El Diablo had started letting teens prospect in cases like Ben's, and the first thing he'd instilled in them was respect. Whether or not someone had earned it. When they were old enough to know the difference, they were to treat everyone they met with respect. No matter what. Both of his street brothers as well as Ben had taken to that lesson with gusto. Even if I'd dressed Gloria down and called her every derogatory name in the urban dictionary I could come up with, I doubt any of those three young men would have followed suit. It wasn't who they were. And they'd have called my ass out on my treatment of her, too.

"You should be careful in those heels, ma'am," Ben offered helpfully as he made sure she was steady on her feet before he let her go and stepped away from her. "At your age, you could easily break a hip." I never said the kid was smart.

"Excuse me?" Gloria clenched her hands into fists and took an angry step toward Ben. "What exactly does that mean?" She gave him a saccharine smile.

He blinked at her guilelessly. "Just that as you get older, your bones get fragile. I'm surprised you didn't break something when you fell this time." Ben looked so distressed I nearly missed the way his lips twitched as he fought a grin.

"I'm not that old!" Gloria screeched and struck out at poor Ben. The kid didn't miss a beat but caught her swing with a level expression. He didn't retain his hold, but let her go and stepped back again, ceding his ground but also letting her know he wouldn't let her abuse him. Gloria gasped, turning to me immediately, cradling her wrist in her other hand, her lip trembling. "Did you see him? He crushed my wrist, Colm! Is this the kind of people you run with? You'd stand by while he hurt an innocent woman?"

I glanced at Ben who just grinned and shrugged. He was willing to take the fall. Kid was definitely smarter than he looked.

"If I say yes, will you be scared and go away?" I hadn't meant to say that out loud, but I couldn't take it back. Ben, who might not be smarter than he looked after all, laughed unapologetically. He didn't even try to cough or anything to cover up his laughter.

"Sorry, Angel. I know it's not polite. I swear I'll get on my knees and apologize later, but I can't help it right now."

"Don't worry, kid. I got your back with El Diablo."

"Who's El Diablo?" Gloria demanded. Probably more to bring my attention back to her. Granted, I didn't know the woman. I might be married to her, but I'd spent less than twenty-four hours with her in total. Probably closer to twelve than twenty-four, and most of that time was in Vegas where I was passed out. I couldn't even remember how I got back to the hotel room that night.

I took a breath to explain El Diablo, but before I could say anything, Ben's street brother, Gray, answered for me. "He's the Devil." Simple. Straightforward. And the truth. It was right there in his name.

Gloria rolled her eyes. "Does he own this place? Seems really big." I could practically hear the wheels turning in her mind. I almost wanted to see what happened if she tried to get her claws into El Diablo. It wasn't the Devil she had to worry about. El Diablo's wife, Jezebel, was just as deadly as her husband. And El Diablo was an assassin.

"He does," Ben answered cheerfully. I was beginning to see I needed to keep a closer eye on this kid. "It's really huge. Several buildings and all kinds of private homes for the club members who don't want to stay at the clubhouse. El Diablo owns all of it."

If we'd been in a cartoon, Gloria's eyes would have lit up with solid gold dollar signs. "Ben…" I practically groaned his name. "You're gonna cause so much fucking trouble."

Kid shrugged. "Sorry, not sorry."

"I demand to see El Diablo about my treatment!" Gloria had an almost gleeful look in her eyes.

"Ma'am," Gray had come closer, putting himself between Gloria and everyone, He guided her back to her car with a hand in the middle of her back. "I think it might be best if you leave."

"I can't leave!" she yelled at the younger man. "I don't have anywhere else to go!"

Ben, who it seemed loved stirring the shit, peered around Gray to grin and wave at her. "You got a nice vehicle, ma'am."

Still eyeing trying to get around Gray, she straightened but stayed near the car where Gray had opened the door and was trying to urge her inside. "It was a gift! I don't have to give it back!" The car was clearly a point of contention with her and whatever had happened.

"Didn't say you had to, ma'am," the prospect continued. "Just… I mean, you could sell it. Get a more practical vehicle and probably a nice house." The look of abject horror on Gloria's face sealed her fate with me. But not before I got what I needed from her.

"Bring her and that fucking ostentatious car to the clubhouse. Keep her outside until I come for her. She tries to get past you, fuckin' *shoot her*." I didn't wait to see what Gloria's reaction was, but I was riding a fine line between keeping the peace and killing the bitch because she'd upset my woman. Except that it was more my fault than Gloria's. Sort of.

No. You know what? *Hell* no. If I'd had an inkling of what my future held, I'd have taken care of this little problem with Gloria and told Sonya everything from the very beginning. Before I'd been in a situation to be alone with her. So this wasn't my fault in the way it was handled. What *was* my fault was letting it go on this long.

I stomped inside the main clubhouse, not even bothering to calm myself. Bandit was behind the bar and gave me a chin lift when I shut the door. Took him a second to register the look on my face because when he did, he raised an eyebrow and picked up his phone. Probably to give Samson a heads-up there might be trouble.

"Shotgun!" I yelled as I went deeper into the structure toward the tech officer's command center, as he loved calling it.

"Yo, Angel. In here," Shotgun called from the room across from his office. Looked like he was expanding or something. Or could be he and his kids needed a bigger game room. Could go either way.

"I need you to look into someone. Right now."

Shotgun gave me a curious look but was also all business. He led the way across the hall and sat at his desk, clicking a few keys on his keyboard. "Wassup?"

"Gloria Turcot." I gave Shotgun her birthdate and social security number. "Look her up."

He typed as he talked. "She the viper out front?"

"Yep." I waited to explain further until Shotgun glanced at the initial results.

"The fuck? Colm Flynn? Gloria Turcot is... *your wife*?" Shotgun shoved back from the desk and stood so fast he nearly knocked over his chair. "Your fuckin' *wife*? And you and Sonya --"

"Keep looking." I pointed at the computer screen, interrupting him before he could give me the beating he thought I deserved. "You tell me what you find, then we'll talk about my beatin'."

Shotgun gave me a wary look. "How'd you know I was gonna throw you a beatin'?"

I gave him an exasperated look. "'Cause it's what I would fuckin' do."

He narrowed his gaze at me, but rolled his chair back over to his desk, sat, and got to work without questioning me further. It didn't take him long to lean in closer to the monitors, that frown on his face deepening.

"The date on this marriage license is fifteen years ago." Shotgun punched some buttons and clicked his mouse or whatever. "Two-thirds of your pay goes to her. Even what you make here."

I tilted my head to the side. "Two-thirds?" I

frowned. "I thought it was half." I scrubbed a hand over the back of my neck and groaned.

"Well, sixty-five percent. This started the next deposit after the license was issued. No other withdrawals other than normal bank fees. Only major withdrawals come every May and November. Women's shelters in the spring, children's charities in the winter." He kept typing, clicking, and reading. Then he looked up at me again. "Have you even seen this woman since you married her?"

"Not after my first mission. Not until I came back. I'd been in deep fuckin' cover. So it was a couple years before I even had the chance to contact her. To be honest, I kind of forgot about her. Yeah, there was a piece of paper with our names on it saying we were married, but she was a drunk hook-up for me. Only reminder I had of her was the missing part of my paycheck. I didn't need money for myself. I lived the job. Anything I needed was provided for me. It's why I give so much money away. I don't need it, and there are plenty of people who do." I sighed. "Anyway, the last time I talked to her was about four or five years ago. She was supposed to meet me to sign divorce papers, but never showed up. There was no indication anything was wrong, then El Diablo needed me in Argentina and I was gone another year."

Shotgun stared at the screen for a long time. "So… what you're saying is, you… forgot? You were married?"

"My life isn't normal, Shotgun, and I don't have to explain myself to you. What I want is simple. I want to *not* be married to her anymore. I don't give a rat's ass about the money, but she's not a nice person and I don't want to give her any more."

"No, I can see that." Shotgun squinted at the

screen just about the time Eden, his wife, stormed into the room, an angry frown on her face.

"Archangel? Does that woman out there in the expensive-looking car belong to you? Because she says she does and that you're expecting her to be waiting on you in the common room to introduce her to El Diablo." Eden huffed and stomped over to me, pointing a finger in my chest. I figured I was going to get yet another dressing down. Fuck my life.

"No," I said, then shook my head. "Well, technically yes, but not for any longer than it takes Shotgun to make her *not* belong to me."

"Already done," Shotgun said, his fingers moving again. "Dissolving your marriage was way easier than fixing the money issue, but I can get Ripper to help. Breaking into a government system, while not out of my reach, isn't something I want to do without backup."

"Understood. The money's not worth exposing you or the club. If it's too risky, leave it. I'll go through the old-fashioned way."

"Nah, I can get it. Do you want anything taken out of her accounts? Any of the money she already has?"

"No. Just stop any more payments from going to her."

"On it, Angel."

"Never mind that." Eden waved Shotgun off. "If that woman belongs to you, bring her inside. That way, when you spank her, no one will come to investigate." Eden crossed her arms over her chest. "That one is rude. Teach her some manners."

"Oh, I'm fixin' to. Just not the kind of lesson she's gonna want."

"You need anything else from me?" Shotgun

pulled out a lollipop and stuck it in his mouth.

"Yes. I want to know where Gloria's been all this time. She indicated she had a rich man keeping her up and that they no longer have that sort of arrangement."

"Yeah," Shotgun grinned, talking around the sucker. "Looks like her boyfriend is some kind of oil billionaire. It'll take me a while to find out everything -- they weren't married, and therefore no legal documents. Give me a few hours and I should be able to find something."

"Main thing I want to know is if the guy's dangerous and likely to come looking for her, or would hurt her physically. I'm not taking care of the woman anymore, but I'm not a bastard either." I took out my phone. "I need to talk to El Diablo," I muttered.

"And, as luck would have it, Archangel, I'm here." El Diablo, the president of Black Reign MC, stood at the door to Shotgun's office and he didn't look happy. "Come with me, please. My office is quieter." His light English accent was deceptively calm.

"Good news travels fast, huh?" I sighed and stalked after my president and friend. El Diablo was the man I'd sworn to follow without question for the better part of my adult life. I'd met him in the middle of my first mission and I knew beyond any doubt, he was the only reason I survived. Now, he might be the reason I died right there.

"Indeed." His clipped tone told me he was, *indeed*, pissed to shit and back.

He led the way, stepping into his office and behind his desk while I sprawled in the chair in front of him, scrubbing a hand over my face.

"Why don't you start from the beginning." El Diablo didn't believe in wasting time. He wasn't above toying with someone before the real interrogation began, but only for his own amusement. Not when the conversation was this important.

"Of which story? Because I have more than one you need to hear."

"Start with the woman outside. Not how you being with her came about or all the circumstances surrounding the meet. That's between you and Sonya. What I want to know is the plan for her and her involvement with you up to this point."

"I haven't seen or communicated in any way with her in at least four years. Probably closer to five. We were supposed to meet to sign papers to get our marriage dissolved, but she never showed."

"Who had the papers? You or her?"

"I did. Still have them in my footlocker."

"I'm assuming Shotgun is taking care of everything with regard to the divorce? Or are you staying with her now that she's come home?"

"No, I'm not staying with her. I did everything in my power to make sure she was taken care of. I reached out to her once after she didn't turn up. I was kind of concerned something had happened to her. All she said was that she was fine and would call me later. After that, nothing. I was too busy to worry about her after that. There was no expectation I'd ever want a woman of my own since my life was too damned dangerous to bring anyone else into it."

"Then you met Sonya."

"Then Sonya met me." I wanted to make this perfectly clear. "I had no intention of ever going after her, El Diablo. The second I realized I saw her as more than a child, I kept as far away from her as I could."

"Why?" There was no mistaking I didn't have the option of not answering his question.

"You know the life I've led. Why would I want to

expose any woman to that kind of life?"

"Not what I want to know. Why would you believe you'd be exposing her to your past life?" I knew exactly where the bastard was going. He was going to make me admit my feelings for Sonya and to gauge how deep they ran.

"Because the first time I saw her after she came home from her first semester of college, I knew I'd never look at another woman the way I looked at Sonya. I couldn't have her, and she'd never want me. Seeing her living her life and playing around with some hapless boy unable to resist her would have… not ended well. For the boy."

"So, you're telling me you stayed away from her because you wanted her to be yours. Am I understanding you correctly?"

"Yes."

"Why did you agree to bring her to the Oasis when Thorn asked you to help her channel her energies and find her future?"

"What was I supposed to say, Liam?" I snapped angrily. "'Sorry, Thorn. I can't help your daughter out because I'd rather be fuckin' her'? I can imagine how fuckin' well that'd go over."

To my surprise, El Diablo laughed. Not a sinister laugh that said I was getting ready to die, but one of genuine humor. "Yes. I can see where that would have been a problem. So, what about you and Sonya?"

"She's going to be mine."

"Unless Thorn kills you first."

"There's that."

El Diablo studied me for a long time, then sighed. "Only you could ever get so caught up in something you forgot you were married." There were equal parts irritation and amusement in his expression.

"But I suppose it never had an occasion to come up."

"It did not. After she didn't show to sign the papers and basically said don't call me, I'll call you, I didn't try to contact her again. She knew how to find me, as evidenced by her showing up here for her bad timing award, and I had more important things to worry about."

"Yes. As I recall you were hunting a particularly nasty drug lord."

"Which is yet another reason I suppressed it all. I have no family, Liam. Only you and Black Reign. If the tie between Gloria and me had gotten out back then, she'd have been as good as dead."

"And Sonya?"

I stood abruptly, glaring down at the man I considered a brother. "I'll kill anyone who comes near her."

El Diablo raised an eyebrow. "Don't growl at me. I'd never hurt that girl."

That's when I realized I had bared my teeth and tensed to spring. At El Diablo. I cleared my throat and straightened. "Sorry." I sat and gave him a sheepish grin. "I should say, I will protect her with my life and God help anyone who comes between me and her."

"I'd expect nothing less. Now. Next question. What are you doing to do about little Miss Sunshine out there?"

"Who the fuck let in that skank ho in the car compensating for her personality?"

"Ah, my sweet Jezebel." El Diablo held out a hand to his wife. She flounced to him and plopped down in his lap. "You sound displeased." He frowned at her, but winked at me when she spoke.

"The bitch is flirting with anything with a dick. Which, I could care less about. What I do mind is how she keeps asking for El Diablo. President of this club."

"Me?"

"Oh, yes. Apparently, she wants to be the woman of the president because everyone else is beneath her."

El Diablo gave me a look. "I think I'm beginning to see why you forgot her so completely."

I shrugged. "Apparently, it was a defense mechanism. As to my plan, Shotgun is going through everything he can find. Given Eden had about as good an encounter with Gloria as you did, Jezebel, she'll help him. He's doing the divorce as well as redirecting my payment deposits. Once that's done, he's looking into her life and the man she was in a relationship with until recently."

"How long does Shotgun think that's gonna take?" Jezebel obviously wasn't liking where this was going. The woman had good instincts.

"Not sure. Several hours at minimum, but I'm sure he'll want a little more time than that. She can be confined to a room in the club whores' wing. Lock her in. Give her food and some clean clothes. Though from the looks of her, I'm sure she'd bitch about anything we gave her."

Jezebel huffed out a laugh. "Do you honestly care?"

I grinned. "Not in the least."

There was a chime and a buzz as both El Diablo and Jezebel got messages. Jezebel pulled hers out and read the message before handing it to her husband. Neither of them gave anything away with their expression. I checked my phone in case I'd missed the thing buzzing. If Shotgun had sent out a club message, I needed to check. Nothing.

"Everything OK?" I asked, looking from El

Diablo to his woman and back.

"Yep." Jezebel gave me a friendly smile that made me entirely too uneasy. "Just got a couple of things to take care of." She stood, then leaned down to kiss her husband. "I'll start working on this now and meet you later tonight. I'm sure she'll need all this sooner rather than later."

"This is your forte, my dear. Spare no expense. Funding your good deeds is my forte." He grinned at Jezebel and she gave him a merry laugh before kissing him once more, then hurrying out of the office, closing the door behind her.

Chapter Eleven

Sonya

I didn't make it the first twelve hours waiting on Archangel. Me and Linnie and Bella had pizza and beer until we were stuffed, then passed out for a couple of hours. They left right at dark at my insistence.

"There's no use you guys staying here when you could be at home in your own bed. I'll have Ripper send me the bill because I think I want to chill here for another day."

"Stay as long as you like. You know your dad won't mind."

"I just want to be away from both clubs for a few hours so I can think without everyone wanting to know what happened. That'll come soon enough. I need to have time to process."

"You sure you don't want one of us to stay with you, Sonya?" Bella gripped my hand in hers. "I don't mind."

"I appreciate it, Bella, but I'm good. Really. Besides, you guys have work to do." We all three burst into giggles again.

"God, I'm full," Linnie groaned. "Got Lock and Poison headed here with a cage. One will drive my car home and the other will take us home. He might have brought someone with them to get Bella's car too, but I'm not sure." She shrugged. "Someone'll get it for her."

"You guys are the best," I said again. "I know I said it before, but I mean it."

"You feel better?" Bella gave me a hopeful look.

I thought about my answer before nodding. "Yeah. I actually do feel better. I also realize you were right, Bella."

"Oh?" Her eyes widened in surprise. "Er, I mean, of course, I'm right. But what was I right about this time?"

I laughed, pulling my friend into my arms for a hug. "About Archangel." I pulled back and smiled at them both. "I might have overreacted just a touch." I tried to grin, but I knew my expression looked as forced as it was.

"You were protecting yourself," Bella said softly. "You weren't leaving because you didn't want him. You were leaving because you wanted him too much. When that woman showed up… Well, that was the feeling you were trying to avoid. By leaving before he could convince you to stay." Of course, Bella knew what I was feeling. Felt like the three of us had been friends forever.

"I'm still going to look at what Ripper finds before I talk with Archangel. But I'm not going to assume the worst. He told me what happened, and I believe him. His next actions will tell me all I need to know."

Linnie nodded. "I think that's a good assessment. Take all the time you need. I'll call you tomorrow and bring food."

"Make it tomorrow evening. I'm going to try some of that meditation shit Angel was trying to teach me."

"Seriously?" Linnie traded a look with Bella. "She's got it pretty bad, Bella."

"Meditation? Who are you and what did you do with Sonya?"

"Shut up." I grinned. "I'm going to be all right. In fact, now that I've decided to grow the fuck up and stop acting like a sulking teenager, I feel better about the whole situation."

"You just tell us what you need and we'll make it happen. If that means we drag Archangel here by his hair, that's what we'll do." Bella was the sweet one, but she was also fierce as a dragon when someone messed with her family.

"I got this, Bella. Thank you, guys, so much." We group hugged. "You're the best friends ever."

"We love you, Sonya. You need us, you call or text. We'll come with reinforcements."

"I will, Linnie."

After they'd gone, I'd soaked in the jetted tub for the better part of an hour. Thinking. Meditating. Trying to find my inner peace like Archangel had taught me. I was surprised, but I had a measure of success. I managed to float in a sea of calm until my mind was quiet and I could find my inner strength once again. The first thought when I came back to the here and now was that Archangel would be proud of me. That was when I realized I was torturing us both by not talking with him.

I got out of the bath and dried off, wrapping a towel around myself. My hair was still up in a messy bun to keep it out of the water so I didn't have to dry it. I picked up my phone and opened my texting app. I stared at Archangel's name for a long moment before opening the last messages we'd traded. I took another unsteady breath and texted him with shaking fingers.

Me: *Archangel? Are you up*?

Immediately, the dots of an incoming text flashed.

Archangel: *Always*.

Crap. The guy was smooth. I couldn't help but smile. The butterflies in my stomach made me shiver.

Me: *If you're not busy, would you like to talk*?

Archangel: *When and where?*

Me: *The girls got me a suite in Palm Beach. You could come here whenever you have time. I'll share the key with you on the app.*

There was a whirr as the door to the room opened and Archangel stepped inside. He put the Do Not Disturb sign on the door, then shut it, turning the lock as well as closing the safety latch.

"Angel!" I jumped up and took a couple reflexive steps back. "You asshole! You scared me to death!" I tried to be mad. I really did. But all I felt was relief. I grinned and threw myself at him, wrapping my arms and legs around him.

He chuckled. "Ah, baby. I missed you."

"Were you sitting outside my door? That's a little fuckin' creepy." I laughed. Because he was waiting for me to call him. He was watching over me. And he respected my privacy by not coming in before I invited him. Yeah. I was a goner on this man.

"Like I said. I missed you."

"I was only gone a few hours."

"Way the fuck too long." He hugged me as hard as I hugged him. "Though I confess I hadn't expected this kind of greeting."

I pulled back to grab him and kiss him all over his face. He laughed until our lips finally met.

Archangel responded to my eager kisses with equal passion, his hands sliding down to cup my towel-clad bottom as he held me against him. Our lips moved together hungrily, tongues tangling. I felt like I was starved for a taste of him. Angel had given me a small bite and I wanted the whole fucking pie.

When we broke apart, both of us were breathing heavily. Archangel rested his forehead against mine. "I'm so sorry, Sonya. I don't care if it was my fault or not. I will take full responsibility and beg your forgiveness and mean every fucking word. Just please let me explain."

"It's OK. I swear. I just needed a bit to calm down. I'm sorry for making an idiot of myself in front of... uh... your..."

"*Ex*-wife. Emphasis on the *ex*." He slid me a sheepish grin. "Shotgun fixed that first thing. She's still at the Black Reign compound because I want to make sure whoever she was with before isn't still a threat to her. While there's no way I'm continuing a relationship with her, if she's on the run from someone, I can't kick her out until I'm sure she's not in danger."

"Nor would I expect you to." I smiled up at him, still cupping his face in my hands. "You're not that kind of man. You're a protector. A fixer. You can't go against your nature. Not like that."

He pulled me close again, this time turning to sit on the bed. My knees were beside his hips and I clung to him. He sighed and so did I, both of us content to just sit there and hold each other.

When he finally pushed me away from him enough to look at me, he brushed a few strands from my forehead and tucked them behind my ear. "I fucked this up to hell and back. I'll tell you everything you want to know. But I swear to you, I don't remember half of what happened that night."

"I think you explained that part well enough. What I want to know most is what happens from here? You said she was now your ex-wife, but that she was staying at Black Reign until you knew she was safe. What will your obligation be to her?"

"Nothing." His answer was immediate and firm. "El Diablo said Jezebel was taking care of her. If she wants to stay, they'll find work for her. If not, they'll settle her somewhere else if she needs help."

"Like financial help? I thought she had all kinds of money."

"No financial help. She's got all the money she's getting from me or the club. But if she needs help moving her stuff, the prospects will help her out."

"No one is that much of a saint, Angel. While I think it's admirable and I wouldn't want it any other way, why would you do that after she deceived you?"

He moved us farther onto the bed and rolled over so he laid on top of me. I loved the tender smile he gave me. He looked… younger, or something. Maybe carefree? Contented? Whatever he was feeling certainly agreed with him and I wanted to always see that expression on his face when he looked at me.

"When I first met El Diablo, he told me something I took to heart and I try my best to live by. He said to treat everyone with respect, even if they hadn't earned it. He said, when you understand the difference between granting respect to someone you don't know and making someone you do know earn your respect, then you had the right to choose which applied. If you aren't sure, you err on the side of caution. It costs nothing to be nice. You might make an ally."

"Sounds like something he'd say." I smiled up at him.

"So I'm going to assume she thought she had a good reason for what she did. To be honest, I don't care why she thought tricking someone into marrying her was a good idea. All I care about is getting that marriage dissolved -- which it has been -- and getting back to figuring out *us*."

"Speaking of us. What exactly do you see happening here? How do we end up?"

"I want you to be my old lady. I want to spend the rest of my life making you happy. I see us ending up very old, very wrinkled, and very happy in a beach house surrounded by grandkids and great-grandkids. And before you tell me how much older I am than you, I plan on living to be at least a hundred and twenty."

I chuckled, shaking my head. "You're so full of shit."

"Am not." He leaned down to kiss me again, tenderly. Gently. With so much love it made my heart clench. "What I am, is so in love with you, I'll defy any god to take me from you before I'm ready." He spoke so fiercely, I actually believed he could make good on his word.

Then I registered everything he'd said. "You're… in love with me?" The words were barely above a whisper.

"Yeah, baby. I love you. With everything that I am."

"Not because of, you know, because we had sex?"

"Sonya, honey. I try to be an honorable man in everything I do. That means I don't lie. Especially not to people I love. I would most certainly make you my old lady to do right by you. But I will never lie to you about my feelings for you. And I'd never tell you I loved you if I didn't mean it."

"You didn't wake up after we had sex and suddenly decide you loved me. I won't believe that." It hurt. Not because I thought he was lying. Because I was hoping like fuck he wasn't. I wanted this so bad! I wanted Archangel for my own so no one else could have him but me. I wanted to ride behind his bike and for him to be proud to have me with him. Because I'd be damned proud to be with him.

He leaned in once more to place a lingering kiss on my lips. "Sonya, when you came home after your first semester of college, I realized you were the most beautiful woman I'd ever imagined. Not only that, you were wicked smart and sexy as fuck." He leaned in again to nip at my neck, making me squeal. "I wasn't in love with you then. But I had a healthy dose of lust aimed squarely at you. No. I fell in love with you when you were telling me about your life in Bane and how you loved everything about living there, even with your father breathing down your neck. You were so passionate and free spirited, you made me feel young again. I remembered a time before I met El Diablo when there was nothing to look forward to but death in battle and wished I'd met you then. Because, in those precious moments when you spoke to me from your heart, I knew you'd have been the person I looked forward to coming home to. And my life would likely have been much, much different."

"Angel." I stroked his beard gently, like I might pet a cat. "I've loved you since I was a teenager. There's no other man I've ever wanted to be with. So I'm all in with this. You're my fantasy. My dream."

"You have me, honey. Everything I am."

"You think you'll be able to handle girls' weekend?"

He stilled where he'd been kissing my palm and narrowed his eyes at me. "What's girls' weekend?"

"Well, you picked me up from one." I gave him a bright smile. "One random weekend a month, we go to Moore Haven to pull pranks. Just to keep Lawdawg on his toes."

"That's your girls' weekend?"

"Yep."

Then he grinned down at me. "Yeah. I can

handle girls' weekend."

"Good. Because I will fight for my right to party."

He did laugh then. Leaning in once again to kiss me. "Yeah, baby. You do. You create havoc, I'll keep the fuzz off your back."

"Sounds like the best of plans. But I have a better one."

"Oh?" He kissed me again. "What's that?"

I pulled him close, so my lips were right at his ear. "I want you to fuck me until I beg for mercy. Then I want you to fuck me some more."

"Christ," he swore, sucking at the delicate skin of my neck. The little sting told me he'd definitely left a mark. Good. I liked him staking a claim. "You're gonna keep me on my toes, aren't you?"

"I'd rather keep your dick in my pussy. Think you can manage that?"

"Oh, little witch. You're playing with fire."

I turned my head and bit his ear with a sharp nip of my teeth. "*Then burn me*!"

Archangel growled low in his throat, a primal sound that sent shivers down my spine. In one swift motion, he yanked the towel from me, taking it with him as he stood. His eyes roamed hungrily over my naked body as he quickly shed his own clothes.

"You want to burn, baby?" he rasped, settling his weight between my thighs. "I'll give you a fuckin' inferno."

He took my lips in a searing kiss as he thrust inside me in one smooth stroke. I cried out at the delicious stretch, digging my nails into his shoulders. Archangel set a punishing pace, driving into me with powerful strokes that had the headboard slamming against the wall.

"Oh god, Angel!" I gasped, wrapping my legs around his waist to pull him deeper. "Yes! Just like that!"

Archangel groaned, burying his face against my neck as he pounded into me relentlessly. His teeth grazed my skin, sending electric shocks of pleasure through my body. I arched up to meet his thrusts, our bodies moving together perfectly.

"Fuck, Sonya," he rasped. "You feel so Goddamned good! So fuckin' tight and wet!"

Arousal flooded me and made my pussy weep for him. I loved how vocal he was during sex, how he told me exactly what I did to him. I loved his dirty fantasies and the way he kept me on edge wondering what he'd say or do next.

"Only for you. Only for you!"

"That's right, baby." He grunted with his efforts as he fucked me harder, giving me everything he had. "And you're gonna take all I have to give you like a good girl, aren't you?"

"Yes! Fuck me, Angel. Fuck me!"

He shifted slightly, hitting the perfect spot inside me with each stroke. My orgasm built rapidly, tension coiling around my insides so I wanted to erupt to release the pressure. "Come for me," he demanded. "Let me feel you come on my cock."

His words pushed me over the edge. I screamed his name, embracing the pleasure he gave me and demanding more. Archangel grunted and buried his face in the pillow beside me and shouted into the fabric. Hot seed erupted inside my pussy, filling me with him.

And then it hit me. "Uh, Angel?"

"Yeah, baby." He was breathing as hard as I was, his heavy weight on top of me the most comforting peace I'd ever had. I didn't care what had just happened. All I wanted to do was lie like this for hours and hours.

"Hmm…"

He chuckled. "That sounded like a contented woman."

"Yeah," I said, stretching. I tightened my legs around him so he knew not to move.

"But I want to know what you were going to say."

"Yeah…" I drew out the word a little. "We… uh… you know. Didn't use…"

"Protection?"

"Yeah. That." I didn't expect him to laugh, but he did. He laughed and kissed the side of my neck. Even when I tried to push him off me in a fit of temper, he still kissed me, his cock staying right where it was, buried deep inside my pussy.

"It's not funny, Angel!"

"Honey, I'm not laughing about that. I'm laughing because you just baited me into hard, rough sex all while yelling at me to fuck you, and you couldn't even say the word condom."

"Shut up."

He continued to chuckle, and I couldn't help but laugh with him. One thing led to another, and I found myself getting railed from behind. And no. He didn't use a condom that time either, and I wasn't at all torn up about it. I knew this was his way of solidifying his claim on me.

"If you're wondering, no. I've never come inside a woman intentionally without a condom. I can't speak to Gloria since I have no idea if we had sex or not, but I knew when I woke up with my dick in your mouth that morning I was never going to tolerate a barrier between us. You're mine and I'm not letting you go. I will use everything I can to make unbreakable ties between us because you are everything to me, Sonya."

"I'm yours, Angel," she whispered. "All yours. Forever."

"Say it again," he demanded hoarsely.

"I'm yours. Only yours, Angel. Always."

Chapter Twelve

Archangel

For the first time in my life, I was at total peace. Me and Sonya spent the night and the next day making love, talking, and getting to know each other. I'd slept with her held tightly in my arms and woke with her lips around my cock, sucking me for all she was worth. Not even going to try to deny I'd love to get used to waking up to that every fucking morning.

Now, she was on the back of my bike and we were headed to Salvation's Bane. Not only did she need to get her stuff, but I had to have a come-to-Jesus meeting with Thorn. President of Salvation's Bane. Sonya's father. I was hoping to be able to ride my bike back to Black Reign after the beating Thorn was likely to give me, but I had Fury at the ready in case I needed some help.

We pulled through the gate. The prospects each threw up a hand in greeting and waved us on toward their clubhouse. The main building was a converted firehouse. There were rooms for guests and most of the club girls were housed there, as well as some offices. Thorn's office was here.

I parked the bike and Sonya hopped off, bouncing with excitement as Caroline and Bella both met her at the door. The three embraced and I couldn't help but smile. I strolled toward the girls and the entrance to the clubhouse. Sonya looked back at me with the happiest smile I'd ever seen from her. And, by God, the woman was so fucking beautiful it hurt.

"Angel!" Mariana, Sonya's mother and Thorn's wife, called out to me from across the room. She had a lovely smile on her face as she greeted me happily and I could see the resemblance between her and Sonya.

"Come in! Thorn's in his office. He said you'd be coming to talk to him." She gestured for me to come with her. The smile seemed genuine, which was confusing as shit. Also, I hadn't talked to Thorn yet or even reached out to him. Not because I didn't want to tell him but because I wasn't sure how I was going to word this. So, how did he know I was coming?

Mariana opened the door to Thorn's office and ushered me inside. "Would you guys like something to drink?" She asked the question like she didn't have a care in the world. I never expected Thorn wouldn't have heard about me and Sonya by now. After the incident at the front gate of Black Reign, all of Reign knew. Someone would have passed it to Thorn. Probably El Diablo himself.

"Get me a beer, if you don't mind, sweetheart." Thorn smiled up at his wife. "Angel, we got anything you want."

"Would it be too much trouble to ask for ice water?" I asked as I gave Mariana a polite smile.

"Of course not. You sure you don't want a beer?" Her smile was polite and I didn't sense a trap, so I tried not to automatically assume she was making a sly reference to the incident with Gloria and how we'd come to be married.

"No thank you, ma'am. I quit drinking a long time ago." I kept my smile serene and in place. I didn't know how much information she had, and just because Thorn knew didn't mean Mariana did.

"I admire anyone who's able to break from unhealthy habits. It shows strength of character."

I dipped my head to her. "Thank you."

"I'll be right back. Anything else, Thorn?"

"No, honey."

I thought the wait for Mariana to return would

be awkward, but Thorn chatted cheerfully about Ripper's triplets and how fast they were growing up. Ripper and his wife, Emmanuelle, had their hands full with the three girls and it amused Thorn to no end.

Mariana returned with the drinks, then left and closed the door behind her. I took a pull of my water before carefully sitting it on the edge of Thorn's desk.

"Tell me how Sonya's doing. I wasn't expecting her home for another couple of days."

I tried not to wince. "Momma always said it's best to just rip the Band-Aid off. Peeling it off slowly prolongs the torture."

Thorn chuckled. "That's not cryptic or anything." He leaned back, putting his feet on his desk and crossing them at the ankles. "What's going on?"

"I'm in love with your daughter, Thorn. I'm going to make her my old lady." I waited for the explosion. When none came, I continued. "She knows that's my intention and has accepted my claim on her." Still nothing. I was getting nervous. Thorn wasn't that much older than me, but I felt like a naughty child being guilted into confessing his every transgression. "I'd like your blessing for this, Thorn. I love Sonya with my whole being, but she's still your daughter. I won't go against your wishes."

"For Christ's sake, Angel. Why the fuck do you think I sent her to you in the first Goddamned place?"

"I… uh, what?" My brain was pulling a four-oh-four on this one.

"She's had a crush on you since she was sixteen! Not a normal crush either. I watched her weigh your pros and cons. She might not have realized what she was doing, but she studied you like she wanted to make damned sure you were worthy of her. I knew before she went to college you would be the only man she'd ever accept. It was you or nobody, and my baby girl isn't gonna live her life by herself."

"Are you fuckin' kiddin' me right now?" I scowled. I stood and paced across the room, unable to process what the fuck just happened. Also, I was really glad I'd hadn't jumped to conclusions with Mariana before.

"Oh, come on, Angel. You're not mad. Well, other than at yourself for sweating bullets when you didn't have to."

"I was ready to take my beatin' from you, Thorn. Now, you might just have to take your beatin' from me."

Thorn laughed, almost falling out of his chair. "And before you start pitchin' a fit over you being married, I knew. I had Ripper dig up everything on you there was before I sent Sonya to you. So I contacted Gloria pretending to be the IRS and asked about her marital status." The man looked entirely too smug. "My guess is, the reminder of you sent her your way. She had all the money in the world until her boyfriend found his next mistress."

That got me thinking. "She forgot she was married same as me. Hell, she forgot all about me *and* the money. Like you said, she had all the money in the world until he cut her loose. She probably hadn't thought about me since the last time we talked."

"If you're in too much trouble over that with Sonya, I'll vouch for you. The whole scene at Black Reign as it was described to me would never have happened if I hadn't been digging into your past."

"You coulda just asked." I glared at him.

The bastard grinned. "Sure. But what fun would that have been?"

We had an early supper at Salvation's Bane.

Everyone laughed at my expense, and Sonya laughed until she had tears rolling down her cheeks and was clutching her stomach. So were all the other women. Especially when Thorn ratted me out with a video complete with very clear audio of the meeting in his office.

Yeah. This was my life now.

It was late afternoon when we rolled into the Black Reign compound. Everyone we met waved and called out to us. Sonya waved back and laughed. I got an itch between my shoulder blades. I couldn't put my finger on the actual problem, but something was off. I began to see almost gleeful enthusiasm in the greetings called out from everyone we met. And I mean everyone. Seemed like every adult in the compound came out of the woodwork to greet us.

By the time I rolled into my parking spot in front of the entrance to the Oasis, there were several bikes pulling in behind me, followed by dozens more people on foot.

"What the fuck?" Instinctively, I pulled Sonya to me, wrapping both arms around her protectively.

"Relax, Captain Caveman." She leaned up to brush a kiss over my lower lip. "They're just being friendly."

"Honey, no one in this compound has ever been this happy to see me."

"Just coming by to welcome Sonya." Jezebel smiled and reached for Sonya. Sonya went willingly, pulling away from me when I didn't really want her to. "Why don't you go unlock your Oasis, and we'll all pitch in to help you move Sonya's stuff into your home."

I smelled a trap. It stank like three-day-old shit, but I could not see it. Instead of questioning Jezebel further, I nodded and went the few steps to my sanctuary to open the gate. This was the place I felt most at peace. I shared it with people from time to time, to help them find the same peace I'd found. It was also the place stacked three mountains high with… sex toys.

There was silence as I stared in disbelief at what I was seeing.

"Um, wow, bruh." That had to be one of the younger prospects. "It's always the quiet ones."

Then the dam burst. Everyone laughed. The guys clapped me on the back, enjoying seeing me uncomfortable. Oh, it wasn't the sex toys. I wasn't a fucking stick in the mud. It was the fact two fucking clubs had got something this big over on me. And I knew without a doubt who had orchestrated the whole thing.

"When this is over, your ass is toast, woman."

"Imma hold you to that."

"Wench."

I kissed my woman while everyone congratulated us and helped move Sonya's things into my house. It was small, but I'd already put in an order to expand my house. I thought we could manage until the new section was complete.

Someone started bringing food, and more someones brought folding tables and chairs. Next thing I knew we were having an impromptu weenie roast. This was one of many reasons I loved club life. I knew Sonya loved it too.

"Hey, Angel!" Shotgun came trotting over to me. I'd seen him earlier in the evening, but he'd disappeared for a while. "Good news. Gloria's in no danger at all from anyone. She never was. No clue why she targeted you other than to get away with it. I believe you were right when you told me earlier you thought she'd completely forgotten about you until Thorn faked that IRS call to her. You could question her if you want. Other than that, there's no reason she needs to stay here."

"Send her on her way, then. Give her any help she needs as long as it doesn't involve money. I'm talking moving shit or whatever. She doesn't get a dime of this club's money. You are only obligated to drop shit off where she says drop it off. No carrying a six-hundred-pound recliner up four flights of stairs. She can take it from there."

"I don't think she has much other than her car and what's in her bank account." Shotgun grinned. "Too bad she tore the side off the car."

"I should see if you'd ask Red and Rosanna at Bane to fix it and send me the bill, but I'm really not feeling that generous. It was her damned fault and she has enough money to fix it, or she could sell it as is."

"You've done more than you should have." Jezebel walked over to us with a smile, arm in arm with Sonya. "She has the means. Don't reward her bad behavior."

"Cut her loose," I said without hesitation. "She'll be fine."

"You want to talk to her first?" Shotgun asked.

"What's the point? If it mattered now, it would have mattered years ago. We're no longer married. That's the only thing I needed from her."

"Good plan." Shotgun clapped me on the shoulder. "I'll escort her outside the gate."

"Well, now that's settled," Jezebel gave me a brief hug. "We'll be leaving. Be good. There's a year's worth of lube under the bathroom sink. Don't forget to wash everything before using it. Bye now." Jezebel waved a cheerful goodbye as El Diablo laughed delightedly as they walked away holding hands.

I put my arm around Sonya as we waved to the last of our friends as they left. "I owe you a spanking," I said, still waving.

"Yep," she agreed, still waving too.

"Thought I saw some bondage equipment near the top of one of those mounds of sex toys." I glanced at her out of the corner of my eye.

"Yep. Middle pile. Jammed between a sex swing and a few dildos." She didn't hesitate with her reply.

"I'll get a stepladder."

"Good idea. If you see a strap-on, grab it, will ya?"

"Yeah, that's not happening."

"Oh, really?" God, I loved that wicked gleam in her eyes. It was a look that said I was well and truly fucked. OK, so not physically. At least, I didn't think so. Then I remembered how this whole situation started.

"You know what, forget I said that."

The grin she threw back my way said her memory was perfect.

As I looked to my future, wondering if I'd always have the peace I enjoyed now, I was sure of two things. First, whatever my future held, it would be with this woman at my side. And second, life would never be dull. I looked forward to every blistering second of what was to come.

Marteeka Karland

International bestselling author Marteeka Karland leads a double life as an action romance writer by evening and a semi-domesticated housewife by day. Known for her down and dirty MC romances, Marteeka takes pleasure in spinning tales of tenacious, protective heroes and spirited heroines. She staunchly advocates that every character deserves a blissful ending.

Marteeka finds joy in baking and gardening with her husband. Make sure to visit her website to stay updated with her most recent projects. Don't forget to register for her newsletter which will pepper you with a potpourri of Teeka's beloved recipes, book suggestions, autograph events, and a plethora of interesting tidbits.

Marteeka at Changeling: changelingpress.com/ marteeka-karland-a-39

Want more? Wanda Violet O. is Teeka's Dark Erotica side.

Bones MC Multiverse

Contemporary MC and Crossovers

- Bones MC
- Shadow Demons
- Salvation's Bane MC
- Black Reign MC
- Iron Tzars MC
- Grim Road MC
- Bones MC Legends
- Kiss of Death MC

Print and Audio

- Bones MC Print Duets
- Bones MC Audio
- Salvation's Bane MC Audio
- Iron Tzars MC Audio
- Grim Road MC Audio
- Kiss of Death MC Audio

Changeling Press LLC

Contemporary Action Adventure, Sci-Fi, Steampunk, Dark Fantasy, Urban Fantasy, Paranormal, and BDSM Romance available in e-book, audio, and print format at ChangelingPress.com -- MC Romance, Werewolves, Vampires, Dragons, Shapeshifters and Horror -- Tales from the edge of your imagination.

Where can I get Changeling Press Books?

Changeling Press e-books are available at ChangelingPress.com, Amazon, Apple Books, Barnes & Noble, Kobo, Smashwords, and other online retailers, including Everand Subscription and Kobo Subscription Services. Print books are available at Amazon, Barnes and Noble, and by ISBN special order through your local bookstores.

ChangelingPress.com